BAD LOVE

MAAME BLUE

JACARANDA

TWENTY
in 2020
Black Writers, British Voices

This edition first published in Great Britain 2020
Jacaranda Books Art Music Ltd
27 Old Gloucester Street,
London WC1N 3AX
www.jacarandabooksartmusic.co.uk

A CIP catalogue record for this book is available from the British
Library

ISBN: 9781913090180
eISBN: 9781913090388

Cover Design: Dapo Adeola
Typeset by: Kamillah Brandes
Printed and bound by CPI Group (UK) Ltd, Croydon, CR0 4YY

For all the bad lovers.

PART ONE

PART ONE

1.

I am not a romantic. I do not know how to tell those kinds of stories, the ones filled with magic and laughter and a purple hue. Romance has never connected with me in that way. But love—hard, bad, rough love—well, I could speak on that all day. And if I did, it would be to speak of my first love: the roughness of his hands, the bristle of his voice, the tender way he kissed me. And it was the kisses most of all that kept me. They were things that began small and playful, growing in depth until we were tracing portraits of each other with our tongues.

At the time it felt like we were creating art, but later when I tried to recall it, it turned in my mind into a mediocre type of pornography; like what we had could only be described as a cheap approximation of what it actually was. But then, my thoughts were often in a tangled mess when it came to him, as I tried to make sense of what we were and what we were not, and how overwhelming it all was.

I remember seeing him once, on a night of no particular importance. He was wearing a blue polo shirt that I liked, with a yellow bird on an imitation pocket. I looked down at his feet, mismatched socks like always, one foot resting on top of the other. He leant against his dining table, arms crossed in a defiant stance, his broad shoulders blocking the crescent moon shining behind him. He was a picture, my picture. I wanted to walk across the room, unfold his arms, place his hands on my face and feel a closeness.

But I knew I wouldn't do it, remaining instead frozen to the spot, not wanting him to know what was going on inside my head because I feared he would find a way to use it against me. So, I stood in his living room doorway, slowly placing my bag on the floor and unzipping my coat. It was past midnight, I was exhausted, and I was certain that he didn't care. A couple of hours ago I had been snug in my bed, looking forward to a good night's sleep. We had exchanged a few text messages, and then it all got a bit hazy. It happened sometimes, our almost two decades of living not yet sufficient enough for us to learn how to communicate properly. He said something, I took it one way, he meant it another, I lashed out at him and he went silent, stopped replying completely. He knew I couldn't stand it when it happened. I used to just fight fire with fire, switch off my phone and respond with the same wall of silence. It caused me nothing but pain, and I could never be sure that he was enduring the same thing. So eventually I decided to cut the bullshit and just go to him.

The journey from my parents' house in Lewisham to Dee's student flat in Holloway hadn't been an easy one. I had had to sneak out, as I was then only a semester break resident, nothing permanent anymore about my status in the house I had grown up in. Plus, catching the bus that late at night was always risky, and I found myself the subject of a verbal barrage from two drunk boys, demanding "show us your bits!" after I dropped my bus pass and bent down to pick it up. I instinctively moved closer to the driver for safety, and thankfully the two pub crawlers got off the bus soon after. I imagined Dee being there, trying to defend my honour, only to have his efforts rebuffed by me telling him I wasn't a damsel in distress. I could hear his response in my head.

"Eh-kwee-ah Dan-kwah! Strong woman, you don't need me eh?"

I smiled in spite of myself at the thought. The echo of his imitated and exaggerated Nigerian accent splitting through his London twang always moved me to warmth. And the way he dragged out the syllables of my name, Ekuah, as if every letter was the most important. My reply was often predictable.

"You're ridiculous."

But none of that had actually happened, and instead we were exchanging silent looks in his living room. I took a seat in the armchair he and his flatmates had found on the street on a night out. He had had the good sense to clean it, germaphobe that he was. I stroked the arms of it as if they were his own, willing him with my eyes to come over to me.

I took a bus in the dead of night to see you, the least you can do is walk across your living room and sit with me.

He wouldn't move though, and I already knew that. He

9

never took his eyes off me, just pulled out one of his dining chairs and sat down. Stubborn bastard. He had this knowing smile on his face too, like he'd won our silent battle and was waiting for me to admit defeat. But I had won the minute he pressed the buzzer and let me into his building. I think he thought I was angry, but I wasn't. This was one of those rare moments between us where I could just enjoy what we were, take a breath, because we were about to make up after a fight, which meant we'd survived another storm. I already knew where the night would end.

So instead, I used the time to study his face, his subtle expressions, his physical habits, miniscule to the untrained eye. He had grown the beginnings of a beard in the days I hadn't seen him, and it cast a faint shadow on his throat. His fingers were making a tight fist, as if he was anxious about something, whilst his eyes said something else. They were bright chocolate-brown pools, with a hunger and hope in them that I suspect was present even when he was a young boy. He used them to survey me: my face, my chest and stomach, and then rested his gaze fully on my hands. I remained settled in the chair, ready to sleep there if needed. I had crossed enough ground that night, it was now his turn.

He continued to stare at my empty hands and I began to feel uncomfortable, like there was something in them that he wanted, needed. And then slowly his face softened, and he ran his hands across the back of his neck in a tiresome motion. I realised that I had never seen that look on his face, in the year or so that we had been in and out of each other's pockets. He looked solemn, resigned, something tired and weary about the way he pulled himself up from the dining chair. He stood as if ready to walk towards me, but paused.

I had been wanting him to yield all evening, but never expected it to happen, it wasn't like him. Usually I would go to his bedroom, climb into his bed, wait for him to follow me, and know that I had that night forfeited the battle between us again. I would initiate the first kiss, the first touch, and lose.

But this time, it was as if there had been a sudden, uncomfortable shift within him that was immediate and all consuming. He took the steps needed towards me finally, before kneeling beside the chair I was now curled into. He gently pulled my hands away from my knees and kissed them, each one in turn. Then he buried his face in my lap, closed his eyes, and remained silent. I ran my hands, now free, along his shoulders, his neck, his black, baby-soft afro hair.

His scent elicited in me the kind of happiness I could never measure or make any real sense of. I loved him so much in that moment that I was unsure how much longer I could stand it for.

2.

I liked to feel needed. I learnt this from the first friend I made at secondary school. During my second week there, a girl named Fifi caught my eye instantly. She was an intimidating presence as the tallest girl in our class with long braids, high cheekbones, a semi-permanent scowl, and a top button that was never done up, in direct defiance of school rules. The only thing we had in common was that she was also Ghanaian. Otherwise she was everything I was not.

During one of our science lessons, a petite girl with pigtails and a lisp was in charge of handing out the textbooks to each table in class. When she arrived at mine and Fifi's, she said something under her breath and then dropped one of the heavy textbooks onto Fifi's head. Fifi was on top of that girl before anyone knew what was happening, scratching at her face, grabbing what hair she could as her own braids were being stretched to their limit. I stood over them in horror, no stranger to witnessing a fight but never having been that close to one before. Everyone else around me began to chant in excited tones.

"FIGHT! FIGHT! FIGHT!"

Within seconds, the science teacher and another one

passing by pulled the two girls apart. I expected to see blood, tears, perhaps even a missing tooth due to the voracity with which they kept hitting at each other's faces, but both had only ruffled shirts and a few hairs out of place. Fifi was dragged to detention with the smaller girl and I grabbed her bag, waiting until after the lunch break to give it to her. She arrived at our next class seemingly unscathed, and thanked me for looking after her things, as if we had been friends all along. I felt awkward asking her for an explanation about the fight, wondering why the girl with the lisp had gone for Fifi in the first place. She did not seem interested in talking about it, so we never did. It was one of those incidents that continues to make little sense, except that it was the beginning of our friendship. Perhaps there was a lesson in it that I never got to learn; it only left the impression that Fifi was not someone to be messed with.

Over the next few years, Fifi would fight physically or verbally with most of the girls in our year group. Except for me. I acted passively with people, avoiding conflict where I could, keeping my opinions to myself unless they were called upon. But secretly I was terrified of hurting someone. I had no siblings, no one to really test my feelings out with at home. So I kept things inside, and often it felt like there was a violence, unexpressed, that I was constantly trying to keep hidden. But my feelings were satiated whenever I witnessed Fifi wielding her aggression freely. I lived vicariously through her, feigning ignorance outwardly, perhaps even giving off the impression that I didn't condone her behaviour, even though I lived for it.

And she was never as angry as she allowed people to believe. She just wasn't afraid of her own power. She had two older brothers who were close to her in age, and she had learnt early on how to stand up for herself. For her, to fight was just to express your feelings, let the other person know who you were, even if that meant having to make them forcibly see it. Despite her propensity for fighting however, people seemed to be drawn to her: her self-assurance, her intelligence, her honesty. She wasn't a bully, she just rubbed people up the wrong way; a bomb thrown in amongst prepubescent girls.

As we came to know each other better, I would tease her about her short temper, the way she let people get to her. She would remind me that I wasn't without my own issues. She had noticed how I often put myself in positions where I would be needed.

"Is that bad?"

She laughed loudly at my question, and then threw a chip my way as we sat at a bus stop after school, eating McDonalds.

"It's just a bit weird. Like, you don't have to insert yourself everywhere. Not everyone deserves it."

For Fifi, she didn't believe that anything came for free, only that there were hidden agendas everywhere and having your guard up was the best way to protect yourself. She viewed the girls challenging and goading her at school as attempting to make her look weak in front of other people, so she had to prove that she wasn't. Walking away wasn't an option. My eagerness to always be helpful confounded her.

"But I like helping people."

Another chip flew at my face, but this time I ducked.

"So naive Ekuah, so naive."

"It doesn't mean anything, is what I'm saying."

"Nah, it means something."

And she was right. I had always reached towards being needed, having a place in the midst of things without having to be the centre. I was too comfortable in a supporting role, and simultaneously I couldn't shake the feeling that stayed with me for most of my adolescence, a sort of dull ache to mean something.

By the time I entered my first year of university, I was no longer ashamed of my desire to become essential to someone. To anyone, really. I let Fifi rub off on me just enough for me to refine the art of independence, and I found it easy. I realised that being an only child had prepared me to be both at the centre of attention and part of an ensemble, depending on how I felt that day. I was able to present as quietly confident, masking my tepid insecurity as I was fuelled—boosted even—time and time again by the acknowledgement of others.

I attempted to imitate what I saw as the strongest parts of Fifi, who was off to a different university, a better one than me after turning her academic life around during our GCSEs. She still fostered an air of "fuck everybody" about her, and I wanted to command that same level of confidence.

But I was misinformed. I learnt years later that Fifi had cared immensely about what other people thought of her, probably even more than I did. What I was imitating was a farce. But for a while, it worked for me. I attempted to reinvent myself, strolling into my halls at London South Bank University, letting my new friend and halls neighbour, Donna, drag me along to a student bar in our fourth week as freshers, to hear her musician boyfriend make his debut at our university.

His name was Dee, and we met in a badly lit basement bar, surrounded by students making the most of the pound-a-pint deal being peddled to them. I spotted him before Donna even pointed him out: about 5"11, wearing a black t-shirt with a picture of Hendrix on it, some kind of brown spirit in the glass he held in his hand, and a look of disdain on his face at the general atmosphere. I had no idea then just how much I would come to love and hate that look, some-times in equal measure.

Donna gave him a chaste kiss on the cheek before intro-ducing him to me. I delivered a half-hearted wave, as if he were far away and not standing directly in front of me. I felt my timidity return briefly, bringing heat to my cheeks and forehead. I didn't care for it, so averted my eyes and headed to the bar for a drink. Donna disappeared to harass some girls who were sat in the corner screaming her name, trying to get her attention. As I took my drink from the bartender, I turned too quickly and watched it splash in slow motion against Dee's chest, unaware that he had followed me and had decided not to keep a safe distance. I apologised in a panic and searched for a napkin, but he seemed unfazed. Instead he looked down at my now half full drink and without saying anything, placed his nose near the rim of it to sniff out the contents. My face didn't hide my confusion, but he ignored it.

"What is that?"

His question was half directed at the cup, half at me.

"Vodka, lemon and lime."

"It smells foul."

"Well, no one asked you to stick your nose in it."

"I just wanted to know what a girl like you drinks."

I scowled at him, taking immediate offence.

"A girl like me? And what kind of girl is that?"

"An interesting one."

"Oh...k."

"Hey, do you—"

Donna suddenly reappeared to tell Dee that it was time to get on stage. We'd only been at university for a few weeks, but she was already friendly with the bouncers, the bar staff and the tech engineers. Dee frowned like Donna had bothered him with something petty, and then disappeared behind a black curtain that acted as a doorway to the stage. Donna nudged me before turning back to the bar so that she could get another drink. I perched next to her as she ordered, and once her drink arrived, she sipped it and raised her eyebrows at me, as if about to ask a question. I smiled back expectantly, and she paused for a few moments before speaking. Then she settled on a pensive look.

"So, what do you think of him?"

"Eh, he's okay, I guess. Seems a bit grumpy though. I mean—"

"No, that's accurate, he's very grumpy. But hot, right?"

"Sure, once you get past the fact that he obviously knows it. No offence to your boyfriend."

"Soon to be an ex one actually—that curmudgeon attitude gets old really fast, trust me."

"Oh. Sorry."

"Don't be. You want him?"

"Uh—"

"I mean, I'm not trying to pimp him out, I just think you guys would make a good couple."

I felt myself snap to attention suddenly. He had stood out to me in large part because I recognised his West African gait; it was my Ghanaian sixth sense amongst a sea of white faces. I wondered if Donna, with her rosy cheeks and auburn-coloured French braid, would be a friend for much longer.

"Why would you think that?"

We were facing the stage, but I turned towards her to ask the question, to be as confronting as I could be in a place that smelled like stale beer and bleach.

"Because of the way he was looking at you. Duh."

She added the 'duh' to remove the confused scowl on my face, the origins of which she had no clue about. She turned back towards the stage to prattle on, ignoring the slump of my shoulders, the unclenching of my fists.

"I'm breaking up with him tonight. I'll give him your

number after that."

"Wait, hang on—"

"Ooh, he's starting!"

That was the end of our discussion on the matter, and I discovered that night that Dee was a gifted musician. He clutched the guitar as if it were someone that he loved, singing melodies that made my stomach drop. The effect he had on the crowd was almost alarming, as he ended his short set to cheers and hoots from a drunken audience. Afterwards, I returned my empty glass to the bar and thought about our brief exchange that had come to nothing.

As people made movements to go on to another drinking spot, I clawed my way through meandering crowds to gasp some fresh air, and found Donna standing outside, smoking and chatting to the bouncer. She had already broken up with Dee, who had swiftly made his exit, returning to his own university in west London. When I asked her how it had gone, she rolled her eyes and told me he was blind if he hadn't seen it coming, and shouldn't we go somewhere else to have a bit of a dance?

Hours later we drunkenly stumbled home, and Donna revealed that she had given Dee my number despite my small protest, swearing that he took it from her with a satisfied smirk on his face.

"I thought it was a nervous twitch because I never saw him smile like that when we went out!"

She followed up her sentence with a snort of laughter, before passing out on her bed. I returned to my own room and tried to curb the excitement in my belly over the thought that he now had my phone number in his possession. I recalled how arrogant, self-assured, beautiful he had seemed.

3.

I was a bag of nervous energy waiting for Dee's call. I sat uncomfortably in the idea that he might never materialise again, that I had imagined the thing between us that lasted mere seconds, the thing I couldn't get out of my head. A whole month passed before I heard from him again. I played it cool and pretended not to remember who he was when he called. He saw right through it of course, and so we began.

Our phone calls set the scene for my falling for him, his voice an ethereal thing that I could mix in with whatever my imagined idea of him was that day. We talked about our friends, our degrees, and briefly, our previous romantic entanglements. I was a novice by most of my peer's standards, dating two boys in secondary school to very little consequence. Dee on the other hand had already slept with four girls, and I pushed down the fear this elicited in me. When it came to love, I imagined that we were equal novices, though he never confirmed this out loud. I felt we were two sides of the same coin; he didn't know how to be alone just as I didn't know how to be with someone. And for all the telephone conversations that we had over many weeks, it wasn't until we saw each other again for the second time that the pieces of him began to come together for me.

It was January, just after the Christmas break. I returned to my halls a few days before lectures were due to begin—partly to get a head start on some reading, partly to get away from the frosty atmosphere between my parents. Dee called me that night as I was warming some tomato soup, saying he was on his way to a local gig and could he crash at mine afterwards, so that he didn't have to do a late-night journey home? He asked it so casually I immediately enquired what time and wondered out loud if he wanted to order some food, as if it were something we had already agreed upon. It had not been, of course, and in fact up until that point we had barely discussed the two of us as any kind of subject, let alone the notion of sleepovers.

Instead I had been fantasising about him: what he was doing on the day to day, what song he heard when he thought of me, whether he told his friends about "the girl from Lewisham"—a moniker he had given me during one phone call that I clung to far too desperately. I noted with vague interest how he had grown larger in my mind during those telephone-wired weeks, with university and friends quickly becoming secondary story arcs that only had half of my attention.

That evening he appeared in front of my building. I watched him park his beat-up Peugeot from the window, butterflies present and accounted for in my gut. I was full of the kind of anxiety that was eventually only reserved for him. It felt like a warning that something dangerous but exciting was about to happen, and nothing was going to stop me from letting it. A kind of gentle madness.

I waited for him to ring the bell, buzzed him up, and then walked to the end of the hallway to let him onto our floor of self-contained bedrooms. We exchanged a brief hello as if we were colleagues not friends, before he followed me to my room. He looked different, unshaven and dishevelled, without that forced air of self-assurance that he had possessed the first time we met. He appeared uneasy as he surveyed my room, removing his coat and running his hand over his whole head before smiling at me weakly. He apologised for the lateness and how tired he was, and I told him I had ordered pizza—having poured my soup away as soon as our phone call had ended.

The pizza arrived twenty minutes later, and we sat on my bed eating it, watching Tom Hanks play a giant piano on my tiny television. We finished eating halfway through the film and although it remained on, there was a silent tension between us that quickly became unbearable. I stood up and picked up the empty pizza box, placing it beside my waste paper basket, afraid of what would happen if I didn't keep my hands busy. He shifted on the bed and then launched into a detailed account of the band that had followed his set that night. They were doing Prince covers and he couldn't decide if he liked them or not. I asked a few questions, trying to remain interested and keeping an eye on the time. Eventually we got onto the subject of his parents and what they thought of his musical aspirations.

"They're musicians, aren't they?"

I tried to recall something from our phone conversations about them, but his response was a frown in my general direction.

"Nah. My mum's in the church choir, that's about it. My dad used to play the piano, or organ or something... I don't know."

"Do you see him much?"

"Not really. He calls my sis sometimes, tells her he wants us to visit him in Lagos. Every few months he'll remember that we exist."

"Oh."

"He's not exactly dad of the year."

"Do you... miss him?"

He hesitated, looking at me, wondering whether I could be trusted with his reply. We hadn't really talked about parents before, nothing beyond me relaying my vague annoyance with my own during that first return home at the Christmas break, my irritation amplified since living away for three months. He said very little about his mum, only that he missed her cooking. I tried to coax more out of him over the phone, but he was monosyllabic. Yet now, sat on the edge of my bed in the middle of the night, he seemed ready to divulge, in his way.

"Not anymore."

"Would you meet up with him, if he came back to visit?"

He looked at me incredulously, like I had uttered something offensive.

"Of course. He's still my dad. He's been crappy but—yeah, he's my dad."

"Okay."

Sitting beside each other, I was acutely aware of how our thighs were pressed lightly together. He looked down at his hands and spoke again, this time in a low voice.

"When I was about 10, he came back to London for a few months, took me and my sis to Maccy D's, we were ecstatic. Then we went to his mate's house, he had all these instruments and my dad was picking up each one and playing them—guitar, piano, did a minute on the drums, bass, it was wild. I genuinely thought he was a superstar. Even made up in my head that that's why he didn't live with us, because he was busy making music. Dumb kids' stuff innit."

"It's not dumb it's—"

"Naively optimistic?"

He raised his eyebrow at me, literally snatching the words from my mouth and causing me to laugh out loud.

"It's not wrong though, is it?"

"Depends on how you look at it."

He pulled a face afterwards, as if he didn't like what was fluttering through his mind but couldn't quite shake it. He rubbed the flat of his palm against his nose suddenly, and then asked quietly if it was alright if he went to sleep as he was knackered. I nodded a little too enthusiastically, switched the TV off and headed into the bathroom to change. When I came out, he was wearing just his boxer shorts and socks. He looked down at the bed and asked me what side I preferred to sleep on. I couldn't tear my eyes away, taking in the whole of him before mumbling something about wanting to be closer to the wall, and then crawling into the bed as if to demonstrate. I felt him slip in after me, our thighs pressing together again before he readjusted his position. There was zero wiggle room in my single bed. I faced the wall and tried to think of anything else but him lying next to me, breathing softly, possibly already asleep. It was a useless effort on my part of course; his toned torso, a maze of muscle and strength, the dark blue boxers with the bulge that was hard to ignore, they mixed with my thoughts and I gave into my urge to leave the bed and run back into the bathroom.

Alone in front of the mirror, I splashed water on my face and took deep breaths, trying to slow my thumping heart, cool down my rapidly heating skin. A storm was brewing inside of me. If I could just touch him, I would be happy. I didn't want anything else but some indication that he felt the same way as I did. I had, thus far, been floating in a stream of uncertainty. He remained that mysterious boy whose text messages I sometimes dissected with girlfriends. He had a sophisticated arrogance that meant other boys my age often paled in comparison. Now he was in my bed and I couldn't deal with it. I would have to kick him out, tell him that he couldn't stay, that it was too much too soon, even though I knew that it wasn't nearly enough.

Eventually I left the bathroom again, and as I climbed back into the bed I felt his hand on my back, guiding me on to the mattress. I resumed my position facing the wall and froze. His hand remained. I closed my eyes and let myself become immersed in darkness for a few moments, and then I turned to face him. We stared at each other in the moonlit room, faces inches apart, until I felt him tug me at the waist and pull me into him, our pelvises colliding awkwardly. I gasped and then heard a small chuckle come from his direction. Instinctively I dropped my head in embarrassment, but felt the warm touch of his lips on mine as if from nowhere, our connection suddenly a real, physical one.

I floated through the motions with a sickly-sweet feeling, painfully aware that I had never done before what I suspected we were about to do. Yet the fact felt unimportant; it was merely something to note, a thing that would very soon become untrue. Nothing was going to stop it from happening, which was the only thing I knew for sure.

His hands were everywhere and so were mine, tugging at my shorts and his boxers, trying to get to the next bit and the next bit, and the bit after that. We were a clunky, glorious mess, fumbling around under my sky-blue sheets, the new ones I'd just bought from IKEA. They had meaning now.

Our clothes were discarded, and he hovered over me, legs spread apart and revealing all of himself as his knees pressed into the mattress and he opened a condom. I lay beneath him and suddenly felt overwhelmed; by him and what was between his legs, as if it were separate to him. An animal I needed to tame, though I was sure I was ill-equipped. But he took control of it himself, guided it where it needed to go, slowly, as I'd asked him to. He obeyed my request with such care that eventually, after the initial pain like a lightning bolt in my pelvis had passed, I pulled him deeper into me with gratitude. Now it was really happening. My mind raced to strange places suddenly: my old English teacher from year 4, the sandwich I wished I'd bought earlier in the day, the pomade smell of Dee's hair every time he lowered his head to kiss my neck. That was when I returned to the room, to him, to that present moment of being completely desired, and the power that comes with it. But it was dangerous too.

I realised too late the risks at stake when letting someone into your space, physically and emotionally. Even in the smallest way, everything after the act is changed in you, as if they leave pieces of themselves behind with you, to germinate. I felt that once I let him enter me, all reason was pushed out. In those long moments smashed together, sweat and skin on more skin, we were one person. I had found what I had been looking for, a search I wasn't even fully aware of, followed by a relief so potent it felt like I was saving my own life. Or, he was.

When morning came, we rose reluctantly from our slumber, as if hungover, strewn across each other in a naked disarray. The room smelt like sex and sweat and lust. I kept my eyes closed a few seconds more, certain that once I opened them, he would return to the surly, brooding boy I had met three months prior. Instead he kissed my shoulder, my neck, indicating an eagerness to repeat our lovemaking. I obliged, more confident in the movement of my body with his now, familiar with how to hold him, where to pause, when to kiss.

I was brand new, a sex Phoenix finally freed, ready to spread my wings and perform wonders. Drunk.

Afterwards, he disappeared into the shower and emerged ten minutes later, wet and naked and looking for a towel. He paraded unfazed around my room in his search. But I found myself covering my eyes as a reflex, afraid that he wasn't really real, and that if I looked too long he might disappear. When he was finally heading out the door he promised to call me, so that we could arrange our next rendezvous.

Once he was gone, I rolled over to his side of the bed, trying to memorise his scent, be imprinted by his ghost. It was the first time I'd had a fantasy come true.

I was thinking, if I could read, to spend my time and buy into whatever I know

4.

I said, I wish I met you when I was young

Dee and I operated under cover of darkness: my room, his room, backstage at gigs he was playing. It felt like we were trying to keep what we had a secret, sometimes even from each other. I rarely invited him out with my friends. I worried about what they might think of him, having only shared with them the filtered, dampened down, more communicative version of him. The one that was less obnoxious and more affectionate. But eventually Fifi met him whilst visiting me on a weekend away from her own university in Oxford. Her opinion of him was expressed swiftly and sharply.

"He's too small for you."

"He's seven inches taller than me."

"I don't mean in stature."

I raised an eyebrow, but she held eye contact with me without blinking. I took the bait.

"What do you mean then?"

She paused and looked away, as if thinking carefully about her next words. Not to spare my feelings necessarily, but to ensure she said exactly what she intended to say.

"He's just not the right size for you. Not the right…

something."

"Well that's clearer."

She smiled and shrugged like that was all she needed to say. I pressed her.

"Well, is there anything you did like about him? His… wit? Sense of humour? Anything?"

"He seems like a taker."

"Fifi, I don't know what that means."

"You're a giver."

"Okay…"

She sighed and then looked at me again, re-engaging our eye contact in the way she always could.

"You can do better."

"Wow."

Her face remained blank, which made me more indignant.

"I would never say that about the guys you date. Or the girls!"

She smirked, seemingly finding my reaction amusing.

"But am I wrong?".

I felt awash with anxiety suddenly, certain that I didn't agree, worried that a smaller part of me did. I could only mumble a response, not strong enough yet in my own convictions.

"You just… shouldn't say things like that to people. So blank like that."

"No, but I can say it to you because you know what I mean."

31

"Yeah, well… I wish I didn't. You know I like him? A lot?"

She gave me a resigned smile and shrugged.

"Yeah. I know."

I had known what her opinion of him was going to be before she said it, and still wasn't prepared to hear it. I told myself that he was just misunderstood, even by Donna who had dated him herself. She never asked me what became of her giving him my phone number, she simply arrived at the conclusion and engaged me in a conversation that seemed to start from the middle.

"I knew you thought he was hot."

"Who?"

"Oh please, as if you don't know. I've seen him sneaking in here at night."

"He doesn't sneak, he just… arrives."

"Listen, he's fun and everything, I mean, I know it was me that got you two—"

She stopped short as she looked around the room, searching for her words. What was it about him that gave everyone pause? Finally, she turned to me with a sincere look.

"Just be careful, okay?"

"Of course."

She gave me a wide smile and then proceeded to prattle on about a rugby player she'd just met.

I had lied. If anything, I was as careless with Dee as I could possibly be with another human being. I floundered from assurance to doubt with him, offering up my feelings again and again, hoping for more and then torturing myself when he didn't immediately reciprocate. And he was a flirt with other women; I had seen it for myself at one of his gigs, when he didn't know I was watching. He seemed to frustrate and attract them in equal measure, purposefully leaving them teetering on the edge, trying to determine if it was worth the fall. Yet I saw myself as the only exception. When it was just the two of us, talking late into the night and huddled together under the covers, I wished that everyone could see what I saw, and then resented my own wish to share him with anyone else. I believed that I knew him best, as a kind, sensitive, insecure soul, different to the person he displayed to others. And I pretended that I did not see how much he liked being regarded as mysterious and difficult, a tough egg to crack, an attractive problem to solve.

I came to bug him about it, annoyed with his perpetual habit of making some things feel more complicated than they needed to be. Especially after he met Fifi—I wanted the two most important people in my life to connect like I did with the two of them, but both were difficult people, set in their ways, unencumbered by my own need to please people. I told him it mattered to me that they get along, that he get on side with Fifi. His reply was swift and judgement-clouding.

"You and me are the only thing that matters."

We lay together at the time, his body heat sustaining me as he whispered it into my ear. I whispered back, unable to stop myself.

"We are?"

I felt him smile, his hands in the small of my back, lips sliding down my neck and over my collar bone.

"You know it. You, me and the music. That's it. Don't worry about the rest."

It was so easy to get lost in him, to not pay close attention to his words, especially when there was barely any physical space between us. In those moments I wanted him all to myself all the time, but his music was already taking off. I had no control over the rapid growth of his fanbase, multiplying as he played at more universities across the country. So, I resigned myself to watching him perform instead, boosted by the knowledge that he would be coming home with me at the end of the night. But in the present, audiences of lust-filled gazes watched him strumming his guitar with partially closed eyes. The girls in the crowd pressed themselves against the edge of the stage, desperate to get a little closer, maybe make eye contact, perhaps get a head nod and a subsequent green light to meet him backstage, and then fumble desperately with this mysterious musician for a meaningful connection.

These were the scenarios I went through in my head, always staying at the furthest point from the stage, watching from the back of the crowd like a wizened owl, convincing myself that I was content. Sometimes I would drag Donna along to his shows, even though she had clearly lost interest in the mystery of Dee.

"Can we at least get closer to the bar? I'd really like to be drunk if I have to watch all these sweaty, model-looking girls fawn over your boyfriend."

"No, I like it back here, we have a seat."

She looked at me like I had said something strange, opening her mouth and then closing it again, changing her mind. I rolled my eyes and asked the question.

"What?"

"Nothing, nothing. How are things going?"

"They're good, why?"

She looked at me skeptically and continued.

"No reason, he's just getting really popular."

"I know, it's insane. But obviously a good thing."

"Yeah, yeah, sure. But I mean, you don't really want to be the girlfriend of a musician, do you?"

"Apparently, *everyone* wants to be the girlfriend of a musician."

I gestured to the gyrating crowd in front of us and she laughed.

"Yeah, but not you."

"Why does that feel like an insult?"

I frowned, trying to dismiss the point I knew she was getting to, before she got there.

"I'm just saying—"

"You're the one who set us up!"

"I know that!"

She leant back in her chair, throwing her chin up in the air, apparently annoyed.

"So, what's the problem?"

I regained my confidence, trying to push her to irritation, show her that I didn't care what she thought even if we both knew that I did.

"You'll always be competing."

"With what? Those girls?"

"With everything."

I stared blankly into my drink, trying not to react, unable to make eye contact. I felt a darkness spreading, like a fresh wound spilling blood from an as yet unidentified injury point. I clutched at straws for solace.

"According to him, I *am* everything."

She nodded, sipping her drink before looking at me with the saddest eyes I'd seen her wear in a long while.

"Yeah, that sounds like something he would say."

I remained silent, picking up my drink again and downing it. I didn't want to be sober for the thoughts that were rushing through my mind in fragments, triggered by her words. She rubbed my shoulder affectionately, a metaphorical rubbing of salt into the wound, from my perspective.

I couldn't see what everyone else could, what I was being warned about. I wondered later, after he had left my place to drive home, what I really knew about him. I believed that I had peeled away several of his protective layers already, taking notes as I got closer to his centre. But I had inadvertently forgotten myself in it all. Now I couldn't remember where he began and my daydreams about us ended. All I had were the moments that we had created together since our first meeting: of sex and pizza and music, keeping the blinds down and bickering. And as the four-month mark crept by, we didn't talk as before; we used half sentences and touch to communicate. We stood at right angles and let our proximity speak for us.

I needed to grasp what was real and began to list facts about him: he studied at the London College of Music. He had a Nigerian father and a Senegalese mother. He called me Eckie, a nickname no one else used. He liked to eat the caramel from a Twix bar before biting into the biscuit. He was a night owl. Sometimes he talked in his sleep. Sometimes I lay awake wishing he would say my name. We had been together, unofficially, for four months, two weeks, four days and approximately fifteen hours. And still, I felt that what I knew about him accounted for almost nothing.

I continued to wonder if he missed me when I wasn't around, if he flirted openly with other girls whilst also thinking of me. I wondered what might happen if he found someone better suited to him, more at ease with their body, musically gifted as he was, who flourished during quiet moments, wasn't as anxious in the silence. Someone who was not as unsettled as I was becoming. What would make him leave me? What could I do so that it never happened? I felt like he was slipping through my fingers, even though nothing had changed between us. I was simply getting and taking in outside feedback, whilst he remained blissfully unaware of what my friends thought of him. I felt like I had something to lose with him, but I didn't know what it was. I thought perhaps I was just getting used to the risk that comes with someone having your heart. And I wanted him to know that he had it, despite the tiny seed of doubt in my head, the one I was trying to eliminate.

I pledged a silent devotion to him and he became all that I could see; and even then, I couldn't see much. It felt as if I only came alive at night, our arms and legs wrapped around each other, shivering sometimes in a cold sweat when our love making was done and we had thrown the covers off our bodies during a sweltering heated rhythm. I called him daily when we weren't together, memorised his gig schedule, showed up over and over again, sometimes cancelling on friends for him. I dreamt about him almost every night, in some form or another. I made myself completely available to him. I cared recklessly.

Once during a particularly passionate night, the condom slipped off with a snap, and he stood in the middle of my room panicked, examining it closely against my light bulb, checking for tears and holes. I remained in bed watching him, feeling completely fine, open to the idea that I could be carrying a new life inside me that was half his and half mine. The thought didn't scare me. If anything, it soothed me to think something could be made from the height of our passion for each other. It turned out to be a false alarm, but my feelings for him overshadowed all reason.

After a time, I lost track of the days and almost missed a coursework deadline. I realised slowly that I needed to force myself out of our self-imposed bunker of sleep and sex and closing off the rest of the world. I began to worry about what my parents would say if I failed my first year, the one I only barely had to pass to get through. They had high expectations; I used to have them too. I sent Dee back to his home, relegated him to phone calls and texts. He was bitter about it, which surprised me. Perhaps it shouldn't have. I managed to finish an assignment within a fraction of the deadline and reviewed my calendar casually. It was my birthday in two days, and I had forgotten.

5.

My parents decided to pay me a birthday visit. My father emerged from the car first, a smile on his face that looked uncomfortable. He always appeared, to me, desperate to convince anyone looking his way that he was perfectly fine. He was a music teacher, obviously disappointed at my lack of affinity for any musical instrument including that of my own voice, which possessed a sort of tone-deaf quality that was hard to imitate. He would often wonder out loud at our genetic dissonance in the area of musical talent, hoping to see himself in me but sadly only seeing someone else. He cared for me, I had no doubt, he just didn't always understand me. Despite that, he relentlessly made attempts to remain a presence in many aspects of my life.

Specifically, a week before my 10th birthday, my father took a substitute teacher role at my school, in what I felt to be a punishment for something I might have said or done to him that was less than charming. The world at the time revolved around me and he was always ruining it. It was only for one term, but to me it felt like an eternity. I avoided him in the corridors and refused to respond when he called out to me with his then thick Ghanaian accent.

"Ek-wee-ah! Ek-wee-ah!"

I hated having him there. I was not an easy child: precocious, verbally challenging him with what looked to the outsider like disrespect, entertaining long periods of stubborn silence when I didn't get my own way, sometimes for days at a time. I spent a lot of my early years with my father when my mother was pulling night shifts at the hospital as a newly qualified doctor, and I often heard aunties tell him that he "let me get away with murder".

His arrival at my school caused me nothing but embarrassment. I didn't question my feelings about this though, certain that my friends would have felt the same way had it been one of their parents. Yet I recall thinking viciously, as I watched him at the teachers' table at lunchtime, that it was not just his presence that bothered me, but that I thought he was weak, and I worried the other kids would notice and make fun of me, or him.

The word 'weak' was one that popped into my head frequently when it came to my father. I had seen him shed more than a few tears during my young life, and I knew that fathers were "not supposed to be that way". They were "supposed to be strong". These were things I had heard my mother say to him on numerous occasions behind a closed door, during a fight in lowered voices, trying to stop me from hearing them. But like any curious child, I often listened anyway, out of sight but well within earshot.

"You cannot keep being this way Kwaku. I can't have it."

"Eh heh, and what will you have?"

"A strong man! The one I thought you were! You have a family, you have to fight for the job you deserve."

"You think I'm not? We cannot all be like you Chrissie, you who wants to be mum and dad but you're not even home to be one of these things."

"Oh, I see, so my career is keeping this roof over our heads and that means I'm a bad mother also? If you want to keep playing babysitter, that one, it's fine. But as for me, I didn't get married to carry a weak man on my back."

I often picked up my thoughts from the ones my mother dropped behind her.

My father was just a sensitive soul, but in a room full of children with short attention spans, he was an easy target. He had little control over my class or the other year five class that he taught that term. We ran riot sometimes—offspring of south east London, three degrees of separation between us and someone on our estate, road, local park who knew someone who had been stabbed. My parents tried to shield me from most of it. But we were not hardened criminals, we were just too familiar with the possibility of violence and chaos. My father wasn't suited for it. He believed in calm voices to instil discipline. My cousins would often tell me they were jealous I had an "easy dad who's not strict". Sometimes I would act out, just to see if I could get a rise out of him, awaken the angry father I always heard about from others. A fool's wish now that I think about it.

A small reaction from him was easy, but the biggest I had ever seen happened that term at my school, and I wished that I could undo it. On a rainy Thursday afternoon, he was teaching my class and a boy named Jed was becoming restless. He decided shooting wet paper pellets at people through the straw from his lunchtime Ribena, was more fun than our class work. He was the resident Naughty Kid, the one who invariably came from a family we all knew was "bad", even though none of us fully knew what that meant, or that we were regurgitating conversations we had overheard from teachers. Rumour had it that his older sister, twenty years Jed's senior, was dating his mother's much younger ex-boyfriend and now they had a baby. They all lived in the same house, looked similar and wore clothes that often appeared grubby.

Usually the thing that triggered Jed to act out was someone commenting on his appearance or how he smelt. They would say it under their breath but loud enough for him to hear, and his tough guy exterior vanished to reveal an angry, snarling animal that clawed at everything in sight. Although shorter and skinnier than everyone else in our year, Jed's bite was often as bad as his bark, through sheer determination and a will to fight anyone who challenged him.

We didn't know then that he belonged to one of the many families in our area living in poverty, a hard life for any 10-year-old made worse by the words of ignorant children. At the time, I knew little of his home life aside from what other kids said on the playground, and kept my distance from him because I hated the way he always disrupted the class and ruined the fun for everyone else.

On the day in question, my father caught Jed with the straw in his mouth and a saliva-ready piece of paper in his hand, and calmly requested that he come to the front of the class. Jed refused, and instead stood up and proceeded to knock over the empty chairs that were around him. My father paused for a few moments, watching him, contemplating his next move. Jed grinned satisfactorily, as he now had everyone's attention, and made a show of grabbing at our artwork that was drying off to the side after a morning painting session. He held each portrait in his hand and spat dramatically on at least five of them before my father had made it across the classroom to snatch away the other untouched pieces. I recognised then, my father's soft spoken but slightly firmer tone as he instructed Jed to go directly to the Head Teacher's office. Jed looked up at him, his expression fixed in complete defiance, and standing only a few inches away, he threw his head back and spat directly into my father's face.

There followed a collective gasp from the class that echoed throughout the room for a few seconds. I was in shock with everyone else and watched my father recoil in slow motion. He wore a look I had never seen before, of pure unfiltered rage. His eyes looked red suddenly, his squared off haircut framing a gently pulsating temple. A storm brewed inside of him, but he refused to let it out. Instead he grabbed Jed roughly by the collar, intent on dragging him to the Head Teacher's office if necessary; a manoeuvre that probably would have lost him his job today.

Jed refused to go and began to kick and punch the air in

resistance. His small body, in full-on tantrum mode, writhed on the floor as my father held his collar firmly. Tears began to spring from Jed's eyes which simultaneously made him angrier and his kicks less effective. My father took it as an opportunity to scoop Jed up with his other hand and carry him out of the class, but suddenly reinvigorated, Jed shoved his foot into my father's neck, causing him to release a short, sharp cry of pain.

But he persisted and got Jed to the classroom door just before the boy was able to swing his newly freed fist in the air and catch my father square in the jaw. My father jerked his head backwards in surprise, involuntarily freeing Jed's other hand, which he then used to angrily yank at the gold chain around my father's neck, the one that had previously been hidden from view before the tussle between them had begun. Jed's pull was so hard that the chain came away from itself in pieces, with the small charm attached, a Ghanaian *fawohodie* symbol, flying through the air and landing amongst our lunch boxes and coats at the front of the room.

Instantly my father let go of Jed and jumped down to his knees, frantically trying to gather what pieces he could find of the gold chain as they shimmered on the grey carpeted floor. His chest was heaving, and I found myself climbing down from my desk to help him in his search. I knew it was important to him; it had been my grandmother's, and he told me once it was the only valuable thing she had been able to give him before he left Ghana. She had died soon after he came to London.

As I crawled on the dust-ridden floor and edged closer to my father, I realised with horror that he was crying. Not quiet sniffles either, but actual gushing tears that were accompanied by deep intakes of breath and the occasional hiccup. I must have been the last one to notice because as I looked up, I was faced with a classroom full of eyes on me, awaiting my reaction. And then Jed, his tantrum over now that he had gotten his way, began pointing down at my father on the floor and laughing maniacally in his direction.

"You're a cry baby, Mr Danquah! Cry baby cry baby cry—"

"GET OUT OF MY CLASSROOM! GET OUT RIGHT NOW!"

My father roared with such power and force that Jed backed towards the doorway in terror, and then ran down the corridor at full speed until he was out of sight and hearing distance. I reclaimed the *fawohodie* charm from the back of the room and held some of the remaining pieces of the chain in the palms of my small hands. Then I walked on my knees back to my father, who sat on the floor with a few more pieces of the chain in a pile in front of him. His face was tear-stained, and he appeared in shock at what had just happened. I sheepishly poured the bits of treasure into his hands, and then rushed back to my seat before he could say anything. He stood up abruptly, shoving what was left of the necklace into his pocket, before wiping his face with one hand and disappearing into the corridor without so much as a goodbye to the class.

During break time the next day, the teasing was merciless as I took on the mantle of Baby Cry, daughter of the official Cry Baby of the school. I appreciated the play on words but that was about it. Naturally, I blamed my father for the whole thing, whilst Jed lived to terrorize another day.

My father and I have never spoken about what happened that day; it felt like there wasn't much left to say. And secretly, I didn't want to give my mother another reason to think that he was weak.

6.

My mother was always in charge. When I was 14 and picking my GCSE subjects, she watched me for days like a hawk, waiting for me to make one misstep in my decision-making so that she could steer me back on the right path again. She hoped out loud that I wasn't choosing the same subjects as my friends just so we could be in the same classes together, because that would be foolish—our futures would not be the same.

She was the keeper of my timetable when I was studying for my A Levels too, ensuring I missed out on as many social events as possible because she refused to let me gamble away my future "messing around with people who only know how to play". She was also the event planner for my sixth form college prom, helping me pick out the dress, the shoes, even my hairstyle for the night. In the lead up, I felt smothered but also desperate for the attention I was getting from her. It felt rare and important.

She was a fiercely driven woman, an established doctor with the right amount of calm and authority necessary for her profession. Her expectations for me were always high, but never higher than the ones I knew she had for herself.

This fed into her struggles with my father however, as she always seemed to want more from him, and he always pushed back with silence and inaction because he wanted to do it on his own terms. Growing up, my house was a place of quiet family dinners, joyful games of make-believe with my father, conversations that felt like intelligence tests with my mother, and a wall between the two of them that I could not knock down, no matter how hard I tried. By the time I was getting ready for university, they were practically estranged. We all lived in the same house, but we did not live together.

So, the day they both arrived to take me out on my 19th birthday, I was a little surprised. It was a hot and sticky day in June, there were flies everywhere, and I was not in the best mood to celebrate over a meal littered with silent exchanges between my parents. But I knew that I had little choice.

We drove to a Ghanaian restaurant in Brixton called Johnny's, which was eventually closed for either bankruptcy or a health violation; rumours of its eventual demise were never really substantiated. At the time it was thriving as a favourite spot for West African Londoners. As I sat opposite my parents, I was sure they hadn't said much of anything to each other since I'd moved out, but perhaps I was wrong. They had arranged this birthday meal after all. I knew they were trying especially hard, because my mother hated restaurants like the one we were sat in. I, on the other hand, loved them.

I couldn't speak Twi or Ga or any of the languages family members in Ghana spoke, but I loved any and all of the food. I would salivate over the prospect of jollof rice, koko, Red-Red, pounded yam and egusi soup, fufu and pepper soup; tell me it was Ghanaian, and I would eat it. My parents loved the food too, but my mother detested what she had to sit through in order to get it.

This was the kind of place where all the wait staff were rude and treated the customer's presence like an inconvenience. You could wait for up to an hour for your food to arrive as you listened to the steady bass from the club in the basement, regardless of what time of day it was. It was my version of dinner and a show, and I liked to make a game out of who would be the rudest waiter or waitress, and which table would get the worst service. My need for drama external to myself never seemed to waver, and my parents only endured it because it entertained me so much.

I was reminded of this fact as I shook myself awake, my chair scraping against the stone floor and causing me to cringe a little. My mother looked around impatiently for someone who might be serving our table, noting out loud that if she wanted bad restaurant service she would have stayed in Accra. It was a sentiment she repeated every single time we went to Johnny's. A waitress appeared after fifteen minutes, loudly chewing a piece of gum as she stood over me, pen and paper barely at the ready.

"I'll have the jollof with chicken and salad please."

I looked at her smiling, holding the menu up for her to take, but she just stared blankly at me before responding in a monotone voice.

"Eh, we haf noh more jollof."

My mother's head whipped round at the waitress, no longer concerned with the menu in front of her. I could see her refined manner morphing into something else, something of her past.

"What do you mean no more jollof? How can you have no more?"

"Hmm madam, we have had som big patties todeh, so we are mehkin more, bot it will be a few few ares."

The waitresses' thick accent and slightly worried look did nothing for my mother's countenance. She muttered under her breath, kissed her teeth and then turned to me.

"Ekuah pick something else, we can't wait all day for rice."

I was disappointed but tried to hide it for fear of further irritating my mother.

"Okay, I'll just have the Red-Red please."

"And don't tell me you don't even have plantain."

My mother quipped at the waitress and then scowled, challenging her as if the way in which Johnny's ran rested entirely upon this waitress' shoulders. The woman simply smiled her least gracious smile and nodded, taking my menu from me. My mother and father ordered the same thing and the waitress finally left us in peace. I began to make small talk about my lectures and the latest albums I had bought, attempting to appeal to both parents' interests. After half an hour, our food still hadn't arrived. We had never been a talkative family; my parents usually communicated through looks, and I fantasised often that they might one day silently agree to divorce, putting each other's happiness first. No such luck however.

My father began to pick at a newly-formed scab on the back of his hand until my mother noticed and gave him a reproachful look. He stopped immediately and then they both turned towards me in unison.

"Your mother and I were talking about our trip to Venice, to see your Uncle Charlie this summer. But I've got some students to tutor now, and your mother will be teaching a summer class to Junior GPs for three months."

My father watched as my face dropped. I couldn't hide my disappointment. I had been looking forward to the trip all year. We rarely went away and when we did, it was always to some long distant relative, with no one my age around to even share my boredom with. But my favourite cousin Amelia was in Venice. My father gave me a reassuring smile and continued.

"But we were thinking, you're an adult now. So instead of cancelling the trip entirely…"

Suddenly his words trailed off and he stared past me to another table, squinting as if to see something far away.

"Ah! Virginia is that you? GENIE!"

He was shouting across the room at a woman sat with two other people. I glanced at my mother whose eyes were wide, so that all you could see were the whites and a dot of a pupil. The woman my father was now frantically waving at was a chestnut-skinned beauty, with long black braids, wearing a green wrap dress and heels. To say that she was stunning would be an understatement. I could not see the faces of her two companions, but she finally located my father with her own eyes and immediately jumped out of her seat to rush over to us. When she reached our table she and my father didn't embrace as I had expected. Instead, they stood looking at each other for what felt like an endless moment. It was as though an invisible wall stood between them, and I suspected it was probably my mother. The woman, Genie, shook my father's hand awkwardly, and he held onto hers with both of his, unable to suppress his smile.

"Ah! Genie, look at you! Can you believe this, Chrissie?!"

He looked down incredulously at my mother where she sat, still stunned. Eventually he let go of Genie's hand as my mother stood up, and to my utter surprise, she and Genie hugged each other warmly. Then my mother stepped back and tapped me on the shoulder so that I too jumped to my feet.

"Ekuah, this is your Auntie Genie. She went to school with your father and I."

"Hello auntie."

She hugged me as if we weren't strangers and then shrieked loudly.

"Ay! How big you've grown! You must be fighting off the boys eh? You should meet my niece and nephew, they're around your age!"

She ran off to grab her fellow diners and bring them to us in a kind of show and tell fashion. Later, she explained that she lived in Maryland and had just moved to London for work, so was staying with her half-sister for the time being. And just as her niece and nephew headed towards us I felt my feet turn to lead. I closed my eyes a few seconds too long, willing myself to stay put and not make a run for it immediately.

When I opened them again, Dee stood square in front of me next to his sister, as Genie introduced them to us. His panicked face matched my own, but none of the adults were paying us any attention. We shook hands as if we had never met, as though his lips hadn't explored practically every inch of my body, as if we hadn't lain in each other's arms dozens of times. I didn't know for a second how to only touch him briefly, how to walk away from him. But somehow, we managed the handshake without tearing each other's clothes off, and I felt an emptiness, a dissatisfaction as he moved to speak to my parents for the first time.

Genie boasted proudly about Dee and his sister Dali, who was the spitting image of him, only more angular, softer in the face and hands, with a wicked laugh that she released regularly. My parents complimented them both, my father particularly intrigued by Dee's musical aspirations. Eventually they returned to their seats and my parents promised to meet Genie later in the week to catch up properly. And then the food arrived and our conversation, what little there was, never quite resumed. It was as if Genie had been a light in a dark room, touching everything as it entered, and leaving a denser darkness in its wake. I sensed her presence three tables away, in-between my parents. It felt important and I had to know why.

"So… you guys were friends with Auntie Genie in Ghana?"

My father nodded but continued eating, almost as if I hadn't said anything, and my mother didn't look up either as she responded.

"Yes, we all went to Achimota together. She was a very good friend."

She gave my father a look I had never seen her give him before, almost wistful. He didn't look back, so she continued.

"She was your father's girlfriend for a while."

I grinned excitedly at this new piece of gossip and raised my eyebrows at my father, looking for confirmation. He remained unresponsive, sliding a finger up the side of his water glass, wiping away the condensation. He obviously didn't want to talk about it, so I decided not to pursue the line of questioning I had already planned in my head. But then he mumbled, barely audibly:

"She was my girlfriend yes, but she was more interested in your mum."

My head snapped back up at him, as did my mother's. There was a pause as they exchanged more looks I didn't understand and then my father exhaled and gave a quiet, sad chuckle at the same time. My mother suddenly and quite involuntarily snorted with laughter. She tossed her head back and waved her hand dismissively.

"Don't mind your father, dramatic as always. Genie and

I were just good friends who did our school work, while he was off trying to become the next Jimi Hendrix."

I smiled but still felt confused, her dismissive hand waving on a perpetual loop in my mind afterwards. My mother shifted gears quickly and asked me about my exams, what my study schedule was like, reminding me that even though it was the first year I still needed to do well. I zoned out and eventually excused myself to go to the bathroom.

I took the steps downstairs, following the sign to the ladies. As I turned a corner, I almost collided with Dee coming from the opposite direction, jolting me into remembering that we were in the same restaurant. I made a movement to step back but he grabbed both my arms and steered me towards the wall until I felt the cool concrete through the thin shirt dress I was wearing. His lips were on mine before I had a chance to speak and I felt myself melting as he pinned me against the wall, making me submit without even having to try. But I was distracted, my parents were too close by. I pushed him away gently and he paused with his eyes closed for a few seconds, as if trying to process what had just happened. I was never the one to pull away first.

"What's wrong?"

He tried to kiss me again before I could reply, and I watched myself duck away from him and then slide out of his embrace.

"My parents are upstairs, it's—"

"It's what?"

"Weird! Sorry, I just can't. Not when they're up there,

plus your auntie! I can't believe they know each other."

He frowned like I had said something irritating and rubbed the back of his neck in frustration. Then he shrugged and gave me this forlorn look. I leant against the wall for a moment, a few feet away from him now, and felt my bladder warning me that it required attention. Dee wasn't looking at me anymore though, he was staring at my shoes, and he took a few steps forward and tapped the front of mine with the front of his. I smirked, in spite of myself.

"I know you wanted space to study and stuff, I get it. But… I miss you."

It had only been a week since we'd last seen each other and my stomach flipped at the sound of this new declaration. I missed him too, in a quiet but constant way. But what would he do with that information? I wasn't sure.

"I… need the loo. Sorry!"

I ran towards the ladies bathroom and avoided the hurt look I was sure he was giving me. Afterwards as I dried my hands, I felt a burn in the pit of my stomach, my regret present and accounted for at the way I had raced away from him telling me how he felt. It didn't happen often and usually I savoured it like a rare jewel. But now I was afraid of losing myself again, of cradling every morsel of emotion he gave me and pretending it was a meal. I wasn't sure which way to go next with him, so I had frozen myself in a sort of awkward meandering.

I wondered if he was still outside waiting for me. Maybe he'd tell me he was angry with me, disappointed even. Maybe he'd ask me what was wrong. I wouldn't want to say though, I already knew that much. Instead I would pull him into the vacant disabled toilet stall. After he pulled down his trousers and sat on the closed toilet seat, I would place a condom on him, now liberated through a few undone buttons on his boxers. Then I would straddle him—I had always wanted to do it in a public place but was too scared to ever suggest it. He would bury his face in my chest as we rocked back and forth to a finely tuned rhythm, and all doubts about us would disappear, despite the graffiti and random phone numbers carved into our surroundings. When we were in it, wherever we were, it felt like we were making love in a palace. His hands would clasp my buttocks and we would do this over and over again, reuniting for as long as our young bodies would allow it.

I stared into the mirror, a smudge of a reflection staring back at me. I smoothed out my dress, took a deep breath and opened the door. He stood in the same place, at the other end of the corridor, leaning, waiting for me. I felt my breath catch in my throat. I hadn't expected him to still be there. The second surprise of the day.

7.

As my second year at university came into view, an eventful summer had left me with a new interest in doing more for my local community. And to some extent this was nothing new, because it fed my desire to feel needed which had never really gone away. I had just learned to hide it better. But now I was taking it public, wanting to talk to friends, family members, strangers even. The refreshing feeling created in the pit of my stomach whenever I did something good for other people, became a thing that needed to be shared and celebrated. Why wasn't everyone doing this? How could I get more people to do it? I towed the line between well-meaning and self-righteous, a toxic combination that Dee was not on board with.

"You think you're hot shit right now, innit?"

He said it to me casually as we lay in bed, propping himself up with some pillows.

"Pssh! No."

I grinned at him unashamedly, comfortable these days in our bedside exchanges.

"You can't even pretend! People don't usually think so much of themselves like that you know."

"What's wrong with being proud of what you're doing?"

He shrugged, like my question was frivolous. I continued.

"So, you don't feel good about your music then?"

"I do, obviously, but I don't know. You're..."

"I'm what?"

I sat up, my defences alerted. He paid no attention and proceeded without caution.

"You're kind of pushing it in people's faces. It's not attractive."

It was a Saturday morning and I was due to have lunch with some friends but had already sent a text to ask if we could meet an hour later, omitting from my message the caveat that I wanted to spend more time with Dee. Now, predictably, I was regretting it.

"Wow, okay. Well I'm sorry my wanting to help people is ruining your hard-on for me. That says more about you than me."

"Why you have to be harsh like that? You know that's not what I mean."

"Then why say it?"

We were both sat up now, and I began to climb out of the bed as he watched me, his annoyance growing.

"Someone has to! You just used to be a bit more... modest. It was cute, is all I'm saying."

"You mean timid."

He screwed up his face suddenly in anger.

"No, I don't. You're not listening to what I'm saying."

"You're right. I'm not. I'm going."

I was sat at the edge of the bed now, jeans on, t-shirt on, one shoe on. He jumped out from under the covers and grabbed my wrist as I stood up to leave.

"Why do you have to be like this? You just walk out when you don't like what I'm saying. Can we not just talk please?"

"I'm not in the mood, Dee."

"So, you really don't have time for me anymore, yeah? You survived Venice so now I'm this small ting? Cool, cool."

I rolled my eyes as I pulled my arm from his now half-hearted grip. His dramatics had long-since stopped affecting me. As I reached his bedroom door and turned to look at him, I got a second wind.

"You know, most people think I've changed for the better."

He smirked in response and stared back at me.

"Right. And what do you think?"

"Fuck you."

I closed the door in his surprised face, aware that our arguments didn't usually escalate that quickly. But things had changed. Now I was purposeful with my words, ensuring they landed the way I wanted them to. I felt that he was raining on my parade and I wouldn't have it. Though what he had inferred was partially correct, surviving Venice had made everything else seem small in comparison.

*

61

My parents had decided that rather than shine a harsh holiday light on the state of their marriage, they would send me to Venice in the summer to visit my Uncle Charlie alone. At least I imagined that was the thinking behind it, though they never told me so.

I didn't tell Dee that I was going, because we just didn't talk about certain things. We conversed about the present, the here and now that stretched between his music, my books, what gig he was playing next, the bars I went to with friends, and where we spent our nights together. Things had quickly become insular between us, and I fretted constantly about becoming "The Girlfriend" who replaces her friends with her boyfriend until it is the only relationship she has. So I kept some things to myself, afraid that he would influence them, subsume their importance until he became the most important thing in my life. I could not admit that he already was. But Venice was something just for me, and it conveniently took place during the summer break whilst Dee was away with his sister in Lagos for four weeks, his father's invite finally coming to fruition.

And when I returned from Venice, I was different. I had been changed in the way only a 19-year-old can be, where every new experience is a catalyst for some other version of yourself; a reshaping of a person that isn't fully formed yet. There were pieces of the trip, memories of it that became smaller as time went by, but also more vibrant and detailed, as if my brain set about to amplify what it felt important for me to keep. Stepping off the plane into the humidity and the sweet smell of lilacs somewhere nearby. Travelling into the city by train, passing the black streaks of cars going the same way, a large blue surrounding us and spreading across the ground until it was all we could see below, a liquid pathway. Sitting in a water taxi, nervous to stand at the front and face the speed and wind of the boat but doing it anyway, breathing in the salty air as if waking for the first time. And sitting on the edge of a taxi dock, the sun going down, feet dangling precariously over the greens, blues and browns that made up the canal water.

A quiet, slow dream engulfed me during those first few days in Venice, and I feared waking up. My tour guide was my cousin Amelia. She too had just finished her first year of university and was excited to have someone to show around. I was a more than willing tourist. We had been thick as thieves as children, when her family still lived in London and we would play hairdresser with our Barbies. Neither of us really cared for our toys properly, so we would often part ways with partially balding Christie dolls under our arms, our mothers scolding and hiding scissors from us, whilst suppressing their laughter at our rough looking salon customers.

When we were 12 years old we each wore black dresses, sitting on a wall outside of her *Nonna's* home in Rome, at her mother's funeral. It had been sudden; a car accident on one of Rome's highways. Even as a child, I had some grasp of how it came to be. I recalled sitting in the back of my Uncle Charlie's car on the motorway many times, feeling like I was on a rollercoaster. The other cars on the road whizzing by, interweaving at a terrifying speed, so that accidents seemed like a frequent inevitability.

That day on the wall, Amelia and I stayed outside in the autumn heat, nibbling sandwiches and listening to Destiny's Child on my Walkman.

And the last time I saw Amelia we were 15, she tagging along on a business trip to London with my Uncle Charlie, us both leaning heavily into our teenage angst and hiding in my bedroom playing My Chemical Romance on repeat. She avoided mirrors back then as I did, frustrated with her unmanageable mane of hair, the loose curls I envied so much.

But meeting her in Venice, she was a new person, completely familiar and unrecognisable all at the same time. Her green eyes were a sparkling mystery, her hair tamed lovingly into four long cornrows, its mocha colour complemented by the scorching sun, and her Italian mother and Ghanaian father present in the way that she moved and spoke, with volume and confidence. She paid little attention to the male gaze that followed her around as we journeyed through small alleyways and cobbled streets, the same gaze that left me uncomfortable and slightly envious.

At the weekend we went exploring, and after thirty minutes in the July sun, I was desperate for a drink. She immediately led me down a passageway that opened out into a courtyard. Colourful but dilapidated apartments were piled on top of each other, forming a circle around the space. There was a drinking fountain off to the right which I rushed to with my bottle, whilst another more ornate fountain stood in the middle of the courtyard, where pigeons were enjoying the sprays of water from it. Amelia made her way to the café off to a left corner, different coloured plastic chairs placed indiscriminately around white plastic tables. Taking a few gulps of the crisp cold water, I walked towards the café and stood beside her as more eyes followed her. She remained oblivious, or perhaps she just did not care. After only a few days of reuniting with her, I couldn't imagine going back home. At least not in the real sense of the act. Dee was always there in the back of my mind like a half-remembered thought, but one that slowly became harder to grasp amidst the blue skies and colourful buildings.

Amelia was staring at the man behind the counter of the café, who eventually came over to talk to us, and I realised that they knew each other. He was the owner's nephew and he and Amelia had been classmates at school. She turned to me to introduce us.

"This is Vio. Vio, this is my cousin Ekuah."

We did the two-cheeked kiss. Mine was awkward and confused, his refined and natural. I felt my face burn as I pulled away from him. He was olive-skinned, and it occurred to me that it was the first time that phrase 'olive-skinned' had made any real sense to me. He was unconventionally handsome, in a way that was hard to look directly at. I hoped that his personality was bland, to offset the pleasing quality of his face, make it easier to talk to him. He corrected Amelia and explained that his full name was Silvio, but everyone called him Vio. Amelia smirked and told him I was visiting from

London. He beamed suddenly, his winning smile causing me to blink as if blinded by sunlight.

"Oh, I love London! Although you are all so grumpy sitting in tunnels like moles! This part is very strange."

I nodded, grinning like an idiot, unable to stop my face from making me look foolish. I hoped saying something might offset the awkwardness I felt just standing next to him.

"Yeah, we love the tube!"

Amelia snorted with laughter next to me and then looped an arm around my shoulder, her slender frame hanging off mine as if I were a tree.

"*Allora* Silvio, you should go back to work and stop trying to fool my cousin into thinking you've visited London before."

She stuck her tongue out at him playfully, and he pulled a face back at her before emitting an exaggerated laugh. Then he turned to me, making a show of paying Amelia no mind.

"Amelia—she doesn't know how to have fun. You should come back tonight, we're having a show here, you will have a good time."

Amelia threw her head back and laughed loudly, making air quotes with her fingers.

"'Show'—okay. We'll come, then Ekuah will see which one of us is more fun."

She smiled at me expectantly and I nodded again, deciding that staying silent was my safest bet. Vio smiled and then suddenly took my hand in his.

"I look forward to seeing you tonight, Ekuah."

I swooned internally, such a cliché of my British tourist self, meeting the cute Italian local, so easily taken by his hazel eyes and correct pronunciation of my name. Amelia just nudged me with her shoulder and rolled her eyes dramatically, before we waved goodbye to him as a queue started to form in front of his unmanned counter. On the train back to Amelia's house to change, she teased me mercilessly about him, and I enjoyed it.

"Ah, so Italian boys are your thing now?"

"I don't have a 'thing' but, I mean, did you not see him?"

She shrugged and looked out the train window.

"He's just Vio."

When we revealed our evening plans to my Uncle Charlie he was enthusiastic and positive, and I was struck by how different he was from my father, who worried often whenever he knew I was out of the house after 7 p.m. My uncle was an English Professor, heavy set, taller than his younger brother, with a stoutness that indicated contentment. My father insisted Uncle Charlie had always been the favourite of the family because of his academic achievements, whereas my father just wanted to have fun. I had not seen much evidence of that side of him thus far.

"Ah that Silvio, he's a good boy, does a lot of work for his uncle's charity—what's it called Li?"

"*Nuovo Modo*—New Way."

Amelia turned to me in the back of the car, her father driving us to the train station.

"I think tonight is to raise money for them. They're

putting on a kind of variety show with poetry readings and music; five Euros entry fee."

"Well that's good. I always feel better knowing you're with Silvio, he's just afraid of me enough that he knows to protect you with his life."

"Ugh Dad, come on."

I chuckled in the background at their exchange, so familiar, jovial and obviously close. It reminded me of my own relationship with my father up until a few years prior, when it was often just the two of us and he knew everything that was going on in my life. He was my protector in his own way. I hadn't realised how much I'd missed it, that thing between us, until that moment. I forced myself back into the conversation.

"So, what does *Nuovo Modo* do exactly?"

My uncle explained that the charity had been set up to help find homes for children who had lost their parents in conflict. When I asked what kind of conflict he meant, Uncle Charlie furrowed his brow and stammered slightly, clearly hesitant to answer my query. Instead he mumbled a reply.

"Politics, you know."

I nodded even though I did not know. Amelia scoffed from the passenger seat and said,

"*Famiglie del crimine.*"

My uncle told her to hush. She smirked and raised her eyebrows at me, assuming I had understood, and then continued to look out the window.

Vio's café had been transformed by the time we returned

to it. The white plastic tables were now draped with blue tablecloths, and fairy lights decorated the bar and walls. A grey-haired man sat in the corner strumming an acoustic guitar, and the melody echoed throughout the courtyard. Some extra chairs had been set in rows outside the café so that it looked like a tiny concert was about to take place, with a few crates covered in a sheet indicating a slightly unstable stage. It was still warm outside, and people were scattered around the courtyard waiting for the show to begin: talking, drinking, laughing, smoking. I felt that I had stepped into an entirely new world, away from the safety net of my life as a student, into a place where men with groomed beards and dark eyes, and women in summer dresses spoke in loud, animated voices, and everyone kissed everyone.

Vio spotted us and planted us in the front row despite our protests. He wore a white shirt and black shorts, his hair a melted chocolate colour, silky and floppy, with a natural curl somehow giving it a style and keeping it in place at the same time. He complimented us both on our outfits and made a quip at Amelia about how strange it was to see her in a dress for once. She used a small fist to punch him in the shoulder, and he almost dropped the two plastic glasses of wine he had for us. When he left, I turned to her.

"Are you two always this way?"

"He knows how to irritate me, that's all."

I raised a doubtful eyebrow at her but she just laughed, shaking her head and sipping her wine. I watched him as he walked away from us, his muscly calves stretching and protracting with each step. I had fast developed a crush on him and was glad for it, simply because it suggested I was still able to feel something outside of Dee, suddenly looking for ways to rally against the strong feelings I had for him.

The show turned out to be an open mic poetry night, and it was the first time I had heard spoken word poetry outside of London. I was enthralled immediately, listening to performances in Italian, some in English, feeling completely taken by it all. I was a long-time fan of the form, favouring it as a topic in my English literature and communications degree, always wanting to read outside my undergraduate syllabus, to find the poets and writers that better resonated with me. That moment, sat in a Venice courtyard listening to rhyme and verse, felt like a personal gift.

After four or five poets had performed, a teenage boy appeared on stage. He was skinny with dirty blonde curly hair and couldn't have been older than 14. He was all long arms and legs, with a long face to boot. He had no paper to read from like the other poets, only piercing eyes like slits in his head, surveying the audience with severity. I felt a cold chill run over me, fearful of what he might expose us to. But his poetry turned out to be some of the most beautiful I had ever heard. In English, he spoke of struggling with himself and his environment, ripping beauty and sadness from the core of his experience, somehow.

If I were a one-man army
I would be both victor and loser
Always at war with myself.

At the end he thanked Vio and his uncle for letting him be a part of *Nuovo Modo* and explained to the audience that he had been a child of conflict. He stood with his hands on his chest, sincerity and fire in his eyes. Then he looked around for a moment before shouting,

"MORTE ALLA MAFIA VENETA!"

And then everything stopped. A collective gasp left an echo of a few seconds of silence, before I heard what sounded like a small drum being beaten with a quick *buft buft buft* rhythm. A blank moment followed before I came to, suddenly on the floor, my plastic chair on top of me as the drum beat became a deafening bash against my ears.

But now my brain began to work harder, and I realised it had not been a drum, but gunshots; the kind that were silenced by something, so that the only sound you heard was the bullets hitting their targets. That same sound continued throughout the courtyard and drowned out the screams from the people around me. I felt the gravel under my face, after I had jumped to the floor on instinct, in an attempt to protect myself. To my right I could see others doing the same, as if we were all in an emergency drill.

I quickly searched for Amelia with just my eyes, my face pressed firmly to the warm ground. Then I felt my wrist being squeezed, the one I was facing away from, and knew that it was her, or at least I hoped it was. Somehow the hand was shaking as it held my wrist, the signal of the terror that I also felt running throughout my body. We lay there as the smell of hot metal and fear lingered in the air. My mind kept replaying the scene: bullets, tiny cylinders of metal flying with purpose throughout the atmosphere in all directions, the size of the space between thumb and forefinger when describing something insignificant. They had shattered everything in my mind's eye—the walls, the ground, even the sky. They had pierced the stars, sent the universe into retrograde, removed the oxygen from the air and reduced us all to weeping children on the floor.

I took a risk, not wanting to be in my own head anymore. I had to know that Amelia was still alive. I turned my head as quickly as I could and came face to face with her, inches away, eyes widened in panic. I mouthed the words *Are you okay?* and she blinked twice whilst squeezing my wrist, a secret signal created on the spot between us that meant *Yes,* and *Are you okay?* I imitated her two blinks and she seemed to breathe a big sigh of relief, muffled as it was into the ground.

We stared at each other, surrounded now by a deadly silence. No one wanted to stand first, afraid this was just a pause, a moment for a reload before more shots flew forth and found unsuspecting, soft skin. And then shoes appeared by our heads and I craned my neck to see Vio smiling down at us weakly, offering two hands to help us up.

"They're gone, nothing to worry."

Nothing to worry. It was comforting in its almost sentence and half-truth. Seeing us stand and remain alive for a few seconds caused other people to slowly stand and then quickly exit the courtyard. Vio embraced Amelia and I in a protective hug as if we had been the intended targets for the bullets, and we held on to each other for a long time in the middle of scattered chairs and debris from the walls. When we separated, I looked at Vio, my voice a shaky, screechy mess, as if I had been screaming. Had I?

"Is the boy okay?"

He looked at me like he didn't understand the question, blinking for a few moments before the words fell into place.

"Oh, the boy...yes...he is okay...I mean, he got caught in the leg but...they will take him to the *ospedale*. The..."

He trailed off as he pointed to some of the bearded men I had seen earlier, now carrying the boy into the back of a car, a bloodied t-shirt tied around his thigh. Or perhaps it was his thigh that was bloodied. I closed my eyes, I couldn't watch. Amelia placed a hand on my shoulder.

"The hospital isn't far away, he'll be okay."

She turned to Vio who gave her a worried look; she said something to him in Italian. He nodded and then guided me towards the bar, my legs wobbling slightly. Amelia hugged me again without saying anything, and then disappeared into the back of the café towards the bathroom. Vio pulled out a chair for me and I sat down, trying to regain my senses, a surreal feeling of being outside of my own body causing me to zone in and out of a conversation that wasn't even happening. All the while my mind was racing with words from the poetry I had heard, coupled with the sounds of a drum beating heavily about my head and the echoes of people screaming. I felt my energy begin to wane.

I looked over at Vio who had returned to the bar and was

preparing hot chocolate for us, humming some inane tune whilst he did it, as if the evening had gone exactly as planned and we were about to enjoy an innocent nightcap.

"This has happened before."

In my head it was a question, but by the time the words reached my lips, it had become a conclusion. Vio paused in his drink making, scrunching up his face as he considered my words.

"Maybe two, three times a year it happens."

"Aren't you afraid?"

"Of course."

"But how can you keep coming back, knowing it could happen again?"

He bought over the hot chocolates and set one down in front of me.

"My Uncle Andreas, he runs *Nuovo Modo*. It has danger around it. But he always says, things without risk, they are not worth doing."

"Even when your own life is at risk?"

"That boy's life was at risk too—so how can we choose to stop now? The criminals, they would have won."

I brought the hot chocolate to my lips but refrained from drinking. My narrow understanding of the important things in life had already been destroyed. I could barely risk my emotions in my relationship, so the prospect of being that close to danger, to possible death on a regular basis, seemed absurd to me. He watched me as I struggled to comprehend what he was saying and placed a hand over mine as it rested on the table, settling it; it had been shaking without my knowledge.

"This thing tonight, it was scary, and I am sorry about that. But...it's worth it. To help the kids. Do you know what I mean?"

He looked at me, like he truly hoped that I understood. I stared back, struggling to connect with the warmth in his eyes, soothing as it was.

"I don't really... no. I don't know what that's like."

He smiled, as if he had expected my lost response, squeezing my hand and then picking up his own hot chocolate to sip it. He took a gulp and then gave me a sincere look.

"I'll show you what I mean."

As Amelia reappeared, all I could do was give him a half smile of uncertainty. The three of us sipped our hot chocolates together in silence, my heartbeat finally back to a slow, steady pace, as I mused over his words and their meaning, feeling more thankful than I had ever been that there would be a tomorrow to find out more.

8.

Amelia and I returned to her home, tiptoeing up the stairs to her room whilst the rest of the house slept. We both got changed in silence and, ignoring my single blow up bed on the floor, I climbed into bed with her. She held the covers open for me, already expecting my entrance. We both lay on our backs staring up at the ceiling, sleep unable to reach us, just a stark awake feeling like exhaustion, restlessness and caffeine. I turned to look at Amelia and saw that her face was wet, one small line of water drawing a path from the corner of her eye down to her pillow. Instinctively I reached over, awkwardly dragging my thumb across the side of her face, trying to wipe away the tears that were in mid-stream. She laughed at my failed attempt and turned her head towards me fully, her big eyes piercing my chest with their intensity.

"I thought we were going to die."

I felt my own eyes welling up but held back, I didn't want to make it worse. Instead I turned my body towards her so that we now both lay on our sides, facing each other, covers bunched up at the end of the bed because it was too hot for all of that.

"But, we didn't."

A big sigh of relief exited my mouth following my own words, as if I had needed to hear it out loud from someone, even just myself. She nodded slightly and closed her eyes, letting small drops of water gather on her eyelashes until she was fully asleep. I lay awake a little longer, still feeling disconnected from things, unable to get back into my body properly. I was too afraid of what might happen with me in it.

*

Amelia and I left the house in the early hours of the following morning, avoiding conversation with her father about how the previous evening had gone for fear of the ramifications, of having to face up to the seriousness of things. Instead we had breakfast at a local café, before travelling back into Venice city, and then taking a boat to Burano to meet up with Vio at his uncle's place. When he opened the door, his beaming smile had returned, still blinding, at least to me. He greeted us both by pulling us into his arms; the embrace an echo of the one we had shared the night before.

His Uncle Andreas showed us around the apartment complex that he lived in and owned. He had inherited it from his great grandmother, a wealthy patron of the town 60 years ago. Having no offspring of his own and content to play uncle to his many nieces and nephews, he opened the house up to orphaned children, a community project that morphed into *Nuovo Modo*.

"My life's work."

He stretched his arms out as we stood in a garden-cum-playground, kids probably no older than six or seven-years-old, screaming and running around with glee, lost in the giddiness that comes with playing pretend. We were then ferried into a small on-site library, older kids sitting in various places on the floor, reading and writing in note-books. Vio's uncle went to get something from an office in the back, and Amelia immediately meandered over to a book with a cover suggesting fantasy fiction. Vio and I remained by the doorway, content to watch the quiet goings on of the library. A few silent moments passed before Vio whispered into my ear.

"Most of the kids come to us when they are very young, too young. Many of them, their parents had borrowed from the Mafia Veneta, and in return they pay back with interest, or they pay back with favours. But too many get caught in the crossfire of Veneta business, and then, their children are just... left."

I turned to him, my eyes wide in shock still, as he reminded me why we were there, why the previous night had gone the way it had. He just looked back at me, almost blankly but for his eyes, glistening with emotion. Amelia appeared beside me suddenly, frowning at him, assuming he'd upset me. In response to her glare, he squeezed my arm gently and gestured for us to go outside, with her following closely behind. When we reached the balmy air, she punched him in the shoulder like she had the day before, only this time with more anger and force. He jumped back but didn't say anything, simply rubbing his arm and giving her a look I couldn't quite decipher. She turned to me and asked if I wanted to go, suggesting that we'd had enough for one day.

"No, I... I'm good. Let's stay, it would be rude to leave now anyway."

I tried my most reassuring tone but knew she wasn't buying it. She turned towards Vio and they began to speak rapidly in Italian, as if both were in a rush. I stood off to the side for a few moments, wondering what was being said as the seriousness of the conversation seemed to suddenly intensify. Amelia seemed really flustered, which was a state I had never seen her in before. She was usually the cooler, calmer of the two of us. But today she had something to expel and Vio was her target. She began to poke him in the chest as her voice grew louder, and a few staff members at the complex glanced their way but kept walking. Vio continued to speak to her in hushed tones, likely trying to get her to calm down, but that seemed to just make her angrier. Now she was shoving him backwards, her two palms slapping his chest every few seconds to emphasise her words, until he was up against the wall, nowhere else for him to back into. I moved towards them at that point, not believing she could do any real damage to his six foot two frame, but also unsure what her end goal was. I remained at a safe distance, calling for her to stop, telling her it was enough. She ignored me and continued yelling until he finally grabbed her wrists, locking her in eye contact and saying the same phrase over and over again loudly.

"*Mi dispiace! Mi dispiace!*"

His apology seemed to break through and she immediately burst into tears, collapsing into his arms. He wrapped himself around her as she shook with sobs and I felt my heart drop into my stomach, finally feeling the depth of my anxiety at the situation after holding my breath for what felt like hours.

Eventually she stopped shaking, wiping her wet face on his t-shirt before pulling away from him. He chuckled as he pinched the material from his chest between two fingers, the wet patch where her face had been making it seem like he had sweat in odd places. She couldn't help but laugh too, and then turned to ask me for a tissue. I obliged, and she turned away from the both of us to blow her nose. When she was done, she walked up to me and put an arm around my shoulder like she had done numerous times before.

"I'm sorry about that. I think... I'm going to go for a little walk. Okay?"

I nodded, squeezing her hand.

"You want me to come with you?"

She shook her head and smiled, wandering off in the direction of the local town, disappearing around a corner and leaving Vio and I standing outside the library. Without letting anymore awkward seconds of silence pass, he led me to the cantina that used to be the old building reception area and ordered us both espressos. I told him it was too late in the day, but he just laughed it off.

"This is your holiday, regular rules do not apply."

I huffed quietly, his words ringing a little too true given the circumstances. We sipped and stared out the window at the boats, the complex a mile or so away from the docks with a clear view to the turquoise water if you were sitting in the right place.

"I saw the boy this morning."

Vio's words interrupted the meandering chaos my mind had become in the last twenty-four hours, and I was glad for it.

"Was he okay? Did his family come—I mean, was it just you?"

The words tumbled out, not really sure what question I was trying to get to.

"It was just me. But he is… okay."

I gave him a smile, weak as it was, and he leaned across the table towards me in response, a loose curl falling in front of his face that he quickly brushed back with his hand. Then he reached over, unclasping my fingers from my espresso cup, my hands clenching it tighter than I'd realised. He wrapped his fingers around my own and looked at me.

"*Mi dispiace*—I mean, I'm sorry about what happened yesterday, truly. Today does not make up for it maybe, but—"

"It—it helped it make a bit more sense, actually."

I looked back at him, my smile a more genuine one this time, my heartbeat increasing in speed as I remained aware of our physical contact.

"I just wanted to make sure you were okay. I think, maybe, I'm too used to things here. I forget, this is not… regular."

"Maybe not but, it's important. I've never been a part of something like that before."

I looked down at our hands, both of his holding my one between them, my thumb grazing his wrist, feeling the gentle pulsation of his quick heartbeat.

"The small things are just as important as the big ones. This is also an Uncle Andreas saying."

He chuckled at his own words, sustaining eye contact with me, and I began to wonder if there was something more he wanted to say. And then immediately after that thought came, I began to panic.

"I'll tell my friend that, he writes songs, he'll like it. My—well he's not my friend, my erm, you know."

My words, a stuttering mess, came out in phases and Vio's face slowly changed from humour to vague amusement.

"You mean, a boyfriend?"

The thud of my hand on the table rang loudly in my ears like that of a chiming church bell that was only metres away. His face hadn't changed, but his body language was something else entirely.

"Yes, sorry, I meant boyfriend. I don't know why I said friend."

His expression was a gracious one somehow, and he looked around, taking a deep breath and stretching his arms as he exhaled, tired suddenly. My heart sank, his change so immediate that I felt despondent. It was not unusual that to hear of Dee was to bring a change into most conversations I had with people, but this one had been rapid and unexpected. I had had no plans for my crush, but I had been enjoying entertaining the idea, even amidst the terror and impact of the previous night. Our flirtatious dalliance had for the most part been in my imagination, but once out in the open I hadn't even been able to maintain it, throwing a spanner, a Dee, into the works as soon as possible. And still, I was upset with Vio for reacting the way he did. I pushed my chair back and stood up, the surprise on his face telling me that I might have done it a bit more dramatically than intended.

"I think I should look for Amelia."

He stood up quickly too, reaching a hand out to me and then changing his mind and rescinding it before I even had time to consider what it meant.

"This one is not a good idea. She just needs some space, then she will be back."

"She's my cousin, I need to look out for her."

"I know, but—"

"What's happened now?"

Amelia appeared as if we had summoned her just by saying her name, walking up to our table, the three of us standing somewhat awkwardly around it. I told her that I was ready to go now, and she gave me a doubtful look. She eyed Vio and he drew his head back slightly, apparently afraid that she might resume her attack from earlier, despite her calm demeanour having returned. She shrugged at the both of us and led the way out.

We said our goodbyes to Vio's uncle, who had become enthralled in paperwork since we'd arrived at the apartment complex an hour earlier, and then Vio walked Amelia and I to the boat that would take us back to Venice city. Not one of us spoke the ten minutes it took to get there, with Amelia looking back and forth between the two of us in mild frustration, wondering what the source of the tension was.

I closed my eyes as we stood waiting for the boat, counting the two days I had left in Venice, anticipating the short plane ride home and the strange shift that had already taken place inside of me since I had first arrived there. When I opened my eyes, Vio was standing in front of me, arms out and waiting for a hug goodbye. I obliged, despite my proficiency for holding on to grudges for too long. As we embraced, he took the chance to whisper in my ear again.

"Sorry for before, I did not know you were with somebody. I did not want to give the wrong impression."

We broke apart and he searched my eyes for understanding. Instead I squeezed the arm I was still holding on to, trying to communicate that the message had been heard, though not entirely understood. The boat had arrived but was still docked, so I stepped on to it whilst Amelia also said goodbye to Vio, the two of them having barely exchanged two words since she pushed him into the wall. I looked out at the water, listening to the small splashes and sprays controlled by the breeze that had drifted towards us in the last few minutes.

The driver announced that the boat would leave in two minutes and I turned to see a moment that became burned into my memory like only a handful had from that trip. Amelia, standing inches apart from Vio, her right hand on his chest, his right hand holding on to her left wrist. The two of them staring into each other's eyes, breathing slowly.

I felt the moment so intensely that I wanted to cry out, but I didn't. Suddenly everything made sense, and nothing did. My fantasies about Vio, my crush from Venice, were extinguished.

As Amelia stepped onto the boat and sat down beside me, I heard her sigh, and smile at me as we briefly caught eyes. She placed a hand on my arm as I tried to turn back towards the water.

"Are you okay, cous?"

"Yeah. You?"

She took a deep breath again, exhaling her reply.

"Yeah, much better."

I bit my bottom lip, careful about my next words, desperate to speak them out loud.

"And...you and Vio, you're okay?"

Her eyes were the twinkling lights when the poetry show had begun; soft and warm, yet somehow bright. She shrugged, a half smile appearing on her face.

"Yeah. He's just Vio, you know."

9.

I returned to London with more stories than I could fit in my mouth, sharing them with anyone who would listen. I embellished some parts of Venice, of course—the way the light bounced off the canal waters, the romantic atmosphere that always surrounded us. Yet it felt less like an exaggeration and more of a reflection of how I had processed the trip.

Amelia and I agreed not to tell our parents about the shooting, but her father found out anyway and shared the news with my parents. They were angry that I hadn't told them when it happened, but their relief at me still being alive seemed to overtake any subsequent scolding they may have wanted to give me. Besides, my decision not to say anything hadn't been because I feared their reaction, but simply because I didn't want to tell anyone about it. I had no desire to relive the moment, doing my best to put the reverberating impact of the night into a compartment in my mind that I hopefully never had to access again. But even so, I did end up telling Dee about it.

I met him unexpectedly on a Friday evening in September. It was the start of a new semester and I had had a day full of lectures and warnings about how much more work this year would be in comparison to the last. I felt the stress already beginning to settle on my shoulders and counted down the hours when I could return to my bed. I made a quick stop at the local supermarket for essentials—food I could immediately stick in the oven to cook—and headed towards the two-bedroom flat I now shared with Donna.

When I arrived home, Dee was sat outside the front of our building, strumming his guitar and sitting cross legged on the floor, doing his best impression of a busker. I rooted around for some change in my pocket and dropped a few ten pence pieces in front of him. He looked up at me and smiled warmly. It had been six weeks since I had seen him last, somehow.

"I missed you."

With that he pulled himself up and kissed me full on the lips, pressing himself against me whilst cars passed by in the early evening. It was the first time he had shown me any kind of affection in public; we didn't really do that. I forgot everything as he ran his tongue along mine, and then pulled away as quickly as he had begun, leaving me wanting more, as usual. He took my shopping bags from me and waited whilst I fumbled with my keys and unlocked the door. As soon as we crossed the threshold of my flat, he dropped the bags and his guitar in the corridor and turned to face me, pulling me towards him again. He smelled so good, that to forget his smell and be reminded of it was a pleasurable experience. Intoxicated, we reverted to our natural state of being together, naked, intertwined, letting time pass without consequence. That was always the calm before the storm for us.

Afterwards, I threw on some clothes and tentatively began telling him about Venice, about Amelia and some of the touristy things I did. His face seemed to be going through the motions of surprise, then annoyance, then anger and finally upset. I was confused for a moment, until I remembered that I hadn't even told him I was going to Venice.

"You really just left the country and didn't tell me."

I feigned surprise at his unhappiness, but I wasn't selling it. So, I went on the defensive.

"You weren't even here, what difference would it have made?"

"All the difference Eckie. You knew I was in Lagos, I thought you were here. What kind of thing is that to do to your... you know."

I stopped and looked at him, the upper hand suddenly mine again.

"Dee, if you can't even call yourself my boyfriend, please don't come at me about not telling you I went to Venice."

He pulled a face, thinking, trying to choose his next words carefully this time.

"You already know what you mean to me. Come on."

I eyed him as he avoided my gaze. I had moved from the bed to my desk chair, the room now too warm to be sitting under covers. He was perched on the edge of the bed.

"If I mean so much, why can't you say it?"

I knew I was opening a can of worms, that we had been

sitting on this conversation for a few months now. I already considered him my boyfriend, had used that fact to shoot down what I thought was someone else's shot in Venice even. My friends thought of him as such, he'd heard other people say it in his presence. But he had never acknowledged it himself, and I never challenged him to, content as I was to just be whatever we were. But I wasn't content anymore. I stared at him, waiting for an answer to my question, hoping that he had one.

"You know I'm not down with all that label shit. It's cool if you are, but I don't think I need to say it for you to know how I feel."

"Well, I think you do need to say it. Otherwise what are we doing?"

He screwed up his face in frustration. Part of me was always a little proud of how easy it was to push his buttons.

"Is this why you didn't tell me you went away? Because of some label?"

I felt stuck. I could have argued back, defended myself, told him that he was being unreasonable and avoiding the real issue. But I felt a tiredness coming over me. I was weary of our fights, one of us always trying to get the upper hand over the other.

"If the label doesn't matter to you, this shouldn't either."

My words were a careless reminder that I was back home, back to self-doubt and knotted butterflies in my stomach because of this boy, this Dee.

"You'd be pissed if I did that to you."

He said it quietly and I felt that pang I always felt when I had pushed him to reveal some vulnerability. Apparently, this time, it was me. I said nothing at first, feeling like I should apologise, but also as if I would be showing my hand if I did. We were still playing some sort of game, somehow. Instead I got up and climbed behind him on the bed, kissed his neck, his back, the cluster of freckles just below his rib cage. There was so much I couldn't say to him that I relied upon our physical closeness for, to fill the gaps we left in our verbal exchanges. He yielded quickly, asking me to tell him more about Venice.

I told him about *Nuovo Modo* and about Vio, the bits about him that I felt were relevant. Perhaps I spoke a little too passionately about him at times. Dee began to smirk whenever I mentioned Vio's name, raising his eyebrows at certain points of my storytelling, grunting at the others. I wondered whether he was truly bothered that I hadn't told him about the trip, or if he was just irked by the fact that I had gone and had a whole experience without him which included another man. This wasn't a common occurrence for me, not like it was for him and other women.

I recalled with bitter clarity those first few weeks between us when we were still testing the water with each other. We often mentioned other potential partners we might have, like a sadistic game of emotional chicken. He told me about an ex-girlfriend who was moving back to London after living in Nigeria for a few years. They had been childhood sweethearts and she had just gotten an internship with a big record label in London. He mused wistfully about meeting up with her, and my stomach turned at the thought of them reuniting. I had no claims to him at that point, nor he to me, but in my head we were practically married. I was constantly running up to the minute replays of the first night we slept together and did not know how to make any of it seem more secure. So, I listened through clenched teeth as he talked about another woman.

"I don't know if I should meet her though, it's been a long time."

"Hmm."

"But she's interned for a few labels now, so she really knows the industry."

"Sure."

"And I know she'll have the hook-ups, she was always cool like that."

I perked up, suddenly catching on to what he was saying.

"So...this is a business transaction?"

"What? No, I'm just saying we're both about the music. She would be a good person to reconnect with."

"And does she know you just want her for her music contacts?"

He paused and then changed track, realising he had been caught out.

"I think it'll be mutually beneficial. Plus, *she* was the one who asked to meet up, so she probably wants something from me too."

"Not everyone works that way, Dee."

"You're being naive if you believe that, Eckie."

"And you're being duplicitous."

"No, I'm being honest. It's what you love about me."

And I did. I did love it. Despite my better judgement, even when he was ruthless it didn't seem to sway me too far away from him. But almost a year later, when the subject was me, my fondness for his attitude towards some things was waning. Venice remained on my tongue as he picked up on the frustration glaring back at him. He stopped rolling his eyes and leant back on the bed.

"So, has it 'changed you'?"

He made very deliberate air quotes with his fingers and then laughed, as if he didn't really care about the answer. But I had been changed by it, by the whole thing. I wanted him to understand, to stop mocking me, to take me a bit more seriously for once. So, I chose that moment to tell him about the shooting, how it had shaken us all, how protective Vio had been and how transformative he had made the experience for me. Dee looked nonplussed, and then quietly angry.

"Then, you liked this guy?"

I shook my head in annoyance.

"Well, you missed the point of my story entirely."

"No, I didn't. You shared a near death experience with some guy who wants to change the world and now you want to do the same. Isn't that it?"

"You're being unfair."

"I'm just trying to understand."

"No. You're not."

I wanted to leave but we were in my room, in my flat. There was nowhere for me to go. I hated being at the beginning of the fight, of sitting with that uncomfortable, rotten feeling in the pit of my stomach that told me it felt so bad because I cared so much. When we were off kilter, so was I, but for some reason I was pushing the bad feelings further forward. He just wanted me to be honest, I wanted to be understood. Neither of us wanted to give the other what they wanted. We were a mess. Eventually, he broke the silence that had been lingering.

"I don't care that you liked him. I'm just glad you didn't die."

I opened my mouth to respond but, as usual, nothing good was going to come out so I closed it again. He seemed to shift tactics.

"So, what are you going to do about it?"

"About what?"

"Well… it seems like you've caught the save-the-world-bug, so shouldn't you, you know, go and do it?"

"You don't think I will?"

"I think you talk a good game about a lot of stuff, Eckie, but you don't really do much of it."

The shock on my face completely unfazed him. He just shrugged as if he couldn't help the words that came out of his mouth, they were entities unto themselves.

"Good to know that's what you think of me. But yeah, I will do something."

"Well, I'd like to see it."

I told myself that his worldview was limited by his own negative experiences, that he couldn't help but cast doubts about me and my motivations because he didn't know any better. I wanted to believe on some misguided level that his pessimistic reactions to the things I did that did not directly involve him were all a backwards way of showing me that he cared. I would watch him from time to time, when I relayed some achievement I had made in his absence. He would sit with it with obvious difficulty. He wanted to keep me in a certain place in time, in his life, for reasons I don't even think he knew.

And I recall that he did meet with his old sweetheart from Nigeria in the end, and he called me before, during and afterwards. I was elated at the time, feeling like he'd chosen me again, somehow.

10.

I began to choose myself, and eventually other people. I started volunteering at an after-school club, helping kids with their reading and writing. Dee's doubts in my ability to follow through on my plans had propelled me into action and into proving to him that he was unequivocally wrong. And I needed the distraction.

Small things had become scary since Venice. I was finding the nights increasingly difficult without Dee. I knew instinctively that he wasn't the reason, that for once my attachment to him wasn't driving things. Instead, something more powerful and frightening was taking over. I would lie in my bed dozing off, sleep gently making its way towards me, until I was interrupted by a *buft buft buft* sound. Faint at first, it would wake me only a little, eventually growing louder than my brain could handle, the sound entering my atmosphere, pushing me awake, forcing a knee jerk reaction of hopping out of the bed, switching the lights on, my face a sheet of fear. After a few seconds my brain would get right, locate the source of the sound in my imagination, send me back to bed again. But sleep never really arrived after that. It was just me in the now too-bright room, unable to switch the lights off, my eyes wide and stinging. I was desperately tired but unable to close them without conjuring images of gravel and blood spattered on a box that used to be a stage.

The days were not as bad, not as jittery, but I made more efforts to coerce Dee into my company, or invite myself into his, covertly so as not to rouse suspicion. Obsession was better than fear. I knew deep down that it was a stop gap, though I wished that it wasn't. And even studying in the evenings became a trial as winter approached and the days got shorter. My heart became a panic alarm as soon as the sun went down, and I worried that I would always be afraid of the dark; an issue I never had as a child, finding me now at the end of my teens, laughing at my belief that I had escaped.

The volunteering job could not have come sooner. I initially assumed it was a response after the many emails I had sent out, offering my lowly, student services, but I discovered later that Genie had arranged it—my parents' high school friend. I was thankful, albeit a little surprised. And my nerves on that first day were also unexpected. I had managed, for the last year or so, to enter a room with confidence, convincing myself that the stakes were not high enough to warrant me stressing about it. But my heart trembled on my sleeve, and I wondered if this was just how things would be now. Forever a bag of nerves post-Venice, never quite the same.

The last time I checked in on Amelia, she told me she had also been sleeping with the light on, keeping company where she could, and that she missed having Vio around "to bug". They had spent the rest of the summer together before heading back to their respective universities, a childhood bond rekindled. I smirked at the pang of envy that still vibrated ever so lightly in my chest when I thought about what was between them, what they hadn't even noticed yet. It warmed and unnerved me, the mystery before the discovery, often the most enjoyable part of things. Still, in thinking of them I was calmed somewhat, knowing that the two other people who had shared what now terrified me were still walking and talking, in another part of the world but still reachable.

I entered the church hall where the after-school club was being held. A double-doored space, with old awning and scratched plastic chairs. I was greeted by Mavis who ran the place, a short Ghanaian woman who looked to be the same age as my maternal grandmother. Her hair, only a few inches long, was jet black with flecks of grey around her temple. I expected a strict auntie I would need to win over with hard work, but her stern countenance revealed only discipline and a tendency towards kindness most of the time. She was direct though, in both speech and instruction.

"Sit with them, you let them pick a book, and you sound out words with them, that's it. We'll move onto writing later, I know that is more your area."

I smiled back as best I could, worried that my abilities might have been oversold by Genie; she seemed the over-enthusiastic sort. But my mother would not be quiet about her disappointment if I showed her up in front of an elder, so I buckled down and tried to learn as much as I could, quickly, from the other volunteers.

Most of the kids were 8 or 9, save for one 11-year-old girl called Danielle who was staggering behind her peers with her reading and writing. But she was a quick learner, always wanting to read more books than she was assigned. She would lean back when she was done with a writing task, clasping her fingers behind her head, her heavily gelled hair slicked back so tightly that it looked like she was wearing a helmet with a ponytail at the end of it. Like the rest of the kids, she had some Ghanaian connection by way of her mother, a devout member of the same church congregation that Mavis also belonged to.

I discovered that the parents at the church paid Mavis a small fee to come out of retirement and use her 30 years of teaching experience to give their children the extra-curricular help they needed. I watched with interest as parents came to collect their kids on Wednesday and Friday evenings, and noted how Danielle was always the last one to leave and make the trek home herself. She would wait inside with us until she heard her bus coming, before bolting out the door to catch it, her yell of "Goodbye!" lost in the speed of her movement and the slam of the door behind her. She quickly became my favourite student, easy to teach with a boisterous personality, I was constantly entertained and kept on my toes. And after two months, her progress was such that I had begun to print off extra tasks outside of the club for her to do, wondering how she had gotten so behind in the first place.

One Friday evening, as Mavis and I watched her run out

of the door, I checked my phone, vaguely registering a text from Dee requesting my presence at one of his three gigs that week. I closed it and turned to Mavis, deciding I had more important things to do that evening, noting my stomach flip in a small way at the thought of blatantly ignoring Dee for the first time.

"Auntie, can I... ask about Danielle?"

Mavis frowned, or smiled, it was still hard to tell with her. We pushed chairs to the edge of the small hall space, starting our usual clearing routine. She nodded.

"Uh huh."

I took a deep breath, knowing I had to be careful with my words. *Come from a place of care, not curiosity.* That's what Mavis had said to me after my second session, when I peppered an eight-year-old boy with questions, assuming it would help him to learn. Instead he burst into tears, his anxiety triggered. I bit my tongue this time and thought about it for a moment.

"She's really smart."

"Uh huh."

Mavis' responses were small, and every new sound she made had the same tone, so I could never really tell what she was thinking.

"I just hope I'm actually helping her, that she's not bored."

"Ekuah. What is your question?"

Mavis had stopped sweeping and instead leant the large broom she was holding against the wall to fully give me her

99

attention.

"I just—I was wondering why she's so behind, that's all."

And then a smile, unmistakable this time. She picked the broom back up and began sweeping the middle of the room, taking her time to respond to my question. When she was done, she scooped up the dust and bits of paper previously scattered about the floor with a dustpan and poured the contents into a bin. Then she took out two of the chairs we had stacked and gestured for me to take a seat as she did the same. It felt almost ceremonial.

"Danielle was always a smart girl, but you know her mother, she has had some… troubles."

"Troubles."

I meant it to be a question but found myself simply repeating the word and imitating her intonation, like a parrot.

"She had to spend some time on a ward, you know? And she was back and forth, since the *obroni* had left. So, we were all praying for her."

I registered the concern on her face, the way she named Danielle's father, the absent white British man, as if he were an apparition or a bad spirit.

"So, what happens to Danielle when her mum's in the hospital?"

Mavis kissed her teeth, shaking her head with more energy than I had ever seen her express before.

"She was with a foster family on and off for a few years, the same one at least, we thought. But hmm, these were wicked people paaah!"

She clapped her hands together after she said it, causing me to jump slightly in my chair, unprepared for the crack of the sound at such a volume. She responded with her own jolt, her face switching to a frown as soon as her hands were clapped. Then she looked at me, shaking her head.

"I don't know if they didn't believe in school or what, but she missed a lot of it when her mother was away. So, when she finally came back, the girl was behind, and was nothing but skin and bones the next time we saw her. Hm!"

She went to smack her hands together again, to align with her exclamation—and I was ready for it this time—but she stopped herself, not wanting to risk scaring me again.

"Anyway, Pastor Vic, he asked us to help where we could, so we enrolled her in this club, free of charge, you know. We do what we can, and her mother, she's grateful."

I stared down at the floor, sliding my foot across it as I pondered over my next question being a smarter one.

"How much school did she miss?"

Mavis shrugged and looked over at me. But there must have been something in my facial expression that tugged at something inside her, because she began to rack her brains out loud.

"Okay, let's see. She came out of year 3 in the middle of the year… and she was around 8 then so… she's now in year 4, but she should be in year 6."

I tried to look nonplussed, but I felt a sadness sitting in the pit of my stomach, wondering what Danielle might have gone through during the last three years, whether she was secretly waiting for her mother to disappear into the hospital again. Mavis stood up, ignoring my increasingly worried face and jangling the keys to the hall in her pocket.

"My dear, don't worry yourself too much. You're doing well with her, and you're the first volunteer who has lasted this long with her in a while, which means she likes you."

She placed a comforting hand on my shoulder, and then ushered me out of the hall so that she could lock up. The next day, a Saturday, Dee sat in my room, fiddling with his guitar strings, humming quiet melodies as I tried to study at my desk. He stopped playing for a few seconds and then made a comment about how I was too quiet lately, almost despondent from his perspective.

"I'm fine."

I replied without looking at him, staring at a highlighted passage in a poetry anthology, unable to decrypt the message.

"Hey!"

I whipped round as he raised his voice unexpectedly. He was squinting at me from across the room, as if trying to see me better.

"What?!"

I really didn't have time for new games, feeling the pressure of my dissertation outline weighing on me.

"What's wrong?"

His tone was demanding suddenly but I had no energy to argue. Instead I put my highlighter down and turned around in my chair a little more.

"Nothing. I'm… I'm just thinking, that's all."

"About what?"

"You know, stuff, life. What happens after uni…"

He leant back into the bean bag chair that now sat in the corner of my room, the one he had purchased and insisted on leaving at my place, so that he always had "his chair". At the time I had laughed, amused and touched that he wanted to leave his things behind with me, that he took us so seriously. But after a few weeks of tripping over it in the dark, I began to resent the space it took up when he wasn't around. Now he held his notebook in his hand, his guitar perched beside the beanbag chair. I watched his fingers clench a little tighter after hearing my words, a tenseness I didn't understand, so I continued.

"Don't you ever think about it? What happens after all this, who we're going to become?"

"Ha, okay preacher Ek-wee-ah."

His chuckle felt false and grated against my ears.

"Well, we can't all be as cavalier as you. I want to do something I care about."

"Well."

He huffed at me in his seat, frowning. Then his face turned into a question.

"I thought you were gonna do something with writing. You care about that, don't you?"

"I don't think I've ever said that exactly."

"Yeah, but you read a lot of books and your course is—"

"I just mean—I'm talking about something bigger than

us, than right now."

He looked like he was pissed, and I didn't know why, but then his face softened. He put his notebook down and hoisted himself up to come and sit beside my desk chair by perching on the bed.

"What do you mean exactly? Like, God stuff?"

I rolled my eyes, aware that my frustration wasn't with him, but unable to stop myself from blaming him for it anyway.

"No, not God exactly. But like, a purpose. I'm just not sure I've found mine yet."

He stroked my bare arm tentatively, possibly wondering if this conversation cancelled out our no-interrupting-my-study-time rule. I didn't pull away, so he kissed my shoulder.

"Can't your purpose just be, being yourself? I love you this way."

"...What?"

We locked eyes, his words hanging in the air like a pendulum, my whole body imperceptibly vibrating with butterflies. *Did he just tell me he loved me?* He immediately averted his gaze and shot up, moving back to the bean bag chair with speed, assessing whether he should reclaim his seat or leave. He stood there, muttering with his back to me, so I only caught scattered chunks of his words.

"...Just like things the way they are, that's all I meant... future's out there... don't need a decision right now is what I'm saying, innit."

His last word was a sputter of familiarity, an attempt at a nonchalance we both knew he didn't feel. I stared at him as he pushed his notebook into his guitar bag with the guitar, before zipping it up, his erratic movements a symptom of the dangerous words that had already left his mouth, entering the coven of my room and unable to be taken back, no matter how much he wanted them to be.

He left shortly afterwards, his phone ringing and providing him with the perfectly timed excuse he needed to get out, telling me he was leaving me to my studies and he had some other gig stuff to sort out. I waved him off with a smile as he chatted on the phone, nodding to me as he went as if I were his buddy. I tried to compel myself to return to study but I couldn't. He had left me with an anchor of emotional significance, one that pulled me down deeper into a new level of affection for him. The word was already out; he loved me, even if he never intended for me to know about it.

Every piece of himself that he gave to me, of intimacy, emotional connection, replaced a small piece of myself. I didn't know why, nor could I figure out how to stop it. Instead I sat there and pondered whether he was right, perhaps I didn't need to focus on the big things in life, on kids like Danielle, on trying to do something better than just exist. Maybe I didn't need anyone or anything else but him, because he loved me. He loved me.

11.

"Oh, she loves it here."

My mother gushed on the phone about Genie, her voice almost unrecognisable as she described how great it was to have an old friend around again. The conversation began as a feedback session; my mother had heard that Mavis was singing my praises, and she wanted to tell me herself that I'd done a good job. The call surprised me, our conversations were usually reserved for exam results and assignment hand-in dates. But since I had returned from Venice, my mother was more open to discussions that didn't revolve entirely around my studies or my immediate future. She continued to provide input into those areas however, letting me know that Genie ran a literacy charity that was offering summer internships that I should apply for. I queried whether it was okay. I told myself I wanted to avoid becoming one of the nepotism stereotypes that me and my friends often made fun of—our attempt to make light of our frustration at not being afforded the same opportunities as our whiter, wealthier peers who were landing internships at companies owned by their parents or grandparents. My mother kissed her teeth in annoyance.

"Oh, it's fine! Take these opportunities where you can. Besides, Genie even keeps asking me if she can take you shopping. Apparently she wants to get to know you, separate from me."

"Why?"

She took a short breath before replying.

"You and her nephew, that Dee boy."

"What about him, Mother?"

I was curt, I couldn't help it. Her tone threatened a lecture and I felt a sudden need to defend myself before she got started. Her response was, in turn, defensive.

"Ah, don't 'Mother' me, did I say anything? But the two of you are… close friends?"

"Well…"

We hadn't spoken about him before, and I saw no reason why we should start now. It had never been an easy topic of conversation for us—me and boys—she having drilled into me early on that they were a distraction from the academic heights she wanted me to reach. But even though we didn't discuss those things, I had already suspected in my heart of hearts that her reaction to him would not be favourable. I refrained from replying to her question fully, but she got the message loud and clear anyway, and continued.

"Well, Genie says he's always talking about you."

"He is?"

"Ekuah, listen. He's a musician—"

"And so was dad when you met him."

The words jumped from my throat, as if I had had them

lined up and ready for this conversation for months. She just sighed.

"Your father was different, he was never going to be... something. Whereas this boy-"

"Dee."

"Yes, *Dee*. Genie tells me he's already meeting with record labels."

"... Okay."

I felt a lump in my throat. My mother paused again, wondering whether she was getting her point across. She decided she wasn't and so continued.

"The two of you, you are going in different directions. You already know this."

"Okay, Mum."

She sighed again and told me to call Genie when I had the chance. I hung up the phone with her discouragement still ringing in my ears. But louder still was the new information she had unintentionally revealed, that Dee was meeting with record labels.

He had been notoriously difficult to get hold of lately, but then again so had I. I assumed he was taking some time, trying to save face after revealing how he really felt. I didn't want to push him, or for him to think it wasn't alright to say. And I enjoyed having the time back, to throw myself into the after school club for a few more weeks, sensing how easy it would have been for me to spiral, to find myself immediately back in his bed, ready to forget my own personal plans because he'd said something I had been wanting to hear for as long as I knew I liked boys.

Yet still, regardless of where we were with each other, we had always kept in touch: phone calls, text messages, sometimes emails, updating each other on our lives, more open about things than we used to be. We hadn't even had a booty call in weeks, a fact I was suddenly realising and missing, despite resenting them a little bit on the nights I just wanted a good night's sleep. Now I wished for my phone to vibrate in the middle of the night on an inconvenient Thursday, his signal that he would come by in an hour, that he needed to see me. And because of this habit of his, I often knew his gig schedule better than I knew my own for studying. I hadn't seen him play in a while, but that didn't stop him from telling me all about them, who he met, what set he did, what his next gig would be.

But now I faced a wall of silence I hadn't even noticed until that phone call with my mother. And the last time we had spoken, it was over text message. It was early evening, he had wanted to come over, but I said no, I had to study and needed to be up early the next day to help at a careers fair the university was putting on, another volunteering event I had offered my services to. He insisted that I skip it, that we hadn't seen each other in three weeks, that volunteering wasn't enough of a reason for us not to meet up. I was tired, frustrated that we hadn't seen each other too, feeling myself missing him, but unable to communicate as such. Instead I was focussed on the either-or scenario he was presenting me with; putting himself between me and the other parts of my life, again. I told him that right now this was my priority, just as his music was for him, and we would see each other another day. He didn't respond. I assumed he was sulking.

I spread myself out on my bed, my fingers tapping against the quilt cover in agitation, my mind racing through questions. *Why didn't he tell me about the labels? Did everyone else know but me? Was he excited? Scared?*

I needed to know exactly where he was at that moment. I knew that if I could just pinpoint his location, then I would feel less like I was losing my grip on him, and on us. I reached for my phone, tossed to the side of the bed after speaking to my mother. My fingers began to look for him in my call history but then I stopped. I wasn't sure it was the right thing to do. Even though I wasn't the first person he had told, it didn't mean that he would never tell me.

My head spun as I hovered over what to do next, aware that I was slipping into game territory with him again, where I tried to guess his reactions and play to my imaginings of what he might say or do. I needed actual human feedback, but still couldn't bring myself to call him, unsure of what I would say without sounding possessive or self-involved, rather than wanting to just hear the good news of someone I cared about. I hopped up from my bed and stepped out into the hallway of the flat, listening out for Donna, but she wasn't home. I dialled her number immediately, perching on the edge of the sofa. I barely let her get a word in before blurting out what was happening. She didn't even attempt to act surprised that he had decided not to share a major event in his life with me.

"You did say you guys don't really talk about the big stuff though, didn't you? And I mean, you left the country and didn't even tell him."

I was taken aback, because I was sure I hadn't told her that detail, aware that she would have laughed and then told me it was a cold thing to do.

"We talk way more than we used to. And yeah, I went on holiday and didn't tell him, but this is a much bigger deal than that! I mean, how could he not tell me?"

"I don't know, maybe... maybe he's not sure you'd care."

I shook my head, as if trying to jolt the confusion out of it.

"Why would he think that?"

"Mate, you've got other stuff going on, that's all. You've barely been around this year, and every time he comes to the flat, you're not home."

I slid down into the sofa, somewhat deflated.

"He comes by when I'm not here? Why doesn't he just call me?"

"I dunno. But—it's only happened a few times."

She registered my anxious silence and cleared her own throat awkwardly. Then she tried perking up her voice to cheer me up.

"I'm sure he just wants to tell you the news face to face. You know what he's like, so dramatic."

I forced a chuckle out and hung up a second call that day that left me feeling hollow. I was unnerved by all the things

I didn't know about Dee, that I hadn't noticed. Were there things he wanted to say to me, that I hadn't been around to hear? I had to know, could no longer stand being apart, with all that was unsaid hanging in the dead air between us.

I took a tube and a bus to his place, going over and over in my head all the conversations we had had in the last few months, where there were hints at information I hadn't picked up on, frustrations I had ignored. And then I thought of all the things I hadn't said to him, things I had wanted to say but didn't know how. Bickering was easy for us, picking at each other had become a natural pastime, but affection when it wasn't physical seemed like a mountain neither of us was ever willing to climb. Someone always had to be pushed into taking the first step.

And when I came to his bus stop, beginning the familiar five-minute walk to his flat, it finally dawned on me, like a mallet to the head, that I hadn't said it back. I had not said *I love you too,* because I felt it in my bones, in the marrow even, and I assumed that it was obvious. I dreamt about it, let it swim around my mind when he was holding me, when I was holding him. And I had been lost in what I felt was a fact: the work to be done had just been waiting for him to say it.

Now I tasted how the words had never actually escaped my lips. Instead I spoke it silently into the air when I saw it glimmer in his eye, too used to words hanging in the silence, impregnating the space between, and leaving us in a thick haze of our own tangled feelings. But I loved him. I adored him, despite my attempts to prove the contrary.

I arrived at his flat, ringing the buzzer twice without an answer. I had already called him on my way there more than a few times, giving up after the tenth try, wondering how panicked he would be when he finally looked at his phone and saw all my missed calls. I leaned on the outside of his building until someone from another flat arrived and let me in. Once outside his front door, I knocked a few times but quickly had my suspicions confirmed that no one was home. I removed my jacket and placed it on the floor to sit on, pulling a book out from my backpack and settling in for the night, suspecting that he was probably at a gig and he would have to come back at some point.

But he never did. I fell asleep after a couple of hours and awoke to the sound of a dog barking outside, the moon shining a silver light through the small window in the building hallway, flashing across my drooping eyelids. I looked at my watch. 3AM. No Dee, a crick in my neck, and dread at the thought of another night-bus journey back to my own flat in Kennington. I dragged myself up on my feet, wrote a quick note on the blank back page of my book, ripped it out and posted it through the letterbox.

I was tired. Tired of everything, of the games and the angry noise between us and the even angrier silences. But I couldn't fix any of it without him. And it was clear to me then that I didn't want to leave things as they were, and I didn't want to leave us. But he didn't know that, and it came to be that that night, or perhaps even weeks earlier, he had already left me.

12.

It's funny what absence can do to you. Not silence though. Silence is an in-between thing, after the thing and before the next thing. With silence, you know that it won't last forever. Absence is something different. Something without a timeline, where you only know half the story. Someone can be absent from your life but still exist in the world, making noise somewhere else, where you are not, and you'd never know. Dee was absent.

Thirty days had passed since my pilgrimage to his flat, since leaving my note, asking him to call me, telling him we needed to talk. It had been thirty days of unanswered phone calls, emails and texts. I had begun to call just so I could hear the quickness of his voice on his outgoing message.

"This is Dee, I'm not around, leave a message."

I filled his mailbox with long silences and sighs, always ending with the same thing.

"Call me back, okay? Call me back."

As if I didn't know he listened to all my messages, probably deleting most. As if I believed that he just hadn't fully understood how voicemails worked, that he needed to be told that he should respond. As if I wasn't getting my message through. I knew that he had gotten them all, loud and clear. His version of what they meant being the only thing that was out of my control.

So, I let thirty days pass, and I hoped, and I wished, and then I just stopped. The day that I did, I got a call from Genie, his auntie, requesting I fulfil my promise of a shopping trip. I couldn't bring myself to tell her that there was no use for it anymore. That my role in her nephew's life was no longer significant, not worth mulling over. But I held my tongue, there was still a politeness game to be played.

When the day arrived, I was beside myself with anxiety, afraid that Dee might pop up with Genie somehow, pretending like we were buddies, as if nothing was wrong, as if I had only imagined his thirty days of absence. His nonchalance was one of the most dangerous things about him. But he did not show, and my stomach felt like a rolling sea as disappointment and relief fought it out.

Genie wore a red flowery dress this time, with a new hairstyle of blonde and brown shoulder-length faux locs. She stood only a few inches taller than me, but her presence was that of an Amazonian. She had a freedom about her that I had not seen in an adult before, and rather than overshadow, she embraced you as if you were the reason she glowed so much. When she spotted me at the entrance of Oxford Circus station, lost in the crowd of tourists and shoppers, she screamed like she had that first time we met in Johnny's restaurant, pulling me from the hoards with a grab of the wrist and encircling me in a warm hug. It was as if she knew what I was going through, without me having to say it. The sweet, citrus smell of her perfume stayed with me all day.

I expected that after exchanging niceties, we would have nothing much left to talk about, but in fact there turned out to be too much. She began telling me about my parents at school, although she may as well have been describing complete strangers.

"Your dad, he was so cool! All the guys wanted to be friends with him, all the girls wanted to be his girlfriend. The way he played the guitar, the piano, the drums. Hm! He could do it all. Every Sunday he did the arrangements, the song transitions, everything."

"My dad did all that?"

"Uh huh! You wouldn't believe it. The church had never seen so many teenage girls attending so frequently!"

"Wow."

I sipped my smoothie in mild shock as she watched my expression change and laughed in response. We were sat in Soho square, the smell of rain still lingering on the grass and in the air after a brief, spring shower. We rested our feet on the warm ground as we sat on benches, watching the occupants of the small square multiply as the sun came out from behind the clouds. I took a mouthful of my chicken salad, feeling like a grown-up having lunch with my cosmopolitan friend in central London, rather than the broke student that I was.

"It's hard to believe that your parents were young once, eh?"

I nodded and stared into the distance. There were a lot of things I was finding hard to believe. She took a swig of her orange juice and continued.

"I was in the choir when I met your dad. I had seen him at school but wasn't brave enough to talk to him there until he approached me during one of my first rehearsals, telling me I had a beautiful voice. We became instant friends after that, and then before you know it, he's my boyfriend. I could feel the hatred from the girls when I walked the halls at school but as for me, I didn't care. I was dating the Maestro, what could they say?"

I choked a little on my drink when I heard her nickname for my father. My amusement couldn't be contained.

"People used to call him *The Maestro*? Really?!"

She gave me a coy smile and then nodded with sincerity.

"He was a man of many talents, Ekuah."

I couldn't suppress my grimace at the innuendo she was making about my father, and her response was to nudge me with her hips and then burst out laughing again. She went on to tell me she and my father had dated throughout most of high school, until my mother entered the scene; a well-travelled 16-year-old whose father was a surgeon. My mother and her siblings had been living in the US for three years before they returned to Ghana on a permanent basis. Genie said my mother stood out immediately at school as she was intelligent, driven and completely indifferent to most people around her. She made only a handful of friends and was very selective with who she let into her inner circle.

117

"She said she only cared about the smart girls. The rest she could do without."

That sounded like my mother, I thought: strong-willed and disliked by some but still a leader. She and Genie became close only after they were introduced by the man who would become my father. At one point the three of them became inseparable. Genie spoke wistfully about it, the way I did when I thought of Fifi and I at school; hopeful about the future and yet wholly concerned with our present.

She lost touch with my parents when she moved to the US, but began to hear from my mother again when she would send her baby pictures of me. The conversation eventually switched to my own education and the future, as it always inevitably did with the parent-aged adults in my life. Genie explained her settling in London was mostly to do with overseeing the setup of a second location for her literacy charity, the head office being in Washington DC. She was passionate about her work and she wanted to know where my own passions lay.

"We have lots of internships coming up this summer you know, in our Washington DC offices…?"

She surveyed my face to get a register on my reaction, and I stared back at her blankly. Suddenly I couldn't picture myself taking up what she was offering, even though only a month or so earlier I would have jumped at the opportunity. But now leaving London felt blasphemous, for reasons I could never admit to her.

"Wow, that sounds amazing but… I don't know if—"

"Okay, okay. Let me stop before you run screaming from here."

"No, I just—"

"You're a London girl, I get it. We have internships here too, it's just a smaller team. But, I will only get you an interview if you promise to go."

She eyed me somewhat sternly for the first time. The pride she had been beaming at me all afternoon was diminished slightly. I was not as much like my mother as she had perhaps hoped, my timidity was of a paternal nature.

"I promise, I will."

"Good, that's what I like to hear."

Her smile returned as if it had never left, and she wrapped an arm around me when we stood up from the bench. In that instant Dee's name was on the tip of my tongue, as if suddenly reminded of their connection, that she might know where he is. But I said nothing, decided it was safer to remain in the euphoria of my time with Genie, she a willing mentor and me an eager student of life. I didn't want to ruin it by revealing who I really was.

We ventured into some of the shops on Oxford Street, and then headed back to my parents' place. I was eager to tell them both about the internship, to see the look of pleasure on my mother's face. I even felt compelled to show my mother what we had bought, even though I knew her interest would be minimal. We had never really bonded over "girly things" as she called them, but I knew that she harboured a secret love of fashion. When I was younger, I would catch her sometimes, flicking through a Vogue, an Ebony, a Marie Claire magazine that I had left lying around, staring intently at the fashion pages when she thought no one else was in sight. But as soon as she spotted me walking into the living room or the kitchen, she would flip the pages closed hastily and push the magazine aside, as if she were only tidying up around it. As I got older, I would try to coax the interest out of her, often searching desperately for some common ground between us beyond the same old back and forth about my school grades.

"I just found this top at H&M, what do you think?"

A brief look up, a nod, and then she would go back to her book. Every so often I would show her a skirt, a pair of shoes, some earrings, and the most I could get out of her was "That's nice" or "It's too short". I always wondered if my mother was interested in fashion but wasn't interested in me. Years later I would wonder if her apprehension was rooted in her fear of what a love of fashion would do to her serious, academic reputation, as if the two could not coexist in harmony within the same person.

When Genie and I arrived at the house, dropping heavy bags and plonking ourselves on the sofa, my mother was sitting at the dining table finishing off some work. She glanced up at us, smiled swiftly, and then went back to her papers. Genie gave me a knowing look; we both recognised my mother's furrowed brow and knew that she shouldn't be disturbed. I could hear my father faintly in the garage, playing music.

When I was about 16, the garage became his safe space. At the time he hadn't been able to find any substitute teaching work, and was averse to looking for something permanent, insistent that he needed the free time to give private music lessons and produce. However, he was not inundated with students for that work either. He and my mother fought daily about my father's unemployment status, and she threatened to sell all his instruments when he wasn't home, seeing as how he wasn't going to try and make money himself. In defiance, my father cleared out the garage one weekend, turned it into his studio and hid the key from her. He now had a permanent place to give music lessons, which he soon began getting more calls for. And my mother was pleased she no longer had to listen to his music, or as I heard her whisper sometimes in anger, "that noise."

I poured Genie and myself a glass of water and eventually my mother came out of her work-trance to talk to us.

"So, what did you buy?"

I couldn't think of a thing to say, so astounded was I at her vocal interest in our purchases. Genie took the reins instead and began laying out each piece of clothing and then holding it up for my mother to see. She mused at each one, made some detailed comments and pointed out which ones she liked the most. I was aghast by this open interest and engagement, remaining silently on the sofa, unable to take my eyes off my mother. Once all the clothes had been reviewed, Genie pulled out a little grey box I couldn't recall her buying and handed it to my mother who took it casually, assuming it was another item we had bought for ourselves that required her opinion. Genie watched her carefully, staring so intensely that it was almost uncomfortable. Then she spoke softly to her.

"I got it for you. It reminded me of that dress you used to wear."

She went silent again as my mother fingered the box for a second before opening it, as if readying herself. She picked out one of the earrings: a satin blue material pulled into a circle over something the shape of a button, with a small silver hook attached to it. She brought it close to her face and smiled inwardly. Genie appeared to be inching closer to my mother, still watching her reaction. She said nothing, just pulled out the other earring and slipped both on. And then just as naturally she pulled Genie into her arms and embraced her warmly. For the briefest of moments, I felt my presence in the room diminish as they stood hugging. Then I heard my mother say,

"I love them."

Astounded still, I sat silently as they stepped away from each other. I had never heard my mother express her love for any kind of material thing before. They both seamlessly went back to a cordial sort of interaction, which now felt wrong, incorrect after that intimate exchange. My father chose that moment to enter the room with a joyful exuberance, playfully poking Genie in the back to get her attention.

"So, you wiped out your bank account trying to spoil Ekuah, eh?"

He looked down at all the bags surrounding my feet and shook his head, chuckling. Genie ignored him and began fishing around in the bags, finally pulling out another secret box that held cufflinks for him. He exclaimed in excitement and hugged her too, but only for a second. Instinctively I looked back for my mother's reaction, but she had already returned to the dining table and her work, as if she had never engaged with us in the first place. I thought I saw her briefly fingering the earrings she now wore, but perhaps she only had an itch.

The rest of the day passed without incident and soon I was heading back to my own flat near campus. Only on the bus, after saying goodbye to Genie, did I reflect on the moment that I did not ask about Dee. I thought I should be proud of myself, for being strong and holding fast, but I didn't feel that way. I was simply making a conscious, and increasingly difficult decision to put him out of my mind. After a month of silence, he did not deserve my asking after him, my showing of any concern for his well-being. Now I wondered what he had meant when he said that he cared about me.

What we had been to each other was by no means perfect, but it should not have been so easy to cast aside. Now it was my turn to do the same. I tried my best to forget him entirely: his face, his hands, his stupid sarcastic laugh. I didn't need any of it. I felt angry and cheated of time, and my mind wandered bitterly back to my parents and the distance between them. Is that what Dee and I would have eventually become, if he had given us a chance? Now I would never know, and my real memories of him had already begun to fade. He was becoming a ghost of my emotions, of what I thought love should be and not what we were.

I believe it was that day that I felt the first cold suggestion that perhaps love does not last. Perhaps my parents had loved each other once, and long ago they had been a patchwork quilt of hopes and adoration. But now they were estranged. They had pulled at a loose thread until they had become almost completely unravelled, and neither seemed to possess the skills to put things back together again.

13.

The next year was a blur of moments. Genie called me to set up the internship interview. She mentioned Dee in passing, that he was on tour, really away this time, university on the backburner. She was surprised I didn't know, and then not surprised at all, cursing him under her breath. I recall sighing but saying very little. I decided my reactions to him now—to hearing of him—needed to be objective, stoic even. He became the compartmentalised thing, significant, impactful, shattering, but only if I let him past the wall I was building inside my own head and heart. Blocking him off made it easier to move on to the next moment, though there were slip ups.

I graduated in melancholy, so used to wearing a pleasant facade by that point, I couldn't really remember what my real face looked like, what my own feelings were even. I stood on the stage holding my fake diploma, seeing my parents out in the audience, my father beaming and my mother with a camera in front of her face so that her expression was hidden. Only then did I find myself searching for him amongst the sea of strangers, a faint wave of hope rising and falling in gushes, until my eyes gave up their back and forth and I left the stage. My disappointment over him marred the pride I felt in my own achievements, but my parents' elation was a welcome distraction. And I was surprised when we returned home to find Genie waiting for us, with a graduation gift for me. Her presence was a constant reminder of Dee, and it pained me to look her in the eye without malice. My mother was in a good mood though. She invited some extended family members over and spent most of the party in the kitchen, cooking and laughing with Genie. I was glad someone was experiencing joy that day.

And then on to the next moment, of my first job, an entry level position as a project admin, at the same literacy charity where I had had my internship. I was the youngest one again, after a final year of university pretending to be wise when freshers came around. Inside me a coldness stirred, and I moved despite it, making friends with the assistants in the office, sitting in on meetings about dynamic ways to educate and inspire, reading all the books I could get my hands on in the organisation's library. I was thankful for this connection. Words had always been a soothing thing. Even with Dee, being privy to his songwriting process became a thing that welded me to him. He had a way with words, a raw talent that captivated without trying too hard to do so. But now when I thought of him, I took a sharp left, playing word association until he was out of my mind again. And this worked for a while, for the most part. Writing worked better though. I began to pen bad, bad poems, lacking structure and finesse, but facilitating a catharsis that I had been desperate for.

I worked on one poem for weeks, about how young we were, writing and rewriting it, as if preparing it for something, for the rest of the world perhaps. But I kept it to myself as I did all the others. They were my version of therapy, of trying to manage the past and face the present at the same time. Things were shifting, yet my anguish over him felt the same, because questions of his absence hung in the air like the scent of damp clothes: enduring, causing a mild irritation that could propel you to rage if you were in the mood for it. I wasn't. I wanted to sit, listen, learn, watch those around me, remember that I wanted to do better, do something that mattered. I was exactly where I had wanted to be after what happened in Venice. And even though the rest of me felt wrong internally, my heart twisted up in memories and endless questions, I knew I was physically in the right place.

I held on to that, pulled it into me in a warm embrace, and began to see a small light at the end of the tunnel. My new friendships with work colleagues were flourishing, I was beginning to receive accolades from my superiors, I was facing prospects. And a big sigh of relief swept through me when Fifi moved back to London from Oxford. She returned to continue her training as a barrister, and I exalted at the prospect of us seeing each other regularly again. My naivety was quickly exposed when I discovered what the schedule of a trainee-lawyer looked like, but she was as excited as me, and we began to look for a place together.

I was still living at home while I tried to save money, and observed with new, slightly older eyes, how my parents remained in the same uncomfortable silence with each other. I worried that they would live out the rest of their lives this way, both too afraid to announce what everyone else was thinking. I wondered if a mutual Stockholm Syndrome was what was keeping them together. But none of my musings were based in fact.

"So, when exactly are you moving out?"

"Erm, I don't know yet."

My mother frowned at my vague answer and waited for me to say more, standing over me and staring as I sat comfortably in my favourite chair in the living room.

"We're still looking, we just haven't found anything in our price range."

"Do you need money?"

I laughed, which seemed to both surprise and irritate her, so I put down the book I had been trying to read.

"I feel like you're trying to kick me out, Mum."

"You were already leaving. I just want a timescale."

"Why? Are you going to rent my room out or something?"

"No, but we are selling the house."

I sat up straight, now fully engaged in the conversation.

"What? Are you joking? To live where?"

"In a smaller place. We don't need all this space anymore."

"Well I don't know if dad would agree, I mean, what about his studio and—"

"It's not for you to worry about. It'll happen after you move out."

"So, it's already been decided then?"

"Yes."

I sat stock still staring up at my mother as she stared back and waited for me to reply again. When I opened my mouth and no sound came out, she gave me a half-hearted smile and left the room, thus ending the discussion. I remained in the living room for another hour, attempting to resume my book but not getting through more than a few pages before the reality of leaving home hit me again. It shouldn't have been such a shock, I knew that. But it shook me in the way every new change had begun to, especially when it affected things that anchored me. And most of these changes were inevitabilities: graduate from university, get a job, find your own place to live. Normalities, steps in life that everyone was taking, that most of my friends seemed to be gliding through.

I was just a very good pretender. Internally I was warring with a tiny terror, small enough to push aside when I needed to, but mostly present and challenging. I had new fears now, ones I hadn't had before. Fear of change, of dying too soon, of sharing my feelings with other people. And they all boiled down to one thing; endings. All things end. Knowing that change was a big part of the process did nothing to calm my nerves. Instead all I saw were inescapable black holes of uncertainty and anxiety dreams ahead. But I still had my game face on, my will to do better than before, my desire to find meaning somewhere during my days, even in the small places. My life was going to move regardless, and I needed to find some way of moving with it. So I began to visit flats with Fifi, and at least act like I was ready for adulthood, even if I wasn't, even if it hurt to do it.

I began to pack up my bedroom, small pieces at a time, slowly and carefully, being sentimental with everything. I picked tenderly through unused Ikea tea lights and thumb tacks I used on my noticeboard, the one that rarely had any timely notices on it, just pictures and a ticket stub from a West End show I had really liked. I took the whole board down eventually, reviewing it as someone's attempt at trying to make the meaningful happen, not sure yet how to capture it.

I made a point to help my parents too, the house already sold by the time I had announced that I had found a place to live. I couldn't help but think my mother timed that a little too well. I tried not to give into the anger I felt towards her as the instigator of change. In hindsight she had never been wrong in making those decisions, but I felt strongly that this move wasn't going to be good for anything, as childish as that seemed even to me. Still, I went through old photos with my father, and helped my mother clean out her office corner in the living room. And although she was in good spirits about the whole thing, my father was becoming the house ghost.

Whenever I bumped into him coming out of the bathroom or eating a snack in the kitchen, he looked forlorn, as if the house were a piece of him that was slowly being over-taken by boxes. I had already suspected that the move wasn't his idea, that he was going along with it anyway, for reasons I couldn't be sure of. I was no longer privy to my parents heated conversations behind closed doors—now they exchanged looks and communicated everything through what I could only assume was telepathy.

And then one day, as I was packing up boxes in my room, he appeared in the doorway, watching me.

"You okay?"

He didn't respond. Instead, he leaned on the door frame and smiled sadly at me. Then he entered the room and sat on my bed.

"Have I told you the story of when we first bought this house?"

I shook my head, putting the parcel tape I was using down.

"Uncle Freddie helped us get it—you remember Freddie? Yes."

He answered the question for me, so I nodded in a small way, noting his liberal use of the word "uncle"; Ghanaian but not literal.

"Yes, you know, he was an estate agent, so he had found this for us and was holding it. We just needed £500 to finish paying the deposit, but we were struggling. Your mother had finished her medical training but now she was taking leave to have you, so mine was the only salary and it was… not good."

He laughed at himself as if recalling a fond memory. Then his face twisted into a frown, serious and still, and I tensed up for what might be coming next.

"I kept telling Freddie, one more week, just one more week, but I knew I was delaying the inevitable, and so did he. But he waited, and your mother and I, we fought constantly about it. She didn't want to raise you in the tiny one bed flat we lived in at the time. I felt responsible, that I wasn't doing my duty as the husband by coming up with the money. I thought, okay, I can't provide for my family, but the state can, so maybe if I leave, they can claim some benefits and…"

He trailed off when he saw my face: a shocked, mostly confused expression that eventually morphed into sadness as I tried to process the information he was giving me. I squinted my eyes at the thought that my father, so steadfast and dependable, had seriously considered making my mother a single parent. He moved closer to me on the bed and put his arm around my waist as I stared at the boxes in front of us.

"I didn't leave, I just thought about doing it. I know that wasn't right, but your mother, she had supported me over the years, made so many sacrifices for me, and I couldn't even do this? No. It could not be this way. So, I sold the two guitars I had at the time. One of them was signed my Fela Kuti, so I got the deposit and the first few months of bills for that."

"Dad!"

He laughed at my outburst, shaking his head and emitting a good-natured chuckle.

"Ah, my dear, it was a good thing, the right thing. If I had not done it, I think your mother would have left me, and we never would have had all those glorious years of raising you together. So, there are no regrets here."

He grinned at me and I found myself smiling back, selfishly happy and grateful for the choices he had made.

"And… I'm guessing moving out wasn't your idea?"

He rubbed his stubbled chin, grey flecks scattered across it that had made an appearance only in the last few years. The symptoms of stress and age becoming a permanent physical presence in his body.

"It was a decision we made together, and it's another good one, I promise. Just like buying this house; we need to move on to the next stage of our lives."

"But you'll miss it?"

"Ah, of course! But mostly, I'll miss you."

He gave me a squeeze and I turned and pulled him into a hug, feeling like a kid again as he managed to encircle me completely in his arms. Even then, I couldn't fully engage with how much I had missed him the last few years. I was seeing for the first time the distance I had put between us, simply by being away and growing up. We talked for the rest of the afternoon, about my job and what music students he was working with. Then he snapped his fingers as if remembering something.

"Ah, I completely forgot to tell you! Your friend, Genie's nephew? He's working on an album and I'm going to produce a couple of the tracks on it, maybe even a few more if it goes well!"

"Wow."

"You see, your old man hasn't lost it yet! I've still got some connections in the industry, old students you know. But when I heard his stuff, I couldn't refuse!"

He was grinning at me, elated with himself. I watched as his face softened when he noticed my own tempered response. A forced smile and rigid head nod were all that I could muster. My insides felt like they were burning. He tilted his head sideways to look at me.

"Is it not good news? You don't want your dad to have a job?"

I nudged him and managed to crack a real smile.

"Of course I do."

"But…?"

"No, it's nothing. I mean, Dee and I aren't exactly friends anymore… I am happy for you though."

He pondered my words for a few seconds and relaxed his shoulder as I rested my head upon it.

"Did something… bad happen between you?"

His question made me want to laugh out loud. I imagined he was thinking the worst and felt his arms tense up beside me. I lifted my head and looked up at him, to reassure him and stop the worry on his face. I had nothing left with Dee for him to worry about.

"No. Just nothing good."

PART TWO

PART TWO

14.

The good thing about time is that it pushes you along, whether you're ready to move on or not. It had been almost two years since I had last laid eyes on Dee. Yet somehow, I still hadn't moved through all of my heartache. I held onto a small anguish reserved only for him, where even smaller parts of me sometimes searched for his face in London crowds.

Things were not helped by my father, who I timidly requested give me no further information on Dee, especially now that they were working together. But he couldn't help but be a small messenger, if only to gush about his own achievements, at the expense of my worn-out heart. Essentially, he didn't know any better.

Dee had self-released an EP that was doing well. He had a full record deal. The recording of his album was being delayed until he returned to London after finishing the UK tour he had started by himself. I dreaded this. It left me quietly anxious, kicking myself whenever I felt excited, hoping that I would sense his arrival before anyone let me know about it.

Almost to distraction, I had been filling my time with

books and bars and new friends. I had moved to Camden. My parents had moved to a two-bedroom house in Greenwich, which I avoided for weeks, not quite ready to see them in a new home, with potentially less breathing space than before. Time became a clean separation between before and after. Before I graduated, after my parents sold my childhood home. Before Dee left, after he disappeared. Memories of him became bearably sporadic, few and far between. But when they did come, they flew by like a freight train, speeding through and causing my heart to jump into my mouth, and then disappearing again just as quickly, leaving the smallest change of atmosphere in their wake. I continued to use prose and poetry, rhymes and verse to work through the bits of my feelings about him that were seeping out of their box. I wanted to deal with them in manageable chunks, slowly and at my own pace, but my mind had other plans. So I settled for filling my notebooks with poetry about him and us and my life now.

Shan, a new work friend, picked up on my love of poetry and invited me to a spoken word night that an old friend of hers ran. It had been a few years since I had last seen poetry performed on a stage, live anyway. Ripples of that night in Venice had managed to keep me away, but my desire to go back had begun to outweigh my fears of what might happen, so I agreed to go along.

Shan was a tall woman of Sri Lankan descent, with blonde highlights in her silky dark brown hair, who spoke with an almost comical lisp. She was five years my senior and had been working in my office for three years, her youthful appearance and liberal use of the word "fuck" in an open plan making her popular amongst the younger members of staff, like myself.

Our singular bonding moment came when I walked in on her in the bathroom, staring tearfully in the mirror, telling me immediately about a huge fight she had just had with her girlfriend, fearing it might be the end of their relationship. I didn't know what to say, so I offered to get her a free lunch, as I was out to buy several sandwich trays for a directors meeting anyway. This was enough for her to take a liking to me. It was nice to be needed again, even in a small way.

Our friendship transformed my work and social life, as she made it her mission to take me to numerous bars, gallery openings and launches of projects from one of her many creative friends. She intended to "expose me to better things" apparently. I had no complaints, only a willingness to follow and see what else was around the corner. As long as I was moving away from what my life used to be, and who it used to be about, I was moving in the right direction.

We arrived fifteen minutes early to the spoken word night and found ourselves in the basement of a pub, the faint smell of bleach wafting throughout the room from a toilet door ajar in the corner. We clutched our drinks and tried to breathe through our mouths as we took our seats. I looked around the basement as more people filed in and I felt my stomach vibrate with nerves. My social anxiety had increased in the previous weeks, in anticipation of attending the event. I still had a sometimes fleeting, sometimes over-whelming fear of small spaces, of words and freedom, and a combination of all these things. I let the anxiety quietly slip under my skin, wondering if it might happen again, if death might almost visit us when we were at our most vulnerable, listening to poets spill the contents of their hearts, only to get one in the leg.

But I pushed it back down, as I always did, usually successfully. Only this time something else came back up. My recent number two fear, bumping into Dee on the streets of London, risking the heart shock of seeing him again, of not knowing what to say. Would I still be angry? Upset? Or just numb, as I had been for so long now? He was not unlike the Venice drum beat, the bullets, the ones that sounded like heavy rain, drowning out all the subsequent good moments we might have.

I sat back and closed my eyes, taking a deep, quiet breath. I tried to focus on something else beyond my anxiety as the room began to fill up with people. The audience looked like creativity personified; a snapshot of London in one room. Women wore fedoras over short bobs or long sandy blonde hair, or colourful headscarves cradling thick, soft natural hair, multi-coloured braids, twists, shaved sides and blonde dyed short afros. Men wore well-kept dreadlocks, twists, fresh fades, clean converse, Doc Martens. Everyone carried a notebook and seemed engaged in scintillating, artistic conversation.

I felt like a voyeur, out of place and time as people in

jeans rolled up just above the ankle, with colourful and whimsical socks exposed, paced the concrete floor, setting up mics at the front of the room where the stage would be. I looked down at my own overly-washed pale pink shirt, blue A-line skirt and imitation brogues; my work attire. I felt at once invisible and lost amongst them. Shan, on the other hand, was well-versed in their lingo, chatting with a few people and introducing me to some of them with names like Whizz and Bongo. I had to stop myself from rolling my eyes when I repeated their names back to them.

One of the dreadlocked men I had seen earlier came over to us and hugged Shan warmly, before introducing himself to me as Jay, the host of the poetry night, *The Light*. He had been running it for a while, and it had become a popular open mic spot on the London poetry scene. We shook hands and I thought he was handsome in an awkward sort of way, as if he had grown into his features without realising it. He was only a couple of inches taller than me, and I heard him curse someone playfully when they called him "pint-sized". He and Shan had gone to university together, and she told him it was my first time at his open mic. In response, Jay looked me over quickly with a curiosity that lingered. He saw me eye the stage with terror as Shan made a joke about getting me up there, and then he chuckled before leaving us to it.

He approached the stage as the packed room grew quiet and we took our seats at the front again. Jay was animated and charismatic with the microphone, making jokes in the breaks between each open mic poet, putting newcomers at ease, warming up the crowd with a deep, sometimes booming voice that rumbled the floor under our feet. Even my empty chest felt stirred by his vibrato. He performed two poems, both of which I recalled later when I was alone, almost word for word. And I remembered the goose bumps I felt as he spoke, little circles of skin protruding from my forearms, a code for each word that he performed. I was enthralled before his second poem was over.

Although reluctant at first to sit in the front row of another poetry show, I was thankful that I could experience so clearly every syllable, intonation and breath of each poet that took the stage. I fell in love with the written word all over again, in witnessing the magic that comes from the writer performing the message as they intended it to be received, the deep pull of a voice speaking of those things that sit within our core, that we often cannot make verbal sense of. And I studied Jay up close too, wondered at the meaning behind his poems, and even his jokes. He had a quality that drew people to him, an openness that didn't seem to question your intentions; these were things that continued to intrigue me long after he had left the stage.

Afterwards, Shan and I discussed getting another drink somewhere else when Jay appeared, helping to clear some of the chairs away around us.

"Ekuah… right?"

He pointed at me, waiting for confirmation, and I nodded, smiling a little too brightly.

"I just wanted to say, it was so nice to look out into the audience and see someone listening so intensely to my words."

I felt my face heat up, my embarrassment palpable in the dimly lit room. I clutched my jacket for comfort and attempted a response as Shan stood beside me, snickering.

"Well you were great! Your poetry was so… hmm. I mean, you're a natural, is what I'm saying. Obviously, because you're the host…"

I trailed off, wincing at the cacophony of words that had tumbled out of my mouth with little regard for sense. He simply smiled graciously and shook his head in a dismissive fashion.

"I don't know about that, but I appreciate the compliment."

There was a pause as we held eye contact in the now nearly empty room, as people were heading upstairs, and then Shan nudged me, reminding me she was still there.

"He's just being modest, he's won loads of slams before."

I looked back at him, my eyes wide with surprise. I was impressed.

"Slams, really?"

"A few here and there."

He grinned at me and I felt the goose bumps again, for different reasons this time.

"Cool."

Shan cleared her throat dramatically, obviously wanting me to say more but knowing that I wouldn't, so she took over.

"Jay, weren't you saying there was a slam next week you were doing? We should all go!"

Jay looked at her blankly for a moment, as if mulling over a decision, and then gave a grateful smile.

"Yeah, great idea. If you're up for it, Ekuah?"

"I'm definitely up for it!"

My almost exclaim was enough to make Shan snort hilariously, at which point she excused herself to go to the bathroom, leaving Jay and I in a sort of awkward silence that I didn't know how to fill. But he did.

"So, it's next Saturday night, in Brixton, but no pressure if you can't make it."

I could make it, and I was interested. But I hesitated, tried to think of an excuse not to go. I was suddenly aware of how close he stood to me, and it felt strange to be attempting an interaction with the potential for intimacy with someone new. Up close, Jay's face appeared slightly asymmetric. He was stout but strong, with a wide, purposeful smile. He had a boundless charm that didn't overwhelm, and the size of his personality was such that I could forget how standing on my tiptoes made me taller than him. He was not the antithesis to Dee, as I imagined I needed at that point; he was just different. I didn't know what to do with different, but after that night, Jay became persistent with his desire to form a friendship with me.

We ended up attending the slam competition together, Shan having conveniently double booked herself. On the busy tube ride home, my ears still buzzing from all the poetry I had heard, Jay turned to me as we stood by the doors that linked one carriage to another.

"So, you've not said—what did you think of tonight?"

I tried to keep my composure relaxed as I leant against the door, though I was too aware of how close he stood, holding onto the train via a metal bar to his left.

"I'm… still processing."

He looked at me amused, unsure if I was serious.

"Even me? I know I didn't win, but—"

"No, no, you were great! I just mean… it's like the words are still floating around my head, you know?"

He laughed and then suddenly moved closer to me, our faces inches apart as people squeezed themselves off the tube, struggling to step around us and all the other bodies out late that night. He smelt like cocoa butter and I smiled in spite of myself. When the tube doors closed again, Jay only stepped back slightly, so that now we were closer than we had been before.

"So, you're a thinker, yeah?"

I tipped my head from side to side, trying to decide if that was accurate.

"I mean, I guess."

"Yeah, you are."

I shrugged but stayed looking at him, at the deep green jumper that he wore over dark denim jeans and scuffed Nikes, all finishing off a look of cool nonchalance. The train jerked again and this time we collided, his dreadlocks tangling momentarily with my braids, before loosening themselves as more people exited the train. I hoped our stop never came, and then winced with embarrassment internally at how hard I had wished for it.

To my relief, Jay insisted on taking me all the way home, his residence just a fifteen-minute bus ride away. On the way we talked poetry and life and moving through the city. I wished I could hold on to the depth of the conversation for later; something close to the bone was being accessed by him and I wanted to know how he was doing it, whether I should make it stop.

"But you write, don't you?"

I shrugged and was sure I felt him frown beside me, as streetlights warmed our path and I failed at trying to bring the conversation to surface level. He remained silent, waiting for me verbalise things.

"I mostly just write as a sort of catharsis. To get stuff out."

"What stuff?"

The question came a millisecond after I had finished my sentence. Honesty was knocking on my teeth, begging to get out. So, I let it.

"Painful stuff, ex stuff."

"Ah yes, the ex stuff. Yeah, poetry is good for that."

"Sometimes. Sometimes it's just... hard."

We stopped outside my front door.

"Maybe it's hard because you haven't got all the bad stuff out yet. Or, you're not over it?"

He was asking me a question without directly asking, and I wasn't sure that the true answer was what I wanted to give. I didn't want him to disappear too.

"Or maybe it's just complicated."

"Is that your thing, complicated?"

I frowned, and then searched for his fingers in the dark with my own, our hands clasping briefly, awkwardly as he stepped closer to me and we stared at each other again. I willed him to move a few more inches forward, to kiss me so that I didn't have to think any more about what we were talking about. So that Dee could be erased from the moment, and I could feel, or at least pretend to feel, like what I was doing was tantamount to moving on.

But Jay just smiled softly, squeezing my hand before stepping away and walking sideways down the steps away from my flat. He waved goodbye as he backed away from me, now on the street, before disappearing around a corner. A minute later I got a text message on my phone.

JAY: We're going to see each other again soon, right? :-)

15.

Jay and I were, for a while, inseparable. I began to frequent spoken word nights throughout the city. If he was performing, I was usually there in the audience watching. I was vaguely aware of the parallels in my behaviour, of watching him like I had watched Dee so many times before. But there was no obsession in my motivation this time, no desire to insert myself, to fulfil that need of mattering. Instead, Jay became a way to feed my curiosity. He was a doorway back into the love I had for other things before Dee, like poetry and connecting with people. I slipped into his poetic, artistic life so easily, it was like I had always been there. And I never got tired of seeing him perform, of watching him captivate crowds in singular moments.

He let me into his circle of writers and poets and creatives with no hesitation. He was patient with me too, as I wrestled with the growing affection I had for him and my potent fear of getting hurt again, the same fear that reset itself within me every time I saw him. I stayed feeling safest in the cocoon of our friendship, aware that something more hovered, but without any real urgency to find out what.

As Jay's poetry night came up to its three-year anniversary, we bounced ideas around about what it should be. He made it easy to give opinions on his work, to feedback and debate; he believed that collaboration could always make something better. It was what he taught to his students in his day job as a secondary school English teacher. And discovering this fact about him only made it harder for me to stay away. There was something honest about imagining him imparting wisdom tentatively, exposing himself to the harsh and sometimes quick mouths of teenagers, some eager and others not so eager to learn. I understood it, mentioned I had done a little teaching myself in the after-school club. I think he laughed, not unkindly at me, but he told me that was cute, that they were almost the same, but not quite. When it was something he was good at, that he had been doing for a while, his arrogance made him buzz, adding to the line of electricity between us that snapped awake my dormant attraction to him.

I would brush such thoughts aside often though, to pay better attention to the task at hand: his anniversary show. He wanted to have music there, maybe even a dance performance, though there was hardly the space, and I took my turn to laugh at this. We talked about it for a full week before any real plans started to formulate. I discovered that talking to him was fast becoming one of my favourite things to do. We were in full conversation swing after seeing a film in Hackney: I had found it too dense, but Jay raved about the beauty of its depth as we sat down in the café afterwards. He had especially liked the music which brought back conversation about his show.

"Right, for music I'm thinking someone new and rising but not so much that they wouldn't consider doing it for a low, low price."

"Does that person exist?"

He responded with a shocked look, as if my question was a ridiculous one.

"This is London, every kind of person exists."

He stretched out an arm dramatically, gesturing to the café as if the people inside it represented the whole city he was referring to. I chuckled and rolled my eyes as he continued.

"You know I'm right. Like erm… this guy Whizz told me about—Naija brother, bad guitar skills, has an EP out—hang on."

He pulled his phone out of his pocket and began scrolling, looking for the musician he was trying to place. I was aware that I felt stuck suddenly, frozen on the outside whilst my insides were circus snakes, knotted and pulsating. *It couldn't be him. That's crazy.* I tried to talk myself out of believing what I already knew to be true, my lips taking the shape of his name, my tongue spring boarding from the roof of my mouth, the volume of my voice increasing with a simple, short breath.

"Dee."

Jay looked up, puzzled at first and then pointing a finger at me from across the table, grinning as if I had won something.

"Yes! D—something."

"No. His name is Dee. Dee Emeka."

He raised an eyebrow, puzzled once more, then glanced at his phone.

"Yeah, you're right. How'd you know that?"

I shook my head, though it was not an appropriate response. He didn't notice however as his phone buzzed with a text and he looked back down to read the message. I gulped my juice and felt cool relief slide down my throat. There wasn't time for that conversation, the one about Dee. I didn't want to make time for it. He was enough as 'the ex', more wasn't necessary. As my heartbeat tried to return to its usual steady jig, I didn't notice Jay smiling, punching a few keys on his phone, and then bringing up YouTube.

"This is the one that got me. I was like, what?!"

He grinned and slid his chair closer to my side of the small table so that we could listen to the song without disturbing the other patrons of the cinema café. But I couldn't do it. He was about to press play when I grabbed his hand suddenly, gripping it tightly, so that his fingers hovered over the play button. He looked at me, an eyebrow raised but with an embarrassed smile on his face, questioning. I stared at our clasped hands for a few more seconds, and then dropped his, resting my own in seemingly relaxed fists on the table. I spoke then, in a low voice.

"You don't need to play it, I know who he is."

He nodded, as if contemplating asking for more information before putting his phone away. But he didn't. He just continued to talk, as if he knew it wasn't time to go there. Not yet. I knew I had made it awkward but had no idea how to fix it. He took the reins and diffused the bad energy again.

"Well, he might not be right for it anyway, and I'm not even sure he's back in London so…"

The rest of the conversation faded into the background of my newly reawakened thoughts. I could only nod replies, unable to sufficiently suppress whatever was happening inside of me. Jay knew something was wrong but did not press me about it. The rest of the afternoon was quieter between us and I knew that eventually I would have to explain myself.

When I finally did, it was a week later in his flat in Borough; a one-bed that he had been saving up for from the age of 18. After receiving his first pay slip, he realised that he wanted a place he could call his own, something he and his mother had never had whilst growing up on council estates. It took him nine years but eventually he did it. He was the proud homeowner of what he called his "very own dump", a place that was anything but from my perspective. I marvelled at his attention to detail, the artwork from friends on the walls, the succulents around the living room, a corner that he used as an office. It felt like a home.

We perched on the living room floor, surrounded by open notebooks filled with poetry belonging to both of us, which we had begun to share with each other. It had become a semi-regular ritual for us, and one of my favourite parts of the week. We would give each other feedback and talk in depth about the meanings behind what we were trying to write. More recently, Jay had been compiling a chapbook of poetry and I was helping him choose his best poems for the collection. But now he didn't want my input.

"No not that one, it's not finished."

He snatched a sheet of paper from my hands and then began shuffling through the notebooks that surrounded us, searching for something that I wasn't sure existed. I refrained from commenting on his snappiness.

"Okay, is there anything you *do* want me to read?"

"No. You know what actually? I'm not really in the mood for this today."

He stood up and looked at his front door, and then down at me as I remained cross-legged on the floor. He was clearly irritated by something. I wanted to know what it was.

"What's wrong?"

"What's wrong with you?!"

I screwed up my face as the tone of his voice took on an edge I wasn't used to. I tried to calm myself before replying.

"Nothing. Do I seem like something's wrong?"

"The other day you got weird after the cinema, why?"

I frowned, taken aback, thinking I had gotten away with not having to address it. He stared down at me impatiently.

"I don't know, I wasn't feeling great…"

He began shaking his head and chuckling in an exaggerated way, as if my words were a farce. Then he walked to his front door, his voice suddenly deflated of the charisma it usually carried.

"Look. You don't wanna talk about it? Fine. But we can't

really do this—"

He gestured to the room and the notebooks on the floor.

"- if we're not going to be honest with each other."

I looked up at him, pensive. His eyes had that same glisten they always did, as if he was about to cry but never quite got there. And it was just as well, because whatever he felt was always written all over his face. He didn't shield like Dee, saw no reason to hide. I wondered if that came with age, the ability to give over to what you were feeling, even if it hurt a little. I dropped eye contact with him to look at the notebooks. I began to close each one, piling them up in one place, but I made no effort to move. Instead I looked back up at him and couldn't help but smile; the way he stood purposefully by the door, suggesting I make use of the exit without saying it. I ignored the subliminal message and patted the floor beside me instead.

"I'm sorry. Please come and sit down."

He hesitated, squinting his eyes, distrusting. After a moment he stepped back across the room and knelt opposite me, uncomfortably close. The scent of shea butter and coconut oil filled my nostrils. Internally I warmed, having mentioned a few weeks prior my obsession with the smell of coconuts. I wanted to grab his hand again in the clumsy way I had that first outing that we took, but I didn't. Instead he leant back slightly and put on a semi-serious face.

"Listen, I'm only staying if you explain. No more silent staring."

I laughed aloud and affixed my gaze on to the shoulder of

his t-shirt, avoiding direct eye contact as I explained, as best I could, my history with Dee. When I was finished Jay showed no surprise, just curiosity. He asked the questions I expected.

"Were you together long?"

"About a year and a half."

"Was he your first...?"

I felt like smiling, not for the memory, but for the way Jay asked about it.

"He was my first real relationship, yeah."

"So, what happened? Why did you break up?"

"We didn't, exactly. He just kind of disappeared."

"Oh. Well that's shit."

A laugh exploded from my throat, both for his quizzical look and his understatement. He just shrugged and gave me a sad sort of grin, sitting up on his knees now, and then twisting himself around until he was back on his buttocks, fully on the ground again.

"Can I say something?"

I felt tentatively open for comments.

"Always."

"I didn't expect him to be a musician."

"Why not?"

"It's just not the kind of guy I pictured you with, that's all."

"You've pictured me with other guys?"

He frowned and then stuck out his tongue, reminding me for a moment of Vio and Amelia, their interactions, a playful, immature comfort between them. Jay sat back and made an exaggerated thinking face before replying.

"I pictured someone creative but, I don't know, also someone with their shit together. Passionate but sensible. That sort of thing."

I nodded, breathing quietly as I contemplated his words and my next ones.

"And who's to say Dee wasn't all those things?"

His response was swift and measured and left me without breath.

"You. The way you are. The fact that you're here with me."

"Wow."

He caught a glimpse of my face and remorse immediately overshadowed his own.

"Shit, that didn't sound as harsh in my head, sorry."

I laughed. His face was suddenly so distraught at my feelings being a little bit hurt, I couldn't help but enjoy it.

"No, no, you're right. It's hard to hear but, yeah. Not wrong."

"Yeah, but I'm sorry, still. I think, maybe… my ego's a bit bruised, finding out you dated a musician of all people. How can I compete?"

I looked at him sceptically, unsure if he was being serious. I could only tease it away, not quite ready to have that conversation either.

"Wow, you really don't rate musicians at all do you?"

I grinned, poking him playfully in the arm. He just raised one eyebrow, rubbing the arm in question as if my physical touch were painful. Then he moved the pile of notebooks from the side back to the middle of the floor, in between us.

"I rate you. Isn't that enough?"

He smiled at me as he said it, and I felt in my stomach a feeling I hadn't felt in a long time; a flutter. We returned to our Sunday task and said no more about it.

We spent many more days and weeks like this. I learnt things about him, like the way his brow furrowed when reading something that didn't make sense to him. How his eyes, a light hazel colour, glinted in excitement when he found something funny, or wrote poetry, or heard poetry that he liked. How he could strike up a conversation with anyone and have them laughing by the end of it.

I felt closer to him as time enveloped us. And I had never had it that way before with a guy. His empathy was a giant thing that brought me so much comfort I worried that I was taking advantage. He reassured me that it wasn't so, that I made him steady. I didn't really understand how I could have that effect on anyone but decided not to question it out loud.

I pondered often about our conversation in his flat that day, wondering if who he described as my imagined suitor was just how he saw himself. I wasn't oblivious to the facts, but I was in no rush to re-engage with that romantic side of myself again. The side that gave everything without knowing what she was giving away, without knowing whether she would get it back.

16.

Jay's poetry night anniversary was upon us. An hour before it was due to begin, I arrived at the pub and took the steps down to the basement, ready to help set up as I had been doing for the last few months. Jay arrived a few minutes later and approached me, a concerned look on his face. He explained that Whizz had decided to do him a favour and got in touch with Dee directly. He was due to come and play a set after the first two feature poets were done. He said that it was too late to cancel, but that he would understand if I didn't want to stay. I tried to laugh it off, shaking my head and saying it was fine, that it would be great for the show. I squeezed his arm lightly in an attempt at reassurance before returning to my task of putting out chairs, ignoring the anxious stare he was giving my back. He stayed watching me for a few moments more, and then stepped onto the stage to test the mics.

Soon the room was buzzing with conversation and we were dimming the lights. Shan turned up after spending three weeks in Sri Lanka, sitting beside me and lamenting about her wedding-hungry relatives and their persistent questions about why she hadn't yet found a good Tamil man to marry. She had assuaged most of their concerns by saying she was actively on the hunt, but not being herself fully had taken its toll after three weeks. Now all she wanted to do was drink her troubles away.

I listened as attentively as I could, all the while feeling Jay's eyes on me from the stage. Perhaps he was waiting for me to spontaneously combust with anxiety? I turned slightly to look at him as Shan took a sip of her drink, mouthing the word *smile* in his direction, which he responded to with a smirk and a quick poke out of his tongue.

Shan noticed and leaned towards me to whisper in my ear.

"Is he alright?"

I nodded slowly, frowning as I thought the question through. In fact, I hadn't even considered it before that moment; whether he was okay and how he was doing with all the awkward moments I kept exposing him to. Maybe we needed to talk about it some more, because the Dee thing obviously wasn't going away.

Jay spoke into the microphone and the night began with powerful verse, of which I could recall very little once it was over. I was too busy focussing on the sparkle in his eyes as he surveyed the room, the sporadic warmth of him beside me as he left and returned to the stage, and the white noise of anxiety that sat permanently in the back of my mind. I found myself looking around at the audience, wondering as quietly as possible if everyone else was waiting for the same thing as me. For Dee to arrive. Was it crazy to wonder if they too knew what it felt like to be left behind by him?

Just before the second half of the night was about to begin, Jay disappeared upstairs and I felt my breath catch in the way it does when food has been inhaled too quickly; soon I would be choking unless I cleared my airway. I stayed seated and watched the steps as if my eyes were microscopes, focussed completely on a spec of something no one else could see. Eventually Jay returned, his face suddenly bright, glowing even. The shadow that had been hovering over his brow all night had disappeared. I should have been happy about this, but I knew what it meant. I hated myself for not feeling relief.

He made a beeline towards me, sitting next to me for a moment, a look of contentment on his face. He leaned in and whispered in my ear.

"You okay?"

They weren't the words I was expecting, so my nod was slow and quizzical. He smiled softly in response and then stepped onto the stage, reuniting with the mic.

"Hi everyone, before we get back to it, we did have a musical guest scheduled but he had to cancel at the last minute, so the mic is still open for the rest of you eager poets!"

He grinned, satisfied as a line began to form behind the registration desk to his right. He turned his gaze quickly towards me, moving the mic away from his mouth, his voice a silky assurance.

"Could you—?"

He pointed his head towards the desk and I jumped up quickly despite my disappointment at his announcement, and my unhappiness at how happy he was about it. I signed up the extra people and the rest of the evening's line up was quickly scheduled. I told myself I wasn't surprised that Dee hadn't made it. But I was angry, angry for reasons that only Dee might understand. His absence once again weighed heavy on my shoulders.

After the show was over, Shan invited me to a party but I declined. Jay and I had already planned to have a celebratory drink in honour of his three-year success. But once she had left, Jay asked if we could postpone, telling me the night had taken a lot out of him and he was tired. I said I understood, ignoring how the shadow had returned once he saw that I did not share his elation at Dee not turning up after all. I couldn't blame him for expecting a better reaction from me. But I hoped at least that he wouldn't see the relief on my face after we postponed our drinks. I already felt exhausted from having to pretend I wasn't feeling what I had been all night. Because I was ashamed of it.

*

I took the long way home, walking through the London fog of drink and merriment that feels so familiar for a Saturday night. I wanted to clear my head, make sense of the constant noise. And to face the fact that I still missed Dee, stupidly and hopelessly. Because to miss him was to also acknowledge the never-quite-disappearing sadness I felt, much like an injury I had gotten used to. What was I without my broken leg, arm, heart? What else would define me now? I tried to recap on almost two years of my life without him; I felt on my way to fulfilment. Yet there were still parts of me left that could not move forward from him, and stubbornly so.

I saw clearly the possibility of Jay, the many signs that he was not likely to realign me with the pain of heartbreak that I had come to know well. This was not his M.O. And yet, I hesitated like a scared child. I was Esther Greenwood of *The Bell Jar*, staring at a fig tree, watching my choices wilt and die in front of my eyes because I was so unwilling to commit myself to something. I wanted to move through everything, skip all this hardness and get straight to being well-adjusted, to trusting someone, to choosing Jay and happiness. I felt that I was dwelling in feelings that were against my best interests, but I needed to see them through to their end, even if I had to do it alone.

And then I came upon my flat after two hours of walking and musing, and I spotted Dee. He appeared as if in a vacuum of pitch-black night; he and I the only two lights in the atmosphere. He was sitting on the front steps of my building, under a streetlight, looking at his phone. His hair was different, freshly shaven, fashionable. His clothes, his shoes, even his forehead looked slightly changed. What a miraculous new thing he appeared to be. I could walk no further, frozen to the spot, eyes unable to look anywhere else; watching and hoping, somewhere inside, that he was not real. That he was merely a manifestation of my hopeless mind, tormenting me with delusions of what I had wanted six, twelve, eighteen months ago. And then he looked up with a blank expression of shock, as if surprised to see me, as if unaware that he had come to camp outside of *my* home, to wait for me.

"Eckie."

The familiar sound left his lips and crept into my ears, settling there too comfortably. I had no response. I could only move forward towards the door and past him, keys in hand. He stood up quickly. I imagined him staring at the back of my head. Or perhaps he was only stood behind me, his eyes focussed on nothing at all. I unlocked my building door and stopped, feeling the pulse of his body heat at my back. He was already too close. I pushed open the door and walked through it, holding it a second longer than usual, knowing it would allow him to follow me. We walked up two flights of stairs before reaching my flat, his fingers tapping against the bannister that led up to more floors, to more people and more complex interactions. I wished to be anyone else in that moment, to avoid what I knew I would soon be facing. But I wanted him to stay. And I wanted him to leave too. I slipped my key into the door, ignoring the running commentary in my head for just a few more seconds. But the lock wouldn't budge; it needed a precise jiggle to shake the mechanism loose. I told myself that I had no jiggle left in me. Instead I held the key in the door and stared at it. And then words began to drop from my mouth like small stones.

"I think you should go."

I said it almost too quietly, so that I barely even heard myself. But he heard me.

"Eckie—"

"Stop."

I jiggled the key, the door opened. I walked into the flat. Dee followed. Autopilot. Fifi wasn't home, I realised with a wash of relief. Dee asked to use the bathroom, a sheepish request made amid a thick silence between us. I hung up my coat, pretended he wasn't there. Resentfully I gestured towards an open door on the left. He entered, and I walked into the kitchen. I poured two glasses of water and brought them into the living room, placing them on the coffee table and taking a seat on the sofa, unsure what I was readying myself for. He joined me a few minutes later, sitting down tentatively on the other end of the sofa, the space of another person between us. He looked at me, his eyes wondering if he was too close, too far away. I gave him no indication of either. I couldn't look directly at him. I was as unnerved as I had felt the first time we spent the night together. And I felt rage, insurmountable and long overdue, like him.

He gulped down his water quickly, before muttering a breathy gratitude, as if he had just returned from a long walk in the desert. I glanced at him and saw that his hands were shaking slightly as he held his empty glass. I stared into my own water, holding it in my hands without drinking any of it.

"My Auntie Genie gave me your address. I told her I

wanted to send you something."

I said nothing so he continued, his words almost prattle-like and unrecognisable.

"So, I thought I'd send myself."

He forced a nervous chuckle out and I felt him shift ever so slightly beside me, causing a sudden fear to rise in my throat.

"What are you doing here?"

My voice, though clear, trembled as my anger quietly bubbled within the undertones of it.

"I wanted to see you—"

"Ha!"

The sound exited me unexpectedly, a ridiculous pitch that was a force unto itself. I thought maybe I was laughing, or at least grinning maniacally at nothing, my eyes darting around the room as I tried to gather my senses. I couldn't think about his reaction to me, only how I might regain control over things. My eyes found my glass again, following the light from the living room bulb as it bounced and flashed off the edge of it, my hands a tight grip of anxiety. I heard him sigh and it triggered me, causing more words to fly from the back of my throat.

"You want what you want. No one else matters. Tonight was no different."

"What?"

He looked at me blankly, his eyes creased in a hovering question.

"My friend, he booked you for a spoken word gig tonight

and you didn't show up. You haven't changed."

"What are you—wait. That thing tonight, you were there? I didn't know, I would have come..."

He trailed off, realising there wasn't any point in continuing. Then he started again.

"So, you're friends with this guy? The poetry guy?"

I looked at him fully for the first time and felt an odd pain in my chest.

"Why do you care?"

He squinted his eyes again, gripping me in a piercing stare I suddenly couldn't look away from.

"You know why Eckie. And… look I'm here—"

"After almost two years."

I silently cursed myself for revealing my monitoring of the time that had passed between us, as if further exposing my vulnerabilities.

"I know, I fucked up. I'm not even gonna say sorry, 'cos I know it's not enough."

It dawned on me then, that he had been practising this. He had run through our conversation perhaps dozens of times by himself, unsure what my reaction might be, what countenance he would find me in. He had tried to prepare for every eventuality, and I was unprepared for all of them. I leant back on the sofa, dropping my eyes down to examine my hands, buy myself some composure time. Eventually I turned back towards him, looking instead at his clothes, avoiding his face.

"You look different. Grown up."

"In a good way?"

I caught a glimpse of his grin, the one that made his eyes bright and his presence a welcome thing, and I resisted every urge to punch him in his perfect face. Perfect still to me, somehow. I pursed my lips and shrugged, feeling a tiredness coursing through my veins. It was already past midnight.

"Just different. More like yourself. Like you know who you are now."

He gave me a look of sincerity in response, his hand reaching towards me but stopping before it touched me, landing on the space between us instead.

"I do, you know, know who I am. What you always knew about me I guess."

"And yet I stuck around anyway."

He paused, unsure how much I meant it, until I burst out laughing callously, trying to cackle away my anger and replace it with bitterness. I hoped that eventually a sweetness would follow, because the alternative had been taking something good from me. He took it in his stride, clutching his chest dramatically.

"Ouch."

I gave a more genuine satisfied smile this time, and finally took a sip of my water, lukewarm now from my sweaty palms. Perhaps something had shifted between us. He continued to watch me with familiar eyes, and I continued to look down into my glass.

"I really missed you Eckie."

I wanted to tell him that his words could not begin to

repair the damage that had long since been done. That for a time I had felt helpless without him, and at times I still did, in a secret, self-destructive way. And so, I had locked up that part of me, hoping I would never have to release it again, that the other, stronger bits of me would prevail. But just the sight of him had let the helpless me out, running rampant across my feelings, touching parts of me that no longer felt that way. So him telling me he missed me only reminded me of what was already lost, of damage already done, of heartbreak that felt irreparable.

But instead, I sipped my water.

17.

His body looked almost exactly the same. Taut and toned, but not as effortlessly kept anymore. I laughed when Dee said he was going to the gym now to "work on his core". I found it funny that he cared about such things. I coupled my remarks with a squeeze of his flexed bicep; it was like holding a warm, grainy stone in my hand.

We lay together again, naked and full. He was the colour of dark mahogany these days, strong and weathered but more beautiful for it, from weekend trips to sunnier climes throughout Europe. After a myriad of intoxicating moments between us, I did not care where he had been, only that he was back. I pushed down the voice that told me this was a mistake, one that I had made so easily because it felt like returning to a desperate habit whilst it was happening.

*

A long moment of silence had passed between us on the sofa, and I found myself finishing my water, taking both our empty glasses to the kitchen. I had needed to busy myself, fill my hands with something other than him again. But he followed me, stepping over a few broken kitchen floor tiles, ignoring them. We'd been waiting for the landlord to fix them for weeks. I thought about this and other irrelevant things as I washed the glasses, listening to him breathing quietly behind me, leaning on the side of the kitchen counter. I dried my hands, slowly turning to face him. He looked as though he was trying to figure something out in his head before he articulated it. He lifted his face slightly, his eyes pointed to the top corner of the kitchen window, so as not to look at me, I supposed.

"I haven't—"

He stopped, stroking his smooth face as he continued thinking, the absence of a beard giving him some of his youth back.

"I haven't written any new songs, for a long time."

I sighed, waiting for more, not knowing what words I was meant to use in response.

"I think my music and us became sort of, linked. Like, my inspiration I mean, it came from…"

He gestured to me with his hand, a kind of slow swat in the air in my general direction.

"You think?"

I couldn't help myself, my words the only defence I had in trying to cull his attempts to infiltrate my space. The same space I had let him back into, I reminded myself bitterly. But he ignored the sting in my voice.

"Yeah, I do. Especially after we would… you know."

His face crept into a smirk, a small but arrogant one

that I knew he couldn't help. I scoffed loudly, my own smile one of disbelief as I backed away from him, out of my tiny kitchen and back into the living room.

"So *that's* why you're here!"

Livid, I felt my rage finally able to stretch its legs. It had been waiting with bated breath for him to say anything that sounded remotely like the wrong thing. Which is to say, I had been waiting for him to open his mouth fully. I picked up his jacket from the sofa, crumpling the leather in my fist and then hurling it in his general direction. He jumped back and twisted his body away from me so that it hit his shoulder and landed in a heap on the floor at his feet. For some reason this made me even angrier. And him too apparently.

"Jesus, Eckie!"

"Don't call me that! Just, please—leave now before you make it worse."

I sighed big and stayed standing in the middle of the room, my arms folded in a last-ditch attempt at protecting myself. He remained, just as defiantly, in the same spot.

"No."

My eyes widened as if catching sight of a blaze.

"No? Are you joking?"

"I'm not going. And I know you don't really want me to. We need to talk."

"Oh, *now* we need to talk? Because you've decided? Because you have no idea what you even did… I mean— what the fuck, Dee?!"

"I'm saying that I'm sorry! I shouldn't have left like that, okay? But like, you were done with us already, before that. I wasn't enough for you, like, I get it now. But I… I missed you everyday, Eckie. Every day, okay? So yeah. That's it."

I felt my whole body deflate against my will, the words I had lined up for retaliation losing their power and becoming just a jumble of letters in my head. Why didn't this feel like a fight anymore? I thought I should defend myself from his accusations, but I couldn't muster it. I didn't want it to be true.

"I don't believe you."

He stepped closer immediately, again anticipating my response, stepping over his jacket and moving towards me until there was nothing but a couple of inches of space between us. Then he tipped his head to one side, placing a hand to my neck gently and bringing his lips to my ear, so that his whisper was a loudspeaker in my head.

"Yes, you do."

I felt the warmth of his breath on my face and the crackle of electricity between us, that spark that had never quite gone out. He pulled his head back to look at me, to see how his words had landed, but I couldn't focus on anything but the thunderous roar in my chest. And his hand was still on my neck, and I wondered how the hell I had let him get this close again, and I knew that it was too late. His words were already poised, his audience already captive.

"I know you've missed me too, Eckie. Haven't you?"

"No."

The word escaped my mouth as more of a moan, my lie

so blatant, so transparent, that he surged forwards and our lips melted together in a blur of a moment that felt like wood on bone. My vision was in and out of focus as I struggled to keep my eyes off him. He pulled my arms around him, my body responding quickly, betraying what I knew to be logical. That once resolute voice of certainty, the one that had kept me going for almost two years, was still present but growing weaker by the minute.

He left you. He's going to leave again. Don't do this.

But that message was lost in the tangle and twist of our bodies, already naked together on the sofa, muscle memory taking over completely. My hands still remembered the backs of his thighs, the strong buttocks to hold onto, the face to kiss. The voice in my head became a faint whisper, and then suddenly changed in tone and direction, reclaiming its volume.

Keep going. You want this. You missed him so much.

*

Eventually we ended up in my bed. Afterwards, he told me that I smelt like poetry and I laughed, asking him how many other women he had said that to. He frowned and told me I was the only one, as if I should have assumed as much. I didn't say anymore, just continued sliding my finger up and down his arm, the hairs responding to my touch, somehow. He wondered out loud how much time I had been spending in the poetry community, and what new things I had learnt since he had last seen me. I told him I was writing more, that I had been working with someone creatively, with Jay. Slowly he slid his arm out from behind my shoulders, propping himself up in my bed. How familiar that movement felt.

"So, you write with this guy?"

His face was an uncomfortable sight. My mentioning of Jay had bothered him, as part of me knew that it would.

"Sometimes yeah, we're friends. We share stuff."

"You never shared stuff with me before."

"Well. You weren't here."

He gave me a childish frown, as if mentioning his absence was now forbidden. I was never going to agree to that.

"Well… I'm here now. Show me something."

I eyed him suspiciously, before sliding out of the bed and rifling through my pile of notebooks, naked in the lamplight; no longer shy around him, only cautious. It was almost two in the morning, but I resisted sleep. I feared closing my eyes and losing sight of him again. I showed him an old poem called *Young Life*, the one I had written after he had left. He said he liked it, asked me what it was about. I sat down beside him and rested my forehead on his shoulder, saying nothing. He watched me as realisation gently crawled across his face.

"Oh. Right."

He threw the covers back over us and then pulled me towards him, letting the notebook of poems rest on the other end of the bed. He kissed my shoulder lightly, sliding his nose across it. I didn't want any of it to end, despite knowing it was a bubble, a moment of a dream, where we were close and comfortable with each other as if nothing had happened and no time had passed. He reached for the notebook again and opened the page where the poem was written.

"Can I make a copy of it? It's so… you. A reminder of you, when we're away from each other."

"Otherwise you'd forget me?"

He looked up, disappointed in my commitment to hold onto my distrust of him, despite the way his legs were tangled with mine under the sheets.

"Come on, you know what I mean."

"You can have it, if it means that much to you."

"*You* mean that much. You don't know that by now?"

My face confirmed his suspicion, but no words left my lips, so he kissed them passionately, causing a breathy sound to escape both our mouths afterwards. We stared at each other and I saw again the glimmer of something I was far too familiar with.

"You're going, aren't you?"

He hesitated, watching my face change slowly.

"I… have a thing in the morning, I…"

I pulled away from his embrace methodically, as if I had been planning to all along, as if I was just waiting for the right trigger word. I climbed out of the bed and grabbed the dressing gown that hung on the back of my door. Once I was fully wrapped up in it, I began picking up his clothes from my bedroom floor. I handed them to him.

"You don't need to stay over then."

I felt things inside me, things that had opened up just hours earlier for the first time in months, slowly begin to close again. He grabbed my hand and ignored the clothes.

"It's late, let's not do this now."

"Are you refusing to leave my bed?"

I pulled my hand from his half-hearted grip, but he clutched the belt of my dressing gown instead.

"No, I'll go if you want me to… do you want me to?"

"No."

"Then what—"

"I don't want you to go and not come back again for another two years. You either stay if you're going to stay, or go now, for good."

"We can't just take it one night at a time?"

"Which night to which? Today until another month down the line? Next year?"

"I want you, Eckie. Why isn't that enough?"

I exhaled loudly, felt my composure slipping gradually from my grasp. He held on firmly to my belt, looking up at me with that sincere but misguided expression. I held fast, as if I was unfazed by it.

"Stay or go, which one?"

He continued to stare at me, realising my question was a serious one, that it was entirely his decision to make. He used his other hand to cradle my lower back, and gently pulled me to him until his nose touched my stomach.

"Stay, of course."

"Okay then."

I crawled back into the bed. He scooped me up in his arms and I felt my eyes droop, exhausted from the way he had ravished me, physically, emotionally, maybe even spiritually. I felt spent. My reserves were depleted as his warm skin sustained my own, heated my flesh, my bones. I wanted to relax into him again, to fully feel the close way that he held me, but I could not. At my core I felt a cold chill. I knew that we were doing this again, that we were different people than the last time and yet, we were doing this again.

Only this time we had the knowledge that if one of us left, we would still survive. We hadn't known that before.

18.

My time was Dee's again, and after a handful of weeks, I felt that things were good. He was back. And I had my eyes wide open this time, taking in everything around me with a fuller consciousness. I noticed the way he watched me when a small flash of creativity struck me, and I scribbled out bits of poetry in my notebook before leaving for work. The way he now handled me with care when we said goodbye to each other, his chaste kisses and prolonged hugs a reassurance that he would be back later. The way he checked in regularly with text messages when we were apart to tell me he was thinking about me. On principle alone, I appreciated the gestures, though they felt strange as they were happening.

He also began to spend most nights at my place, often arriving when the sun had gone down, after Fifi had retired to her room following a long day of work and study. I considered trying to manoeuvre things so that they never crossed paths, and then decided against it. What could Fifi say that I did not already know? He eventually bumped into us outside of my building, Fifi and I on our way out to share her first Saturday afternoon in a while that would not involve work.

Dee greeted her sheepishly, as if apologising for his presence before she made him. She simply raised her eyebrows, surprised to see him—I hadn't exactly announced his return. Then she suggested meeting me at the bus stop and disappeared around the corner before I could protest.

"Sorry, we're on our way to a thing."

"That's cool, I just had a few hours before a label meeting so… yeah."

We stood a few inches apart, not touching. I felt the pull to him but was aware of how much safer I felt not being in his embrace in that moment. He seemed to sense this, my withdrawal and imminent departure, and tugged me towards him by grabbing the zip side of my jacket. I let him move me, let him kiss me with a passion and control I could never fully detach myself from, until he was ready to let me. Only this time I did, and my stomach dropped as I forced myself to pull away from him, a mixture of frustration and sadness levelling my gut. He smiled at me satisfied, as if he had won the moment, successfully reminding me of what I would be missing if I left now. And then I left.

I waited for Fifi to say something when I caught up with her again, but she refused to engage, choosing instead to talk about the new job she had gotten, clerking in the youth justice department whilst she continued studying for her full licence to practice. I played along for approximately five minutes until I couldn't hold it in any longer.

"I'm sorry I didn't tell you he was back, but—"

"You know I don't care. Not like you think."

"Oh, well. Great."

She gave me a look of annoyance, as if I was being deliberately obtuse, which I was. I needed a reaction from her, even if it was the reality check I wasn't ready to hear.

"Listen, I care if you're happy, that's it. So, are you?"

I frowned at her, her question unexpected, even though I should have seen it coming.

"I don't know yet."

She exhaled a big sigh, as if the conversation were a tiresome one.

"Don't you think that's something you should already know?"

She was looking at me uncharacteristically, with sincerity. I realised that she was worried about me, about the precarious situation I had found myself in again. All I could do was shrug, so alarmed was I by her open show of emotion, an action so counter to what I was used to from her. I knew then that I was expected to take this a bit more seriously.

Instead I waited for him at night with my eyes wide open, lying in bed, staring into darkness. My mind was awake once his thighs pressed against mine, his hand on my back or shoulder or waist, things whispered to me until I eventually gave into distraction for an hour. Then we would separate from each other and he would fall asleep. At some point I would struggle into my own broken sleep, my head full of a buzzing nothing.

Soon enough I found myself regularly waking up in the early hours of the morning, too early to start getting ready for work, leaving the routine of limbs intertwined in sleep that we had fallen into. Once away, I would tiptoe into the kitchen and open the tap, watching the stream of water as it disappeared into my cup, the street lamp outside the window making the liquid twinkle. I was a shadow in the night, warmed by the thought of Dee in my bed but still wrestling internally with something. I wanted contentment to come, needed it to, if for no other reason than to get a good night's sleep. But the thing that was getting in the way had grown over the last few weeks, and finally it had begun to show its face. I stared out of the window and found my guilty thoughts wandering back to Jay.

We hadn't seen each other since Dee had returned. Jay had called me a few days after his anniversary show, but I couldn't bring myself to answer. I knew that if I spoke to him, I would have to tell the truth, admit that what was blossoming between us was secondary, that I wasn't done with my first thing yet. Not yet. Eventually I mustered up the courage to call Jay back and found myself explaining my absence in a vague, less than truthful way. His voice only met my excuses with sincerity and friendliness, without a hint of hostility. I promised to meet up with him soon, to resume our poetry review sessions, once I squared away this new thing that had arisen. In the meantime, I tried to bridge the new gap between us, the one that I had created with infrequent text messages filled with nothing at all. I failed at relieving my own guilt over disappearing, by trying to enforce a normality and falseness that hadn't previously haunted our friendship. Jay's text replies were in turn enthusiastic at first, before reducing in length as the exchanges went on, increasingly leaving me wanting more. He was an accomplished poet, published in anthologies, a teacher of English, guiding children in how to communicate, analyse, understand words. But he no longer gave me the privilege of his language skills, and I could not blame him for any of it. I sensed that he was giving me a way out before I had to ask for it. And so, the days turned into weeks without us speaking, and I was left alone with my anger at the mess I had caused, at the loss I felt over my friend.

I didn't mention any of it to Dee. Instead I waited, for what I wasn't sure. But then a time came when he had to be away for a week, to play a festival up north. He held onto me tightly in the days leading up to his trip, even turning up outside my office to take me to lunch, a thing we never used to do. He was attentive and interested, and I was suspicious. I found myself counting down the hours until he left, to give me a week off, to sit and think about the whirlwind we had thrown ourselves back into. And I suspected that he knew it, that he didn't want me to have time to ponder over things in case I changed my mind, saw the light. But he had to leave and said goodbye to me somewhat reluctantly the morning of.

"I'll call you when I get there, yeah?"

A kiss, him kneeling by the bed after tying his laces, his hand on my neck, possessive and passionate.

"You're only going for a week."

Another kiss, this time on my shoulder, and then his face pressed into my neck, his hands moving to my waist, wrapping his arms around me.

"Yeah well, I don't want you to forget about me."

I turned my face towards him, causing him to lift his own to look at me. I bent my head to kiss his cheek and he gave me a smile that made my heart leap a little. And this scared me.

"I'll see you next Friday."

He grinned and then made a growling noise, pushing his face back into my neck and causing me to scream out in laughter. I pushed him off me and he jumped up, picking up his duffle bag and guitar, hanging one off each shoulder. I lay back down, closing my eyes and hoping to get thirty minutes more sleep before I had to get ready for work. But I sensed he wasn't gone yet and opened them again to find him still standing in the doorway, watching me.

"Dee, you're doing that weird thing we talked about."

He laughed, looking down at the floor before lifting his face towards me and landing on a soft smile.

"I just love you, that's all."

I sat up with a speed that made the bed creak, but he was already at the front door, already opening and closing it quickly, as if seeing my reaction might have ended his life. I remained where I sat, hopes of sleep a distant memory now, behind all the trouble I seemed to have gathered around me. Things were suddenly very real, and exhilarating and terrifying. I checked my phone, as if I did not already know the answer to the question I was about to ask. Jay's poetry night was on as scheduled the following evening, so I decided to venture there.

When I got to the pub basement, I took a seat at the back as Jay stood on the stage, comfortable and in his element. My ego was a little bruised. I had been hoping for some small sign that he was broken without me, not quite himself. In reality, he was exactly as he had always been, just as I also was. Perhaps a part of me was convinced that we could only know we meant something to someone when we could see evidence of the pain we had caused them.

He approached me afterwards. I had been waiting for him to say goodbye to some younger women, university students lusting after the well-read older poet, with lovingly kept locks who smelt clean and cared for. I inhaled a sigh and watched him interact with his adoring fans, irked that I was irked by it at all. Once they left, I stood up from my chair as Jay came towards me, and we instantly began to stack chairs and place them in the corners of the basement room without even greeting each other. It was a quiet task we had long since grown accustomed to doing together. Afterwards we sat on the edge of the stage. I didn't know what should be addressed first but, as always, he did.

"Where have you been?"

I looked at him, wondering if he was trying to test me, to see if I would lie. My paranoia was becoming habitual.

"Nowhere. I mean, I've been somewhere, obviously. With… with my ex, with Dee. I'm sorry. I should have just told you."

"The guy who disappeared?"

I nodded, a reminder of Dee's sins hitting me harder somehow because they were coming from Jay. He laughed in apparent bewilderment and shook his head at me.

"Why?"

"Because... he's back? Honestly, I don't know yet. I wish I had more of an explanation than that."

"Yeah well, so do I."

He wasn't reproachful, just contemplative when he said it, like he also wanted to solve the puzzle of Dee and I. He stood up quickly and brushed away the dust that had travelled from the stage to his jeans, causing a brief shower of it to sprinkle onto my own still-seated thighs. I squinted and then looked up at him.

"I missed you though."

It had sounded pathetic falling from my lips, but I felt like a liar all the time I didn't say it.

"Well, I missed you too, obviously."

He held out his hand and pulled me up from the floor jovially. He suggested we get a drink together and I agreed. We headed upstairs to the pub, settling into a corner booth and talking until it was last orders. Once the pub closed, we walked and talked some more. Jay had a way of pulling fond childhood memories from me like no one else could, not even Dee. He made me feel as though all my words were precious and they mattered, even the ones I stuttered over and rephrased. I had almost forgotten how completely important I always felt with him. Upon reaching my bus stop, we said goodbye. I promised to call him, meaning it sincerely at the time. I think he smirked at me, and then kissed me on the cheek before saying something like,

"Yeah, see you around, Ekuah."

It had been wonderfully cool and nonchalant in the face of my still simmering need to feel needed.

*

In the days after, I still couldn't sleep properly. I still arose in the early hours, even on the nights when Dee wasn't there, staring out the window into the darkness, trying to reckon with the shapeshifting sense I had. I felt like I was betraying someone and held the unsettling feeling that perhaps it was myself. Soon enough, my doubts began to ruffle Dee's feathers too.

We had been going for five months before the fighting began again. It came in short and frustrating bursts, sometimes ending in cold silence, other times a door slam, and most times, sex. I wondered frequently how I could want to be so close and so far away from one person all at the same time. It was an irritating state that was fuelled by tiny habits: he ground his teeth sometimes when he slept, or he peed with the door open, or sometimes he slept as far away as anyone sleeping in the same bed could be.

The last one hurt the most. I would lie awake at night, wondering what he was dreaming about, talking myself out of rolling over to his side of the bed. I was still afraid of him, of his potential to emotionally ruin me, and my propensity for continuing to let him. I found myself laying frozen in my own body, pretending to sleep, waiting night after night for him to leave again. The anticipation and the dread crippled me, crippled us.

19.

I was dog-tired. There hadn't been proper sleep for weeks, not for me anyway. Between fighting with Dee that was becoming a weekly routine, and new responsibilities at work, I was emotionally spent. I needed a break from Dee, and denying the fact only took more energy from me. So, I began to sneak around, to keep certain things from him, especially things about myself. I began to show up at more poetry shows again, specifically the ones I knew Jay would also be at. I told myself that I deserved it, that I had a life before Dee decided to bless me with his presence again, and I was going to make sure I had one once he was gone. And I believed that it was only a matter of time before he was gone again.

Jay was happy to see me back to the old routines we had established with each other, though he was a little guarded at first. He wondered out loud what the deal was, if I had "sorted out my problem". I told him I hadn't and didn't reproach him for referring to Dee that way—I was sure I was to blame for it. I distracted myself from the guilt I felt by spending more time with Jay, helping him make plans for the summer break and the golden few weeks he had off as a teacher. He was reluctant to follow through on any of my suggestions however, and the following week I discovered why.

Jay had been commissioned by the International Education Foundation to run poetry workshops in Accra, Ghana for a month over the summer. I was the first one he told. He had invited me to his place, explaining cryptically over the phone the day before that he had something to share with me. Just the idea made me nervous and I considered rescinding my initial agreement, for fear of finding myself in an awkward situation with us alone in his flat. But I went anyway, looking back at Dee that morning, still asleep in my bed. He stirred when he heard me picking up my bag.

"Where are you going?"

His voice was filled with confusion, as if it were the middle of the night rather than ten in the morning.

"To a friend's place. Will you be around later?"

He reached out to take my hand, but I moved to open the bedroom door, narrowly avoiding his touch in my hurry. He didn't notice, yawning instead in my general direction and rubbing his eyes.

"Nah I told you, I'm in the studio this week, finishing off the album."

I was facing away from him, desperate to leave. I turned back, feeling numb suddenly.

"Okay. Well, see you later-later, then."

"Later."

His reply reached me as a muffled sound just as the door closed behind me. I felt the distance between us like a sharp pain. But I had found a way to separate out my feelings for both Dee and Jay, somehow switching from dull melancholy to bright energy. So when I reached Jay's place, I was okay again.

"Come with me."

Jay said it with a straight face, as if asking me if I wanted a drink, or to check out a film that weekend, and not whether I wanted to travel to Ghana with him. I was speechless for a moment. He took another breath, sensing my silence was hesitation and not necessarily refusal.

"They're letting me bring someone with me, I think it should be you."

His confidence moved me, but I found myself laughing it off, batting it away as if he was making a bad joke.

"But… I'm not a teacher, or a poet, or in any position to afford a flight to Ghana right now—"

He placed a hand on my lower arm. It had the desired effect, pausing my protests, weakly delivered as they were. I looked up at him and sighed. We hadn't sat like this, alone together, in what felt like a long while. He was still handsome. His dreadlocks were tied into a tight bun, emphasising the jut of his jawline, the permanent five o'clock shadow on the lower half of his face, the reassuring crooked smile that made a regular appearance. As I looked at him and the smile crept through, I marvelled at the way it lit up his whole face, and something in me. Perhaps he could tell because he chuckled as if we were sharing a private joke, never dropping eye contact, my stomach a wave of butterflies again. Intellectually I knew this was a betrayal to Dee and what we were currently trying to war through, but I also knew that I had no plans to leave Jay's flat. Jay knew it too and continued his campaign to get me to leave the country with him instead.

He explained that he needed someone to help him organise the workshops, someone with my project skills, who was good with people and got things done. He would deliver them, I shouldn't worry about that part. He also emphasised repeatedly that it would be an all-expenses paid trip, and that if he recalled correctly, I had a lot of leave left that I hadn't yet taken. How could I say no to this opportunity?

The 'yes' escaped my lips before I had any further chances to silence myself.

After we had talked through the details, my first thought was to call my parents. I hadn't been to Ghana since I was a child, and my parents had not either, choosing to use the money others might buy a plane ticket with, to pay for after school activities and late bills, especially during the years when my father's employment was less than stable. I knew they would want to know that I was going.

I called my mother first, hoping to catch them both together, though that hadn't happened since they'd moved to Greenwich. She was oddly apprehensive about me going to Ghana, peppering me with a million questions.

"Where are you staying? Did you have your vaccinations? Have you told your Nana Gertrude that you're coming? You know what she's like. Who is this Jay man? A friend or who? And what even will you be doing for a whole month? Are you allowed that much time off?"

I was bothered by her disjointed speech. She was usually direct, purposeful with her words. There was something foreign in her voice as our exchange continued. It felt wrong. I wondered in my head whether she was okay but could not bring myself to ask the question out loud—it had never been necessary. And then she paused between her follow up questions and I heard the buzz of a television in the background. She didn't watch television.

"Are you... watching TV?"

I couldn't hide the concern in my voice but, true to form, she ignored it.

"It's just on in the background. Your father, he's not here."

I waited for her to continue, to explain the connection between her doing something she never did, and my father's whereabouts, but she said nothing more. I promised to give him a call next, and that seemed to satisfy her. But he was just as elusive and out of it as she was, and I realised that something was happening with them, though I didn't know what. I tried to press my father, but he just wanted to talk about Ghana.

"This will be a good trip for you dear. I hope this Jay boy is a good one?"

"Yes Dad, he's good."

"That's all I wanted to hear."

"Dad... what's going on—at home I mean?"

"At home? Nothing, why? Did your mother say something?"

I was sure his question wasn't intended to arouse suspicion, but it did. I closed my eyes and considered a different tact.

"She just didn't seem like herself. I just wanted to check things were okay?"

He sighed quietly, in a tone that matched my own.

"We're okay dear, don't worry about us."

"Dad…"

"Really Ekuah, this one is okay. I'm away working for a few days to do some backing on an album, so I'm not home. But your Auntie Genie is around so… yes."

"So, things are—"

"Everything is fine. Yes."

I thought I heard him smiling softly on the phone, as if trying to will me into reassurance unsuccessfully, because we both knew what he meant when he said, "Everything is fine". It was a phrase I had heard him utter often throughout my childhood, specifically for the times when everything was not fine. When my parents were fighting and caught me listening. When my father's bank card got rejected at the supermarket during the period when he couldn't find work. When I awoke one morning to find him sleeping on the sofa, a suitcase open and half packed on the floor.

Every time, he had reassured me with what we both knew to be a false platitude, and then somehow, he managed to fix it and made everything truly seem fine again. But this time I was not convinced. I told him I would call him in the next week or so when my trip was finalised. Then I hung up the phone.

I had fantasised often that they would split up, because I could not understand how two people so at odds could continue to stay together. And I was no longer an excuse for why they kept going because I didn't live at home anymore. But the real possibility of it hit me hard. I had held on too tightly to the times when everything went back to the awkward normal that was between them. If anything, a big part of me relied upon their staying in a settled, slightly unhappy state. There was something about it that made my own uneasiness in my relationship more bearable. Or perhaps it was just giving me an excuse to keep going with Dee.

So, I waited too long to tell him about Ghana, about flying off under the wing of someone else, and about the nagging feeling that I wanted to be anywhere but where we were. The guilt of it, of delaying what I knew to be inevitable, kept me up for too many nights. I tried reaching for solace in Dee's warm body beside me, rarely spending a night apart from me anymore, as if he knew we were losing something. It felt like he wanted to make his presence known, get me to understand that he wasn't going anywhere. But we both knew I couldn't be convinced. Or, I didn't want to be. Ghana went from being weeks away to days, and an attempt at a secret trip to the Ghanaian embassy in Archway caused me to slip up in sharing my whereabouts with Dee. So I confessed it all in a vomiting mess of words and apologies for not telling him sooner. He paused for a long time before responding to my monologue. Standing up slowly from the bed, the sun's rays from the window giving him a halo, he leaned on the window sill and looked down at me. I sat upright on top of the quilt covers, one leg folded, the other outstretched, my hands tapping nervously against my thigh, waiting for a verdict.

"That's a lot, Eckie."

I nodded, unsure if I should say anything more. He watched me, thinking. Maybe trying to figure out what had been going on in my head all this time. I thought it was obvious what was happening. But it wasn't.

"Okay… okay then. I'll be here, innit. When you come back."

He attempted a smile, small and friendly. I wasn't used to seeing it on his face, so I looked away, mumbling the words that were scrambling to get out.

"I don't think… maybe you shouldn't be here. When I come back, I mean."

"Are you serious?"

I hadn't expected bewilderment. I thought I was still looking at the boy who never responded to the note I posted through his door. I didn't know how to deal with this new version of Dee, and I was only just realising that was the problem.

I managed to lift my face up towards him again, the shock on his own having quickly changed to anger. Something I was familiar with.

"This isn't working, Dee. You know it, I know it, why keep pretending—"

"Please don't give me none of this rehearsed bullshit. You say we're done? We're done. Boom."

His joggers were already done up, and I watched the muscles on his back bend and flex as he searched for a t-shirt to throw on. The urge to reach out and touch him suddenly flared up, and doubts about my decision began to scream loudly in my ears.

"I just need some time, a break, that's all."

It wasn't even true, couldn't have been, because in that moment I felt far away from him, further even than when he had disappeared and his whereabouts were simply: unknown. In my mind we had already broken up and my heart was starting the work to piece itself back together again. But the formality of it all, of exchanging the words that formed the end, felt cruel. His face said about the same thing. He quit trying to leave abruptly, as if remembering himself, that he was a changed man.

"I knew it you know. I'm not dumb. And when I told you how I felt, you never actually said it back, plus... well, we're always playing that game aren't we? It was gonna be my turn at some point."

He sighed big, like the day was already done and he had long been tired and weary. This time I reached over for real, let my fingers make contact with his shoulder, his back to me as I pressed my own into the headboard. *Not too close,* seemed to be my mantra these days.

"What game?"

He turned to look at me, no recognition on his face, just mild surprise to still find me there, realising he wasn't just talking to himself. And then that chuckle came, the one he gave before he hit me with some 'truth' about myself. I braced before I knew I was holding my breath.

"Tit for tat. I wrong you, you wrong me. I left, you're leaving. It's always something with us, right?"

I opened my mouth to speak but we both knew I had nothing left to say. I closed my eyes as he opened the bedroom door to leave, listening to him gather up his things in the living room. I heard the twang of his guitar as he slipped it into its case, and the click of something on the coffee table, that I later discovered was my spare key. He hadn't put up a fight, and I wasn't sure if I had wanted him to. But I felt the burden shift, even if the ground beneath me still felt unsafe to walk on without him.

*

The following week, Jay and I caught a plane to Accra. Inside I felt like liquid, feeling myself shifting, unsure of what my final form would be. Or whether it even mattered. As we went through security, I removed my watch and pulled out my phone from my back pocket, placing it in a plastic tray and watching as it vibrated with a new message. Once I'd been full body x-rayed, I wondered if my organs showed up on the monitor as one big blob, or if I was more intact than

I thought. I retrieved my phone knowing full well what I would find there. The text message from Dee sat comfortably in my inbox, my finger hovering over it, almost afraid that the words would challenge the resolve I was trying to gather over leaving him. Instead, he had left me with a snapshot of the old Dee, a figure I could rely on for his nonchalance and mask of apathy during moments that commanded so much more.

DEE: Have fun. x

The rage and hurt I had been suppressing since his return showed itself briefly. I took a sharp breath and my fingertips turned white as I tried to squeeze the life out of the phone. But as quickly as it had arrived, the feeling left, and I held down the power button and dropped the phone into the bottom of my bag. He had given me exactly what I had wanted; the old Dee. The one who would always let me down, always just out of reach for me to connect with fully.

To be presented with something other than that, something that promised to stay around, that warranted affection and gave it willingly, in the body of someone who had broken me so significantly, was too much for me to comprehend. Perhaps I wasn't strong enough or mature enough to take that new journey. Not with him.

Sitting on the plane, I looked over at Jay and saw, curiously, that there were still big chunks of me that wanted to hurt Dee, and other parts that wanted to see what could happen with Jay. I wasn't sure yet where the line of distinction lay between the two. Or if there was one at all.

I stared out the window at the tarmac as we rolled along it, hoping an ascent would help me to detach from the thread of feelings that still connected me to London. I waited for relief to follow soon after we took off, but instead I sat with a heavy thing, an angst in my stomach for the first few hours of the flight, trying to distract myself with a film. It was only when we hit some turbulence that I was shaken out of my silent brooding, my heart jumping into my mouth as the rumbling and rocking continued for more than a few seconds. I immediately felt Jay clasp my fingers before giving me an open smile.

"You okay?"

I nodded, unnerved for sure, but okay.

20.

Everything was hot. My head, my legs, my armpits, even my elbows were crying out for some cold relief. Lying on the bed directly under a fan in my underwear, trying to think cold thoughts, I barely registered the sound of a key in the door, the gentle click and unclick of the lock. He entered the room and looked down at me laughing, my body making a star shape and covering most of what was supposed to be his bed. I lifted my head slightly to address him in an exasperated voice.

"Why didn't you tell me it was going to be like this?"

"I thought you already knew."

I kicked my leg half-heartedly in his general direction which just made him laugh more. I closed my eyes and tried to blow cold air through my mouth onto my face unsuccessfully. I listened as he removed his clothes and climbed onto the bed with me. As he hovered over me, his proximity did nothing to reduce the sauna-like atmosphere in the room. One of his knees was pressed into the mattress, placed carefully between my legs, the other he balanced on the edge of the bed. He took the whole of me in with his eyes, and then let a few seconds crawl by in our horizontal position before leaning down and gently grazing my lips with his. I found myself whispering his name.

"Jay..."

I grasped the back of his neck and enveloped him in a deep, open-mouthed kiss, our tongues dancing with each other, our bodies pressed together. A few minutes later his lips were on the curve of my neck, then my collar bone, slowly tracing a path of small kisses along the length of my body until he reached my pelvis. He ran both hands down my legs, removing my underwear in the process, before reaching around the backs of my thighs and pushing my legs up into open arches for him to enter face first. I wasn't bothered by the heat anymore. My eyes were closed, my body writhing in humid pleasure.

*

We arrived in Accra tired but excited and were met in the Arrivals hall by a large cardboard sign that read "Mr Stanley and Ms Danquah". It was our driver, Ishmael, who was assigned to us by the foundation for the duration of our stay. He met us with a smile of ivory white teeth and a sun-weathered brow, picking up our suitcases as if they were filled with feather pillows. He had lived in Accra his whole life and only took shortcuts with his driving, whilst his stories were long and detailed; spilling beans about the famous politicians, authors and musicians he had had in the back of his car during his many years as a driver. He explained that he picked up more jobs from the foundation than his taxi colleagues because of the glowing feedback he received and his dapper-like appearance. And the spick and span shine of his Mercedes Benz didn't hurt his business either.

Jay turned towards me from the passenger's seat and we exchanged a look of amusement as I settled in the back and Ishmael nattered on, weaving effortlessly through traffic, over newly tarmacked roads and around the gutters that sat like open mouths on busy corners. I felt myself half dozing listening to the low hum of the engine, only fully awake towards the end of the journey, when we turned into a darkened dust road, lit only by the moon and our car headlights. I expected a dense fear to rise in my throat—something that occurred now whenever I stared out into darkness and couldn't see the end of it—but nothing came. Instead I turned from the window to find Jay staring back at me in the rear-view mirror, a warm smile on his face, unbothered that I had caught him looking.

Eventually the car veered right, and we were back onto a paved road lined with large compounds, all with high gates and lights of their own. Ishmael slowed the car and stopped outside of a red and white brick building with a sign that read *Liana Hotel*. He pulled our bags out of the trunk, and Jay tipped Ishmael as if he were a wealthy man. It made my heart bounce a little, but I said nothing. We checked into our respective rooms next door to one another and said a small goodnight before retiring.

We had the next day free to do some sightseeing before beginning the workshops, so I suggested we take a Tro-Tro—a bus that was more a framework of metal and wheels than an actual people carrier, but that still served as a form of transport for those travelling around the city. We crammed ourselves into the bus with what felt like hundreds of other people. The heat of the morning and everyone's sweat seemed to mix together to create a new collective body odour that left me both nauseated and nostalgic. I recalled being a child and climbing aboard one with my Nana Gertrude, the first time my parents took me to Ghana. They had declined to go with us, but insisted I have the "tourist experience" on the Tro-Tro. I remember loving it, being enthralled by all the colours, the sounds, the different things people were transporting from one place to another.

Jay seemed to be having the same experience as an adult and grinned at me excitedly when he heard a chicken squawking from somewhere in the back of the bus. By the time we hopped off, my back was soaked in sweat, my backpack absorbing most of the moisture but not nearly enough. Jay pulled two bottles of water from his bag and handed one to me.

"We look like we just jumped into a river."

He laughed at himself, wiping his brow with his forearm whilst I took a swig, unable to take my eyes off the small muscle lines that were showing through his t-shirt where the sweat made it cling to him. And we stood like that, watching each other on the side of the road, a few feet away from a market that was everything except quiet. I handed the bottle back to him and he took a deep breath like he was going to say something. I was poised, but he simply exhaled and then wondered out loud where we could get some food. I turned to the task at hand and led us to a woman on the side of the road selling roasted plantain and peanuts, and ice-cold bottles of Fanta which we gulped down too quickly. And then we walked and talked, just like we had in London, only this time under the sun, surrounded by colour and busy people and the constant honking of car horns.

In the afternoon we visited my Nana Gertrude, a thing I had promised my mother I would do. She was an older cousin of my maternal grandmother who had since retired to the US. Although not a blood relation, Nana Gertrude was the niece of a close family friend, growing up with my grandmother and living with my family for a while. This made her family, and a cousin by situation and affection. She was one of many that made up the colourful history of our family; one that was oftentimes a patchwork of stories, some parts unequivocally true, others dramatic embellishments.

Nana Gertrude was in her eighties and had always been a kind but firm matriarch that I remembered from my childhood during the few times we visited Ghana. When Jay and I went to see her, we sat in the guest living room, fancier than the other living room that was further into the house. Her floors were marbled and shiny, and we drank milky tea in relative silence as she surveyed us. She had been chewing on a wooden stick when we arrived, and it sat mangled on the side of the coffee table. Jay began his routine of the small talk that he was so good at when he suspected that awkward silence was around the corner. He didn't know that Ghanaians didn't really do small talk. After a few minutes Nana Gertrude cut him off and said:

"So, you are West Indian."

It was not phrased as a question so Jay didn't reply immediately, instead choosing to smile brightly at her before glancing at me, hoping I would provide clarity. I looked back just as bewildered. She seemed to just be pointing out the things she saw.

"Yeah, Jamaican actually."

She ignored him and addressed me directly.

"Your mother didn't tell me you had a boyfriend. When will you be arranging the marriage?"

Jay jumped in before I could sputter through my tea, clearly amused.

"We're just friends Nana G, we're here to work, to do some teaching."

I worried he was being overly familiar by giving her a nickname, but her face changed instantly, as if it was the best news she had heard all day. Her slow, laboured drawl disappeared, replaced by a faster talking, high-pitched, younger woman. She was eager to share with us stories of her teaching days. She spoke passionately about her old students, about how hard it was at first in a school where all the teachers, but her, were men. How her students adored her, even the ones who misbehaved, and the many cohorts of successful men and women she had taught well into her seventies. Eventually her arthritis made it difficult to walk the two miles to school every day, and she had never cared for cars. So she moved in with her son and daughter-in-law and officially retired.

She was a true storyteller, so earnest in her detail. I watched Jay watching her, both exchanging excited words with curiosity, wanting to know more about the other. I felt a pang in my gut at seeing them this way, the kind of jolt that made me want to shift closer to him, to hold his hand. When we finally left Nana Gertrude's house, we talked non-stop about her until we reached our hotel, and then Jay hugged me tightly in front of my room door, as if I were personally responsible for the life of that 83-year-old woman. I accepted it gladly and held on to him just as tightly, perhaps even a little longer than the moment called for.

After a full day of good food and exploration, we turned our attention to the workshops and I got to see a side of Jay I had never seen before. He held power and calm in a room that many others would have faltered within, standing in front of 12- and 13-year olds, sharing poetry in an attempt to stretch their creativity and their ability to express how they feel. I felt sometimes, like a student, watching from the back of the class, rooting for the teacher to change hearts and minds. One afternoon I was joined by our Ghanaian rep from the foundation, Kwame, who excited the students when he attended a workshop because he was a known Afrobeats DJ around town, who mixed his own music as backing tracks to poetry videos he uploaded to YouTube. By the end of the week, they buzzed around me and Jay in much the same way, and we revelled in it.

High off the success of the first few days of workshops, Kwame offered to take us out. We ended up at a bar on Labadi beach—powdery yellow sand at our feet, cocktails and barbecued chicken fresh from the grill on our tables. It felt like paradise. Kwame told me a little about himself. He had been an intern for the foundation whilst he did his teacher's training. He ended up working with them in Nigeria and South Africa, before returning to Ghana and getting into spoken word. He described it as,

"Tripping and falling into something I knew everything and nothing about".

At the time, his friend was running an open mic variety party, where singers, poets and dancers were welcome to perform at a small bar in East Legon. To help drum up a bigger audience, Kwame offered to bring some of his teacher friends along. He said before that time, he had had little interest in the British poetry of Shakespeare and Lord Byron that he had been taught about at school. But seeing poetry performed raw and unformatted, with people turning their real-life experiences into art that resonated with him, he found himself falling in love with it.

"There's no rhyme or reason to loving something like that, that's what makes it real."

I had inhaled three cocktails by this point and laughed playfully but a little too loudly at his candour, rolling my eyes as I sipped my fourth Pina Colada.

"Poets."

He eyed me, smiling but with curiosity, and responded

as such.

"And you Ms. London, what are you?"

I turned to Jay, half expecting him to answer for me, but he looked back at me smiling, eagerly awaiting my response. I attempted my own clunky words.

"I am a… I'm a poetry appreciator."

"Eh heh. Then you my dear, do not know love, you only know how to watch it."

Kwame's words struck me unexpectedly, and I felt them like a deep cut. Jay meanwhile nodded in agreement, and then seeing my face, affectionately rubbed my back as if to comfort me, trying to laugh the whole thing off. Kwame smiled suspiciously as he watched us both and then leaned across the table to grab Jay by the shoulder and make eye contact.

"And you my brother, you know love far too well."

Then he stood up and excused himself to go to the bathroom. I leant against Jay and tried not to think about what Kwame had meant, and the way that Jay had lowered his eyes in response, rather than retorting with a humorous quip as I had expected.

We didn't go back to the hotel that night; instead Jay, Kwame and I sat on the beach, watching black waves dance with the sand beneath it. They teased us as they came ashore and then quickly retreated. Kwame was a contemplative sort and pulled a tiny notebook from his shirt pocket a few minutes into watching the sea, writing furiously. Eventually he laid down on his back, staring at the sky, his white shirt billowing in the breeze and making gentle ruffling sounds against the sand beneath him.

Jay and I sat huddled together as the breeze picked up and a slight chill ran through us both. He made a "brrrr" sound, the vibrato of his voice rumbling in my chest.

"Today was a great day."

I said it to no one in particular, and he nodded, putting his arm around my shoulder.

"I'm really glad you came. I didn't think we'd actually get here."

He took a deep breath, which caused my own to catch in my throat. I wondered if he was referring to the present, or that other "here" that our friendship had only ever alluded to. And I wondered if he knew that I was still wondering. As if reading my mind, he turned to look at me.

"Do you know what I mean?"

He was so close to me suddenly, and the air smelled like coconuts: my drink, his hair, a mixture of the night, I wasn't sure. Or I was.

"I think I do, yeah."

He kissed me before the words had fully fallen from my lips. So passionately and softly that it somehow felt heavy; there was a weight to it that made it impossible to stop. And something was anchored in that moment too, as the moon shone like a beacon for our lost souls. We had found each other, despite the small anxiety I had that the relief I felt might only be temporary.

21.

Our affair wasn't wild, but it endured. And it carried us through the weeks in a busy, passionate haze. I felt tiny strokes of guilt over Dee whenever I grasped moments alone, wondering quietly what he would say about it all and knowing that I was probably breaking his heart. But my own hurt—nursed obsessively during his absence—continued to push me further away from him. And I couldn't deny how taken I was by Jay's desire for me. It was open and fresh, and I didn't know what else to do with it but give in, lest it leave me, and I never know anything like it again.

During the days, we fulfilled our duties to the foundation. Jay planned and delivered his workshops, I recorded them, made notes on the discussions that took place and the suggestions that came from the young people, turning them into reports and material for future lessons. In the evenings we visited the beach or went to bars with Kwame and his friends: poets, writers, educators, NGO workers and all living room politicians. I joined them in heated discussions about Ghanaian democracy, though I knew a lot less about it than they did of British politics. Most times I was just happy to observe close friends as they intellectually sparred with each other. And I in turn, became braver with my words and opinions, allowing a more outspoken me to emerge.

My newfound confidence showed its face one night at Kwame's family compound. My stomach was filled with red wine and too much Red-Red, the taste of sweet plantain and beans still on my tongue. I stood amongst the dozens of others in Kwame's garden, at the BBQ-turned-party as soon as the sun had gone down. Jay stood at the other end of the garden, engaged in an intense conversation with a slender, curvaceous woman a few years older than me, named Doris. She had big brown eyes under an umbrella of thick lashes. Her hair was a short afro and she often wore a serious frown, alluding to her reputation as a deep thinker and one of the youngest lecturers at the University of Ghana. There seemed to me no look or outfit that she could not pull off, and it was easy to see why many men were drawn to her. She was endearing, and a shared love of British period dramas had made us fast friends. But I resented her displays of arrogance when we were in a group, and her directness was at times cutting. So sometimes we were friendly, and other times we were acquaintances.

Watching her with Jay, I felt an unreasonable but gradually insurmountable stream of jealousy creep through my veins, coupled with a strong will to have possession of him. I had not realised how quickly I had sunk into my feelings for him, how they now swept me up in a strong wind of fury and were no longer the gentle breeze they had been just weeks earlier. But my anguish in that moment was based only on a fiction I had created; Doris' fiancé, an African American officer in the military, was all that she spoke about when she wasn't tangled up in socio-political conversations with her friends.

Even so, she had Jay's attention and I wanted it back. So, I waddled over to Kwame, my shoes sticking to the grass that had recently been showered with rain.

"And how are you doing exactly?"

Slightly slurred speech exited my mouth and surprised me, my thoughts spinning with ineptitude. Kwame peered down from the extra foot that he had on me, with a quizzical but amused look on his face. He appeared to slowly realise just how drunk I was.

"I am doing exactly fine, although clearly not as good as you."

He chuckled good naturedly and then took a swig of his beer. I decided to move closer to him, despite the imbalance I was feeling.

"I am doing pretty good, yes, even if you *do* think I know nothing about love."

He looked taken aback by my comment, his face full of confusion as he tried to decipher what I was talking about. When he'd finally figured it out, he tried to laugh it off.

"I didn't say you knew nothing, just that maybe you like how it looks from afar."

"I like how you look from afar."

I knew that I was making a fool of myself, but I couldn't stop. I tried to lean against the back fence that he stood in front of, whilst also maintaining eye contact. But my attempt to look nonchalant failed as I slipped on the wet grass, my feet almost giving way underneath me completely, until Kwame grabbed my arm tightly and interrupted what would have been a painful and embarrassing fall. He continued to hold my elbow as I pressed my hand into the fence, trying to regain my balance. I would have found the whole thing hilarious if I wasn't so drunk and single-minded. We were almost nose to nose for a few seconds and I continued with my plan for seduction.

"Do you like how I look up close?"

I wasn't sure what I had meant but was certain that leaning in and whispering into his ear would have the desired effect. Instead his eyes widened in embarrassment and he released a nervous laugh. And then Jay appeared as if the interaction were planned, an annoyed and worried look on his face. I had not seen him look at me that way before, and at first he directed his frustration at Kwame. They both paused, exchanging looks that I didn't understand, before Kwame gently removed my vice grip from his arm, smiled awkwardly at us both, and disappeared inside the house. I turned to look at Jay, irritated that he had ruined my fun, and simultaneously happy he was by my side again. He did not appear as pleased to see me, which quickly threw me back to annoyance. I began to saunter away, but he stood in front of me, a lecture at the ready.

"What was that?"

"Nothing, don't worry about it, it's fine."

"No, it's not. And quite frankly neither are you."

"Well *quite frankly*, I've had too much to drink. It's not rocket science."

I attempted to walk around him, but my body was slow moving as the alcohol settled in for the night. I feared the hangover I would have the next day, but he wasn't done talking.

"Were you trying to embarrass me with Kwame?"

"What? No!"

I wasn't really sure what I had been trying to do, but I saw that his expression was not one of anger, only of upset, and for some reason this irritated me further. But he carried on with his questions.

"Then what, you wanted me to be jealous? To look stupid over you?"

"Ugh! No okay! And let's be honest, I'm the only one looking stupid here."

The hurt look on his face was sobering me up and that was making me angrier.

"I'm going to go back to the hotel. Please get out of the way."

I attempted to push by him, poking him in the chest, but he felt like concrete; completely immovable.

"Why are you trying to pick a fight with me?"

His question was thrown at me with a scowl and I felt my head begin to pound. I had had enough.

"YOU'RE PICKING ONE WITH ME!"

My sudden screaming caused him to jerk his head back

with wide eyes, as silence fell upon the garden for a few moments. I felt all eyes on me and searched desperately for a hole to fall into, to no avail. Eventually people went back to their chatter and I grabbed my bag, mortified, sprinting to the back gate. Jay had finally moved out of my way, only to immediately follow me. The compound security guard let us out with a friendly farewell.

"Eh, goodnight sah, goodnight madam!"

I waved goodbye awkwardly as we walked through the gates and continued to chastise Jay as we got further away from Kwame's house.

"Stop trying to engage me Jay, I'm tired and I don't want to talk anymore."

"I'm not trying to talk to you, I just want to make sure you get back to the hotel alive."

His voice was stoic now and I looked ahead of us at the pitch black nothing I hadn't noticed before then, feeling the uneven dust road beneath us. Jay pulled out his phone and used the screen as a torch to guide us along the ten-minute walk back to the hotel. He slipped his fingers into mine without asking and I was glad that he hadn't; I would have stubbornly said no.

Standing in front of my hotel room door, I jammed the key into it, appearing angrier than I felt. I expected him to leave me to it, but instead he followed me in and shut the door behind him. I leant on the wall, watching him walk into the middle of the room and then turn to look at me. I felt a wave of tired embarrassment wash over me when I thought about Kwame and the awkward position I had put him in. I covered my face with my hands as if that would turn back time, and felt Jay a few seconds later gently removing them, linking them with his own before letting my hands drop to my sides.

We didn't talk as he took my bag from me, throwing it gently to the floor. Next, he removed my jacket, and then watching for my reaction, he slowly removed my dress. He said nothing as I pulled off his shirt, unzipped his shorts and slid my hands into his boxers. We exchanged hot tongue kisses, and I pressed him up against the door before letting him remove my underwear. As he opened and slipped on a condom, turning me around and pushing me into the corner between the door and the wall, with the flat of his palm in my hair, I closed my eyes and felt a warmth rush over me as we rapidly made love. My head still felt airy by the time we got to the bed. He wore a piercing, passionate look now that we were face to face, and he was more focussed this second time around, our eyes locked in close contact as if he was trying to delve as deeply into me as he could, while he had me.

Afterwards I felt like I couldn't breathe properly, as if something was trapped in my lungs. But I exhaled with ease when he turned in his shallow slumber and pulled me towards him. I wished for sleep to come, to slow down my constantly busy mind, and I prayed for distraction from the other thoughts. The ones that were known to spill lies, to cast aspersions and doubts on the object of my affection.

Certainly with Dee, they had not all been unfounded. But Jay was different. He was new and loyal and disarming in a way I wasn't sure he realised. I knew something powerful was happening between us, and I wanted to embrace it fully. But that little voice betrayed me, telling me that I wasn't ready yet, and I wasn't worthy. And that in fact, I might not ever be.

22.

The time to leave Ghana came upon us quickly, looming like a dark cloud that I wished I could vanquish with my mind. Jay and I had found a rhythm in just a few short weeks and returning to old routines in London still felt like a faraway possibility. Plus, my insecurities about what it was we were doing together no longer existed. I already knew Jay was mine. He reassured me about his devotion silently, in the way that he pressed himself against me at night, the palm of his hand finding the perfect place in the small of my back, so that he could pull me closer to him, make sure I felt him deeply inside me, solidifying our affection for each other.

When our penultimate day in Ghana came, we tried, at least professionally, to return to business as usual, knowing that it wasn't so. We ran a final showcasing workshop with all the students we had been working with, about thirty of them in total. We invited their parents and guardians along and set the stage for them to perform their best poem, after weeks of writing, edits and practice. And it became the perfect crescendo to our trip, watching the transformation of some of our students from quiet mutterers into confident speakers, churning out poetry that moved me and many of the parents to tears. Afterwards, there was a small reception and the students presented us with a scrapbook they had made, with pictures and pieces of their poems and notes to us both. I felt that swell of emotion that arrives in the chest, a warning that more tears will come, and they will overwhelm.

Later, when everything was done and we had said our goodbyes, I felt drained, and then such a surprising sadness that I didn't know what to do with my hands. Ishmael arrived to take Jay and I back to the hotel to pack for our early flight, but I couldn't bring myself to get into the car. Jay saw the anxious look on my face and told Ishmael we would walk. Then he took my hand and kissed it, and we began the forty-minute trek back to the hotel.

"I'm not ready to go home either."

I looked over to him and smiled. He still knew what to say when I didn't.

"I know we have to, I just don't want this to end."

I spoke softly, listening to the buzz of a bee somewhere nearby, hoping Jay was hearing what I was saying. He continued to stare ahead, pensive, giving my hand a gentle squeeze before he replied.

"You know, it doesn't have to. We could… keep doing things together. Poetry stuff I mean, and…"

He trailed off, sounding unsure of himself for the first time. Then he stopped us mid-walk, pausing in front of a shop selling yams, plantain, brooms and an assortment of things you might find inside a Ghanaian household. He looked at me seriously, checking he had my full attention.

"When we get back home, this isn't going to end, is it?"

He swung his finger from him to me and back again, to indicate exactly what he was referring to, so there was no confusion. I felt under a spotlight, a deserved one but still, it was nerve-wracking and real. I wondered what would happen if I said what I wanted to—would it mean I was promising forever or just for now? I wasn't sure either option was a certainty in my head, but his open face, full of vulnerability and strength, somehow was all the certainty I needed.

"I told you, I don't want this to end."

He smiled, pulling me towards him and kissing me softly on the lips.

"Then it won't."

Once we got back to the hotel we were occupied with practicalities: making sure our bags weren't too heavy, that we had our flight times correct and that Ishmael knew when to come and get us for the last time. Jay finished packing before me and spent the rest of the evening lying on my bed reading a book, as I packed and repacked my things, trying to fit in all the gifts I had bought for friends back home. Every so often he would comment on what I was doing, even though his eyes remained on his book.

"Leave the ornament, take the sugar cane. They'll be grateful."

I chuckled and shook my head as I left the small ornament of a tribal boy sitting cross-legged on the bedside table. I even liked it when he was right, which confused the self-righteous side of me.

We slept restlessly, both anxious about the early flight and the promises we had made to each other. The bond between us would be tested as soon as we touched down in London, and we knew it. So later, hunched together in the back of Ishmael's cab on the way to the airport, I felt Jay's arms tightly around my waist and I snuggled into his chest, wishing that I could freeze time. But it was the click of the radio that brought me back to reality.

As Ishmael fiddled with a knob attempting to find a station with a good signal, I heard a familiar voice singing words that I knew to be my own. My poem, *Young Life,* was flooding the car and the space around me, except that now it had a silky R&B melody backing it up, and the sultry tones of Dee Emeka singing the words, making the message sound like a thing of nostalgia and grace. I wanted to recoil in horror at the shock of him finding me, somehow, in a cab in the middle of Accra at five in the morning. But it wasn't disaster that made me sit up, that pulled my body away from a dozing Jay beside me, who only stirred when he felt my body warmth retreat. No, the thing that struck me, was pride. An unmitigated wave of awe and joy, because Dee was on the radio. And despite everything, I still hoped good things for him, even though he had taken my words to get there. I desperately wanted to be angry about it, but I couldn't. I asked Ishmael to turn it up a little; I wanted to hear it fully. But Jay was awake now, wondering why the music was so loud. I quickly asked Ishmael to turn it back down. I hoped Jay wouldn't recognise Dee's voice, so that I didn't have to explain the smile on my face, the energy coursing through my veins. He wouldn't understand, and that was okay. In fact, it was probably better that way.

23.

My mother summoned me to lunch when I returned to London, staring at me from across the table as if I had been gone for months. We took turns ordering, and then as the waiter walked away, she gave an emphatic sigh.

"We need to talk about your father."

I took a piece of bread from the pile in front of us and passed it between my fingers with no intention of eating it. I was bracing myself.

"Is he okay?"

"Oh, he's fine. But he's been spending a lot of time with your friend."

"My friend? Who... Dee?"

She nodded conspiratorially and sipped her water.

"Well, I know. But it's a work thing and he's happy so..."

"Yes, yes. And now he is out at all hours, gallivanting to this place and that. Can you imagine? A man his age."

She shook her head as I tipped my own to one side with curiosity.

"So, you're worried about him?"

She stared at me blankly as if I were speaking a foreign language, and then sighed, already weary of the conversation she had started.

"Your father can take care of himself, clearly. But it would be nice if he came home occasionally."

I managed to stop myself from rolling my eyes.

"You know what it's like, the music stuff happens at all hours. He's probably exhausted."

I was trying to trigger her empathy, but it wasn't working. I didn't have all the facts.

"Ekuah, I haven't seen your father in over a week."

"What?!"

"Yes, a whole week. And then a day or so here and there. It is… well, what kind of a marriage is that?"

I wondered to myself what kind it had been before, when my father spent all day at home and my mother returned from work and made him feel bad about it. But perhaps that wasn't important now.

"Have you told him that you miss him?"

She frowned at me and kissed her teeth.

"For what? He wouldn't believe it anyway."

I frowned back at her, annoyed at how obstinate she was being. Still, there was some other detail that I was missing, that I knew she would never reveal. This was more than she had ever shared about their relationship with me before. I didn't want to spook her by asking too many questions. I looked down at the table and resolved to keep quiet as she relaxed back into her chair and the waiter arrived with our food.

"Perhaps I am worrying for nothing, but I don't think

that Dee boy is a good influence. On your father or you."

"Mum, you don't even know him."

The words stumbled from my lips, a reflex to defend Dee, even when I knew it was unnecessary. She had rattled me, so I tried to refocus on my father.

"The last time I spoke to dad, he sounded really happy. For the first time in a while…"

I quieted myself, regretting my words instantly. My mother didn't react as I expected however. Instead she chuckled.

"Well, then let him enjoy. Maybe he can call his wife once in a while too."

"Have you called *him*?"

"To what end?"

She asked the question with genuine curiosity, as if I were suggesting something absurd. Time to switch lanes again.

"So how is Auntie Genie? Is she back in the US?"

My mother's face changed immediately, taking on an expression I came to know as one reserved solely for Genie. She softened all over, became less rigid somehow. Even the light from the restaurant window hit her differently. And my heart sank as I wondered if my father had ever received such a look from her before.

"No… she'll be here for the rest of the year, so she's staying with me for a while. With us I mean, your father and I."

I smiled weakly, nodding, before picking up my sandwich and biting into it, the crunch of the lettuce not quite loud enough to distract from the mental math I was doing in my head as pieces of information began to slip into place. I probed tentatively.

"So, you haven't been completely alone, because Auntie Genie's been there, right?"

My mother didn't look up from her pasta dish in response, directing her nod instead towards the table. Nothing more, just a silent agreement, no longer giving me the piercing stare that was reserved for words about my father. I felt the unevenness of things in the air, knowing there was nothing I could do about it, not in that moment. Silence ensued, and I finished my sandwich in relative peace as I looked around the restaurant and watched the people passing outside the window. Once my mother was done with her meal, she placed her fork down slightly diagonally to indicate that she was finished. Then she looked up at me and asked me to tell her about Ghana, which filled me with relief.

I mused about the workshops, the students, getting to know the city, and about Jay, of course. I made sure to mention that he and I were due to meet with the foundation in a few days, to debrief on the trip and discuss the potential for future projects. I realised I was still hungry for her approval.

"This Jay, he sounds sensible, smart."

"He is."

"And Dee… he didn't mind you going away with another man for a month?"

"Well… did you mind?"

She laughed at my response but didn't miss a beat.

"Yes, but then I remembered that I raised you right. And if there was any trouble, your cousins would tell me."

I laughed, assuming she was joking, but she just continued to look at me.

"So, you and this Dee boy, you're finished?"

Why did it sound so finite coming from her? It wasn't inaccurate, but it seemed to solidify a situation that I hadn't fully processed yet.

"Are you asking for you or does Auntie Genie want to know?"

I wasn't really thinking when I asked the question, I just didn't want to be the only one sweating at the table. My mother gave me a look I knew well, one that told me I had spoken out of turn. I looked down at the table, mumbling my words.

"Just that, you don't usually ask about this stuff..."

"You're my daughter. I can ask you whatever I want, can I not?"

Her tone was cutting and reproachful and I felt like a child again, a metamorphosis that happened almost imperceptibly. Only this time, she reacted to it, by lifting my chin with her hand, her version of an olive branch. I replayed the moment in my mind on a loop for days afterwards.

"This Jay, your Nana Gertrude tells me he's a good boy, which means he will be good to you."

"He will be."

"Then you won't need to be seeing Dee again, yes?"

She looked at me with sincerity, hopeful that we were in agreement. It hadn't occurred to me until then that I might have to close the door on Dee for good. And it horrified me a little to note my hesitation, to realise that I wasn't ready to do that yet.

24.

It wasn't impossible to imagine not being with Dee again, not agonizing over everything I was and wasn't feeling for him. But never seeing him again? That was something I felt I had less control over. Which was unnerving in itself. Since his first disappearance from my life, he had entered my father's, connecting with him as a producer and, according to my father, now as a friend. It felt like a personal attack, though if I knew Dee, the impact on me wouldn't have really occurred to him. When it came to his music, he was single-minded, focussed and completely committed. The music was his wife and I was always just the mistress.

Even when he used my ideas to elevate his career, I couldn't find a way to feel cheated, because I had known the score from the beginning. But the budding relationship he had with my father caused me more distress than I was willing to admit. I had spent a lot of Dee's absence pretending it wasn't happening, and avoiding conversations about him with my father where I could, despite seeing how it was bolstering my father's confidence. He had no idea the small ways he too might be breaking my heart by continuing to work with Dee. But I also couldn't completely agree with my mother that Dee was a bad influence, only that he was leaving an impression on my father.

I had been back in London for a few weeks when my father came to see me on my lunch break, full of stories.

"My God, that boy is talented! And his work ethic, wow! He knows where he wants to go."

He spoke evangelically about Dee, as if trying to convince me of something I was vehemently denying. Instead I sat quietly and listened, nodding when appropriate, smiling every now and again. I didn't want to rain on my father's parade, even if it made me uncomfortable. Eventually I found a way to manoeuvre away from the topic slightly.

"So, do I need to book appointments with you, now that you're a big deal producer? Because you'll need an assistant for that."

"You know, the label just gave me an intern actually. He makes a good cup of tea, but that's all. He talks too much."

He pulled a disapproving face, and then a second later he chuckled to himself, thoroughly enjoying his own words as if he had told a great joke. He really was happy, and I considered him for the first time without my mother, no shadow of expectation hanging over him. It left me with a false sense of security, fully aware that my mother was not quite the same without him, even with Genie thrown into the mix. I wondered what my father knew, what he was pretending when it came to the two of them. He jolted me from my thoughts with a proposal.

"How about we do something tonight? It's Dee's birthday and he's hired out this Korean fried chicken place. It could be fun?"

For a moment I was too thrown to speak, trying to consider what he was really asking me to do. To join him in celebrating the birthday of an ex. It was so cliché, mundane even in its detail. But the devil was there too, informing me that my father had a significant relationship with Dee now, suggesting that I no longer held pride or place with either. And the smallest detail being the most obvious, like a slap in the face; I had completely forgotten Dee's birthday. I was no longer counting his days, monitoring his living. The fact penetrated me deeply, emphatically, and I was both proud and bothered by it.

Too long had passed since I had said something, and I zoned back into the conversation, recognising the concerned face my father now wore.

"...Or we can get some food ourselves, we don't need to go to the party at all."

The confidence he had been exuding when we first sat down together seemed to quieten down inside of him and I felt guilt grip my stomach.

"No, no it's fine, let's go."

I hoped my tone was a reassuring one but suspected it was not. He laughed awkwardly and then looked at me with sincerity, and I sensed he was about to console me, to tell me we really didn't need to go, and we could just do something together. But once again, I was wrong. He reached across the table and put his hand on my arm, as if to remind me of who he was.

"I've been working with him for a while now, and I promise you, he's not as bad as you think he is. He means no harm."

I stared at him, a retort already formulating in my mind, venomous and with ill intention.

"Did he tell you that I wrote *Young Life* and that he never told me he was turning it into a song? Or was that just another harmless thing he did?"

I knew that I didn't care about it, about the song or who wrote what or why, that my joy at hearing it on the radio in Ghana had been genuine. But I couldn't take my own father siding with him, trying to appeal to me, ask for forgiveness on behalf of Dee without knowing all the facts. I began to wonder what other half-truths Dee had been whispering into his ear about me, and why my father didn't share the disdain for Dee that my mother had always had.

"He credited you on the song, I have residual cheques for you. I thought you would be happy about it."

He said it so innocently, his hand still warm against my arm, still reaching across the table, trying to get through to me. Suddenly I seemed like the unreasonable one. He smiled graciously at me, his eyes inferring that I just didn't understand the fullness of the situation. All I could do was sigh and take note of the new facets of my father that I didn't recognise, that my mother had only alluded to. He was proud of what he was doing, what he was creating. He was living his dream, and he wanted me to be happy for him, to accept that the man who was helping him do it, was the same one I was trying to remove from my life. So, I found a way to bite my tongue for the time being, to support my father and let him enjoy this moment, as short lived as I hoped it would be.

*

I arrived twenty minutes late to the pop-up-turned-restaurant on the edge of Shoreditch. It was relatively small, with only a few tables and a separate section off to the left that had a bar and a dance floor. My father was sat at a table with Dee and two women in their mid-twenties, glaringly beautiful and very chatty. The whole restaurant was dimly lit with a golden sheen to the lamps that illuminated the black and red walls, with a tiled floor that was identical to that of a chess board. I had never been good at chess, or at seeing what moves might be ahead of me.

I made eye contact with Dee immediately. It had been four and a half months since he'd left my key on the table and closed my front door behind him. He wore a button-down black shirt with a black and white checked pocket, black jacket and trousers to match. He sported a fresh haircut and a fresh new smile when he spotted me in the doorway, even before my father did, and gestured excitedly for me to join their table. I hesitated, wondering if it was too late to turn around and go back home. Why was it still so hard for me to just sit with him, to be in his space and trust that in the shortest of moments, it was almost impossible that I would get hurt? Eventually I walked over to them and slid onto the empty bench seat beside him. He still smelled good and I worried that it would shake me. But it was not a scent that was familiar; it was like new clothes or a shiny new penny. Not like himself.

My father leaned across the table and kissed me on the cheek, asking me how I was and introducing me to the other two women. He too was in a suit I had never seen before, a dark blue one with a light blue open collar shirt underneath, accompanied by shiny new shoes and the fresh scent of expensive aftershave. Everyone appeared changed to me. I wondered if my changes remained on the inside, and outside I was still just a familiar face. Dee was treating me as such, including me in the conversation, providing me with context for stories I had not been a part of. In my short absence he had become a social butterfly and I hated how false it felt to me, and how well it suited him. I smiled along, stayed quiet for the most part, pretended that I wasn't the uninvited guest. And then one of the women, the brunette, asked Dee about his album, and what the inspiration was for his first single, *Young Life*.

I looked down at my drink, hoping to disappear into it. I also hoped that he would lie. That he would tell some well-rehearsed tale about what had inspired him to write it. A lie would have helped me, made me feel more secure in my deciding to leave him, even as he sat beside me. Instead he glanced at me and I glanced back, and a hush fell over the table, and I wanted to both laugh and cry. But I did nothing.

"I didn't write it actually. Not the lyrics. Someone else close to me did. And when I read the words, the melody just came to me, like jigsaw pieces falling into place, you know? Like it was meant to be."

The brunette with small eyes and a pouty expression nodded seriously at him, as if she were taking a mental note of his every word. I began to wonder if this was an interview. She continued her line of questioning.

"So, your first number one was a collaborative effort—will you write something more with this 'close friend'?"

She made a point of doing air quotes with her fingers and Dee smirked. I remained still, clutching my cup as I had done with the water in my living room almost a year earlier, Dee sitting beside me, trying to ask for forgiveness. I watched him now, from the corner of my eye, sure that I saw the edges of his mouth twitch in frustration. A lifetime ago he would not have even entertained this kind of exchange. He would have called it superfluous, self-aggrandising. But he was brand new, and so, he had to be different.

"If she was up for it, definitely. But for now, well…"

He looked down at his drink and silently pressed his thigh against mine. My heart raced in response.

"I'm just waitin' for her to return my calls, innit."

The brunette threw her head back in laughter, as if it was the funniest thing she'd ever heard. Then she locked eyes with him, a flirtatious grin on her face.

"I'm sure if she knows what's good for her, she will."

He smiled back, good natured and friendly, not

completely in on the joke. He dared not glance at me again though, letting our thighs remain pressed together, neither of us disconnecting. Instead he announced loudly that it was time for more drinks, which elicited a hearty cheer from his friends on the surrounding tables. I noted that I didn't know any of them. Then he asked if anyone wanted to join him on the dance floor, because apparently he danced now.

I decided that maybe it was time to go. Jay had already texted to say he was at a nearby bar with friends, so when I wanted to escape I should let him know. He hadn't appeared too bothered when I explained my father's invitation, how awkward but obligated I felt to go along with it. His only words of caution felt sensible.

"Don't stay any longer than you need to."

I looked around and remembered that I hadn't wanted to be there in the first place. I got up to go to the bar, and then pulled on my coat, preparing to exit the restaurant quietly.

"Leaving already?"

I heard Dee's voice behind me suddenly, leaning against the bar, watching me as I slid my bag onto my shoulder. He moved closer as I turned to face him, and I took a decisive step backwards, instinctively searching for my father, uncomfortable with the idea of him seeing us together.

"Your dad's outside on the phone, and you didn't answer my question."

"You're a mind reader now?"

"Only when it comes to you."

I sputtered out a laugh at the irony of his statement,

hoping my reproachful look was effective. He ignored it, choosing instead to once again step closer to me, until I put my hand out in front of me, pressing it against his chest to halt his movement. He immediately placed his hand over mine, applying more pressure so that now I felt his heartbeat pulsating through my fingers.

"Please don't do this. Just let me go."

The words were merely a whisper because he was stood so close. His expression didn't change; he kept staring at me like he was laying eyes on me for the first time. Then his shoulders drooped slightly, and he sighed.

"Aren't you going to wish me happy birthday before you go?"

"Happy birthday."

I said it quickly, looking around the room, nervous that eyes might be on us. He looked down at our shoes and began to lightly knock the tip of his shoe against mine, as if I needed more reminders of how close we were. That he was still holding my hand.

"I heard that Ghana was good."

"It was."

"And did you… get everything you needed from it?"

Finally, I looked up at him, into his face, knowing it was what he had been waiting for.

"Yes. And a lot more."

"I'd ask if you missed me but… you didn't, did you?"

I felt like he was trying to cut me open, and I briefly forgot how to disengage. Distraction was my next best move.

"We heard you on the radio, on the way to the airport."

"We?"

I felt my face screw into confusion, unsure how he'd missed all my other words except that one.

"I—"

"Do you love him?"

He let my hand drop as he said it, as if he had already decided the answer and just wanted to prepare himself. I couldn't do anything but stare at him, afraid that my reply might break him. But his question was a brazen one, and now I realised that we were standing apart, and I had been wishing somewhere within me, that he would kiss me. But how could he?

"Do you really want to know?"

My response wasn't meant to be antagonising but the smile that broke out on his face seemed to say that it was.

"Nah, it's cool. I already know how it is."

Now he was walking away from me as if the conversation were over, and I watched myself pull him back by clutching his arm, trying to avoid drawing more attention to us but also not completely caring anymore if I did. Nothing was resolved.

"Wait. Tell me how it is then?"

He stared at me as if I had insulted him. And then that smile again, telling me I was being ridiculous and none of it was a big deal.

"It's just like before; I'm not enough for you. You want a grown up, so now you've got one. You don't need me anymore. It's calm."

"I never said that—that's all in your head."

"Then why did you leave?"

"Because it wasn't working!"

His eyes narrowed and then relaxed into soft sadness.

"You didn't even give me a chance to fix it."

I had a reply ready, knew a rebuttal was warranted, but the words wouldn't formulate. They hung at the back of my throat, leaving me with a partially opened mouth in apparent stunned silence. Dee watched me and then leant down to kiss me on the cheek, pressing his lips against my face for a few long seconds. Then he whispered into my ear.

"Get home safe."

With that he went back to his table, my father having since returned from outside and now in deep conversation with the two women, oblivious to everything else that might be happening.

I pulled my jacket closed and left the restaurant feeling strange. I knew that Jay was minutes away, probably waiting with open arms, the fullness of what he felt always written on his face, ready to be received by the beholder. I wouldn't tell him what had happened, how the kiss that Dee had left on my face was still burning, as if I had been branded. How I might have left a piece of my heart in a Korean fried chicken restaurant, but that I wanted to save the rest for him.

25.

I hadn't planned what I would do once Jay became a permanent fixture in my life. But I quickly realised that to keep
Dee out of my periphery, I would have to distance myself
from my father. The idea of doing it consciously pained me,
as if I was letting Dee win a battle so that I could eventually win the war. It felt unfair, and I mulled over it unhap-
pily for weeks until it was already happening, as my father's
work began to keep him away from home for longer periods
of time. My mother scoffed every time I asked about him,
laughing at my attempts to use her as my informant on his
comings and goings. She was busy having her own quarrels
with him, refusing to join him at industry-related events
because she couldn't understand how spending time with
people she didn't like was going to be helpful to him or his
budding producing career. My father on the other hand, was
convinced that it was my mother's dislike for Dee that kept
her from showing an interest in his new life.

"I know she doesn't like the boy, but she can't make an
effort for me?"

To some extent, he was right.

"He spends too much time with that boy. He thinks he

too is a young man, doing whatever he pleases."

My mother seemed unnerved by it all, frustrated at my father and the opposite directions their lives were taking. Even I would have liked to finger Dee as the problem with their marriage, but we all knew that ship had begun to sail some years prior, so I stayed out of it.

Instead I faced forward with Jay and experienced the knock-on effect of going to Ghana. The team responsible for organising the trip had been eager to meet me and see what other ideas we had for poetry workshops. In the meeting Jay and I exchanged nervous looks. We hadn't expected such a quick offer of more work, so not much planning had happened between us beforehand. Jay threw out an idea off the top of his head, about his monthly poetry show and making it do more, perhaps something bigger with young people. It was vague, and I wondered if they would buy it, but the feedback from the students and the foundation staff in Ghana had given us a good reputation. And there was an 'Us' now. Something that was more than just a romance, more than the November nights we spent in Jay's flat, hunched together under a quilt watching the first 20 minutes of a film before we became lips on thighs and horizontal rhythms. Even more than the long walks we took along the Southbank, or the browsing we did in Borough market, chomping down on fresh sandwiches and making bets about who could cook a better meal between us.

We were embarking on a working partnership now. We kept talking with the foundation whilst I continued to work and progress at the literacy charity. Jay was up for a Deputy Head role and we spent three consecutive nights talking about all the reasons why he should probably take it. It was good money and it was what grown-ups did. He chuckled at the latter statement, the one I made with confidence.

"Your youth is what makes you say that so easily."

"You're not that much older than me."

I nudged him with my foot, covered in a thick sock that merely sprung off his bare toe as we lounged on his sofa.

"My five more years on this Earth tells me that sensible is fine, but passion is better."

I stayed quiet, pondering his words for a moment. It wasn't really my decision, but he made me feel like I was a part of it.

"Okay, so what do you want to do?"

He tipped his head to one side and looked at me before smiling and planting soft kisses on my neck. He kept his head there, nuzzling until I started to giggle. I pushed his face away with one hand, the other on his collar bone, and brought us eye to eye. He sighed and stared back at me, still with a strange smile on his face.

"This. I want to do this."

"This won't make you money."

He raised an eyebrow, looking serious.

"It might though. It might."

We made a compromise. He would take the job to make more money, that would help us fund some of our own projects if things with the foundation didn't work out.

And that was it. The beginning of taking the things we had been hovering around, a little more seriously. We started reviewing our notes from the Accra workshops, what the kids had liked, what they didn't, what they had wanted more of, what had happened by accident that worked out well. We realised the best parts of the workshops, the bits we had most looked forward to, were what I had termed 'spotlight moments'. Five minutes where a student stood up and introduced themselves and answered three questions from the audience; completely random ones that could have nothing to do with poetry or school. The only two rules were that the questions needed to be something that told you more about that person, and the person needed to answer the questions completely honestly. At first the students didn't take it too seriously of course, asking who had dated who or how much the speaker's trainers really cost. But then they became a little more real, queries that poked at purpose and future hopes, at sad truths about family or kind words about friends. It brought out an unpredictable vulnerability that sometimes shook a whole session, leaving a raw feeling that Jay and I carried with us throughout most of the trip.

We thought through the idea and eventually made it into a plan. I felt like we had birthed something together when the idea for the *Spotlight Shows* came to fruition. The format was simple: one spoken word artist would do a set, 15 to 30 minutes if they had the material. This would then be followed by a 20 to 30-minute question and answer session, where audience members could ask poets anything they wanted;

and personal, artistic, professional or otherwise, the poet promised to answer as honestly as they could. We wanted to cultivate an intimate atmosphere between the poet and the audience, maybe get behind some of the ideas for their work and give people a better understanding of who they were. And we could adapt the idea as workshops for young people. Jay would use his school contacts and get poets to run workshops with a handful of young people over a month or so. At the end of it, the young people would be the features of their own *Spotlight Show*, taking it in turns to perform and answer three questions from their peers. We would work on confidence building, presentation skills, project management, writing and performance.

We presented the idea to the foundation excitedly, anticipating answers to all their questions. They were impressed but wanted to see a real-life example. We scrambled to pull something together at the last minute. None of our poetry friends wanted to do it at first; the feature slot was enticing, but the prospect of having to answer any number of questions about themselves from strangers terrified them. But then Kwame came to London to visit and we roped him in as our guinea pig poet, and he blew us away. It helped that he wasn't afraid of being vulnerable; if anything, it fuelled him. The audience left bewildered but oddly happy, giving us small compliments at the end about how refreshing and scary and eye-opening it was. We proved our worth and were given a small pot of funding to get the workshops going in a handful of east London schools. Alongside that, we began running and funding monthly *Spotlight Shows* ourselves.

I feared the momentum of everything would run away with us, but Jay found a way to keep us both grounded. He had a steadiness about him that never seemed to waver. It allowed me to be flightier, and I felt the need to plan less. Instead I pounced on opportunities as they came up, getting some of my work colleagues on board with the workshops, looking at ways to go at things from the literacy angle. I organised a small *Spotlight* workshop for some of the children we worked with at the charity, running it as a mini-project. It led to a promotion for me, with a little more money and a lot more responsibility. I felt like I was finally finding my stride.

Laying down my head to sleep at night, buzzing with new ideas and hopes for the next workshop or *Spotlight Show* we would run, I barely recognised my own life. Often, Jay slept beside me and I felt my body relax whenever he was there, only ready to sleep when he was. I didn't think about Dee. Or I did, but as an afterthought, not quite from another life but another time. He was in the past now, and that was the best thing. Jay felt like what I hoped the future would look like.

And soon my mother was inviting us to the house for dinner, an invitation she had never had cause to offer until now. He hadn't met my parents yet, and I was prepared for them to never meet, but my mother insisted. Jay played at being nervous at the prospect, but these potentially awkward social situations were where he usually shone. We arrived ten minutes early and my father greeted us at the door, much to my surprise. My mother was running late after stopping into her GP surgery to see an emergency patient. My father made us drinks, asking Jay about himself, where his family was from, what work he did. I frowned for a second as I sat beside him, certain I had already given my father all this information.

"Ah ha Jamaica, okay... and you're a teacher? Did Ekuah tell you I used to teach? Yes, music yes... no not anymore, I'm a hitmaker now."

I didn't even try to hide the large eye roll I gave as my father bragged about his job with a new quality to his voice that I didn't like. He had never been an arrogant man, but I suppose that now he had reason to be, and for him he felt it made him shine a little more brightly. For me, it just made him harder to look at. Jay continued to indulge him however.

"I've heard some of your songs, you're amazing... sir!"

I scoffed over my tea and felt Jay nudge me in the waist. My father just shrugged, throwing a hand in the air as if to defend his modesty. Jay continued.

"I'd love to pick your brain actually, because we've been talking about adding a musical element to our *Spotlight Show* and..."

Jay paused as my father raised his eyebrows discerningly. He assumed it meant that my father wasn't interested; he didn't know that the eyebrow raise was for me.

"Ah! Of course! I made this same suggestion to Ekuah a few weeks ago but she refused."

I tried to appear unbothered, but Jay shot me a look before turning back to my father and grinning somewhat falsely. I closed my eyes for a few seconds and sighed before replying.

"I didn't refuse. I just said it'd depend on which artists you had in mind, that it would need to fit in with the tone of the night—"

"Talent is talent though, right?"

Jay interrupted me and then gently squeezed my thigh under the table, as if to reassure me that he wasn't mad. I gave an unenthusiastic smile in response and my father took it as an opportunity to clarify the situation.

"Oh no, no, I get it. You think I will suggest Dee, but I know better than to do that to you. There are many other artists I work with now, my dear."

My father grinned at Jay as if to reassure him, but Jay's face remained a blank sheet, and I spent the rest of the evening wondering what he was thinking. We didn't say any more about it, and my mother arrived shortly thereafter, regaling us with detailed stories about her patients that week, a topic I don't think I had ever had a full conversation with her about before. The rest of the dinner was relatively pleasant all things considered, and my mother was quite taken with Jay. He, on the other hand, barely said two words directly to me until we were on the way home.

We travelled silently on the tube, me anxious, him quietly brooding. He took my hand as we walked from the station to his flat, and then finally, he spoke.

"Your dad and Dee, they're close?"

I exhaled quietly, preparing myself.

"Industry-wise yeah, I guess they are. But besides that, I don't know."

"Your dad thinks a lot of him."

"My dad thinks a lot of *you*, he told me so himself, don't worry."

He turned to me and we stopped walking.

"I'm not worried about that. But, should I be?"

"What do you mean?"

He looked at me like I knew exactly what he meant. I did, but I needed him to say it.

"You let that guy get in the way of what we're trying to do with the *Spotlight Shows*. Even though he wasn't really involved."

"I know, but..."

"I'm just saying, your dad works with Dee and he loves him or whatever. So, he's going to be in your life whether you want him or not. Are you okay with that?"

I felt annoyed that he was challenging me as if I was the one making things hard. And I was quickly remembering why I never wanted to talk about Dee. It still hurt too much, and I wasn't quite ready to explore why that was.

"No—I'm not okay with it. I don't want him around."

"But you can stand it, right? That's what I'm asking."

I began walking again, not trying to get away, just looking for movement that might help me process. He joined me as if we had never paused.

"But why are you asking that? Would you be okay with it, if you were me?"

"If an ex was cool with my dad? Nah, not really. But if me and that person were done, I'd make sure it didn't ruin the life I was trying to build with someone new. But you know, that's just me."

He chuckled awkwardly, and I smiled back, uncomfortable with the whole moment, feeling a bit suffocated by it. I wasn't sure that the truth was something people often wanted to hear, but he was asking for it.

"You want me to say that I'm over it and I don't feel any kind of way about him working with my dad. But... I can't say that. Not yet, not one hundred percent."

We were outside Jay's flat now and he leaned on the door. I wondered if he was deciding whether to let me in or not, now that I'd said the real thing. He wore a shade of sadness on his face, but there remained that glimmer of hope that nothing seemed able to extinguish. I moved closer to him, tentatively.

"Is that... okay?"

He tugged at my jacket and pulled me towards him, locking me in a full lipped, open-mouthed kiss that made my tongue tingle. The best parts of me were his and I hoped that he knew it. Our faces separated, and he pressed his forehead lightly against mine so that our eyes were locked, no interrupted view from peripheral vision, just our mouths inches apart, making clouds in the cold air every few seconds.

"I love you, you know."

The words hung in the air like a feather, dancing around our faces and edging slowly towards the tip of my own tongue. I was left wishing he knew how deeply, and differently, I felt it with him. I couldn't help but compare it, to think of that tiny piece of my heart, not tiny enough really, that still sat in the palm of Dee's hand, knowing how careless he was with it. But Jay had the rest, the untouched parts, the parts that wanted to get stronger and wiser. So, I said it back, in the way that you might whisper a prayer into the night air, hopeful but never completely sure that it was heard, or at least not in the way you intended. His response was a beaming smile, pulling me closer to him somehow, kissing my neck and whispering into my ear as if his final declaration would cement things.

"Move in with me."

26.

Four weeks later, I was moving in. Although I had already been spending a lot of time at Jay's, thinking of his flat as my new home still felt like playing pretend. And in the background of everything, I was saying goodbye to Fifi in our current capacity, my friend of 13 years and roommate for three. As she began establishing her legal career and I worked in the day and planned the *Spotlight Shows* in the evenings, we had become ships passing in the night, staying updated with each other's lives via text messages and social media updates. When it came to my moving out day, she helped me pack up my kitchen things and leave behind whatever she wanted. She teased Jay as he carried a box out to his car and I felt his chuckle run through me like water, their fondness for each other only re-confirming the things I already knew about him. When he was out of the room, Fifi turned to me. "So, I guess you're off to be a grown up now?"

I nodded with a mock serious face.

"I mean, he's a grown up, I'm… growing. So, yeah."

"Well, whatever you do, don't do it too fast."

I tipped my head to one side as a question, waiting for her to say more. Instead she turned away from me and began closing all the open cupboards and drawers in the kitchen, muttering whilst she did it.

"I will not miss this, always leaving the bloody drawers open, so weird…"

"Hey."

I put my hand lightly on her shoulder, forcing her to turn around and look at me again.

"You don't think this is too fast, right?"

She bit her lip as if she was thinking about it. It was her choose-your-words-carefully face, a new mantra she had adopted for her practice, that I knew she was saying to herself now.

"Do you? Think it's too fast?"

"Come on, Fi."

I threw my arms out to my sides in mild annoyance, just as Jay re-entered the room. He picked up on the tension immediately and asked quietly if things were cool. When I nodded, not making eye contact with Fifi anymore, he leaned in to tell me that my father was downstairs with a van, for some reason. Before I could process that information, Fifi began edging her way out of the room but I stopped her and asked Jay to give us a minute. He disappeared again and Fifi spoke before I could begin.

"Like I said last time, I want you to be happy, and you look… happy. If it's fast, maybe that's not a bad thing."

She shrugged as if replying to herself, while I frowned, perching on the edge of the sofa.

"It's scary. It does feel very… adult. But also, I love him, and I spend a lot of time thinking about the next time we'll hang out. So, this cuts that out, I guess."

Fifi released a loud laugh in response, which made me laugh in turn, both of us shaking our heads, still not confident in the life choices we were making but trying to own them anyway. She grabbed my shoulders from behind and shook them affectionately as we made our way out of the flat and down the stairs to greet my father. He had decided, without warning, to come and help me move; making a big show of the gesture by turning up with a van. However, it ended up being a lot more useful than Jay's little Golf GTI. And as a cherry on top, my father also gifted us a brand-new TV as a moving in present that we did not have the room for. But Jay was excited and determined to mount it on his wall, or at least look up how to do it online and then decide whether it was worth it. I laughed at the thought and then watched like a lady of leisure as they emptied the van of my boxes. Afterwards my father pulled me aside, looking a little uneasy. He said he wanted to talk later, when I was settled. Then he announced loudly so that Jay would hear from the other room, that he needed to get going. I was perplexed, suspicious that what he had to tell me shouldn't wait, so I followed him out as if to say goodbye.

"Dad, what's wrong?"

He sighed so gravely I didn't know what to do with myself, wrapping the long sleeve of my jumper around my hand and into a fist.

"It's not bad, okay? It's just that for ease and for my work,

I'm getting a second place, a flat in East London, that's all. I'll be closer to you now!"

He tried to chuckle half-heartedly once he had gotten his sentence out.

"I thought mum hated East London… oh. Oh, wow. Okay."

He watched as I finally caught on to what he was saying. I didn't know what to do once the penny had dropped, so we stood there for a few seconds more just staring at each other in anguish. A moment later I threw my arms around him tightly, feeling tears in my eyes while he stood like a statue, letting me squeeze him. Eventually I let him go, wiping my face, embarrassed. I expected him to look as forlorn as I felt, but his expression remained unchanged. Instead he reached into his back pocket, pulled out his wallet, and fished out two crisp fifty-pound notes before folding them into my hand. I was audibly confused.

"What is this, why—"

"It's a housewarming present."

"But Jay already lives here."

"Then use it to get take away or something, so you don't have to cook."

"Again, you know that this was already Jay's place, right?"

"Yes, I know but—"

"And no one takes notes this big anymore."

I held one of them up to my face, inspecting it with both hands. He knew I was teasing him, but it wasn't enough to cut through the tension.

"Ekuah, just take it okay? Let me do this one thing."

I swallowed, suddenly regretting my words. He smiled at me, and then pulled me back into a hug for a few seconds before getting in the van and driving away. I stayed outside for too long after he was gone. Eventually I was snapped out of my trance when I felt my phone vibrate in my pocket. It was Jay, probably wondering where I was. I ignored it, glancing back up at the space where my father had been parked, before going back into the building, into my new home.

*

These things happen. I remember my mother saying this to me as a child of four or five, when I was playing with my father and running too fast around the house. I sidled into a table and broke a vase. At first, she towered over me, her face filled with fury, but upon seeing my terror she immediately softened and attempted to console me when I burst into tears.

"Don't worry, these things happen. It's okay."

I spent several days after seeing my father wondering if my mother was okay. I couldn't get hold of her properly, we kept missing each other's calls, and her text messages were often incoherent half sentences. Eventually I just turned up at the house in Greenwich, frustrated and anxious. The visit was just for me. I needed to see her face, to find out what exactly had finally made my father move out of the house. It was a thing that had been threatened silently since I was old enough to realise what was happening between them. I knew that I wasn't supposed to take sides, but I also knew that my mother would expect me to be backing my father and whatever his version of events was. I wanted to give her a chance to be wrong about that. I hoped she was.

I rang the doorbell once, keeping my finger on the button a second too long so that I felt the reverberation in my ears. I heard the jostle of a key in the lock and stepped back in surprise as Genie opened the door in a dressing gown and a headscarf. She looked just as surprised to see me, squinting her eyes at the February sun behind me as if it was too early to be opening front doors. I glanced at my watch; the hands were on 9.30AM and I realised that it was Saturday and maybe this time didn't work for everyone at the weekend.

"Is—is my mum home?"

"What? Yes of course, come in, come in."

She ushered me through the door, making an uncomfortable face as the cold air hit her before she shut the door behind me. I stood awkwardly in the corridor so that she had to squeeze past me, pointing her chin away from me to shout.

"Chrissie, Ekuah *aba*!"

With that she took a left turn and disappeared in the direction of my parents' bedroom. I stayed standing in the corridor, staring at the guest room to my right, the bed made, untouched, almost inviting in its pristineness.

My mother emerged from the bathroom with a cloth wrapped around her, a mixture of purple and green *adinkra* patterns covering her from the top of her armpits all the way down to her ankles. Her braids were tied up in a hasty bun and she smiled at me strangely when she saw me. I smiled back at her and she turned towards the kitchen, indicating with her hand that I should follow.

"Do you want tea or coffee?"

"Tea please."

She pulled a face, grunting softly and flicking the kettle on.

"You're not drinking coffee anymore?"

She pulled out a chair by the kitchen table and we sat there together, listening to the gentle boil of the kettle.

"I'm just trying it out. Jay doesn't drink too much of it, so…"

"So, you're what? His shadow?"

She didn't even say it with energy, she just scoffed and then stood up again to make the tea. I looked down at my hands on the table cloth. It was a pale blue colour, perfectly matching the chairs and the dado board running along the kitchen walls, stopping at the door and the cooker. As a child I always wondered how she found these matching things in different places, and then I discovered later that my father was responsible for most of the decorating in the house I had grown up in.

"I didn't know Auntie Genie was still here."

I heard her scrape one of the cups against the side before bringing them both over to the kitchen table and sitting back down.

"Your father was never here, this way he can sleep in his own bed."

I stared at her, trying to decide if she had ignored my comment or not. I opened my mouth to speak but thought better of it and took a moment instead, blowing on my tea with no intention of sipping it.

"What's wrong with her being here anyway? Do you want me in this house alone?"

"Of course not."

"Well then."

"But mum, dad—"

"Your father felt that other things needed his attention. So, he has gone to attend to them. I can't begrudge him that."

I so desperately wanted to tear into her about Genie, to ask why she was still there, why she wasn't living in her own house, knowing she could afford it. And I wanted to know why she wasn't in the guest room, how my father's presence had been erased so quickly from the house. Why she, my mother, was continuing to pretend we didn't all know exactly what was going on. But her tone and the way she nodded her head as if the matter were done with, meant there was no more talking about it. I would have to feel around for the missing pieces of the puzzle myself, making them fit where I could, knowing I might never have a complete picture.

I returned home, more lost than when I had left that morning, only now I had plastic containers of jollof that Genie had made, and some bottles of Supermalt for Jay because I disliked the smell and refused to buy them whenever I was food shopping. He was ecstatic at the haul I had brought home, but disregarded it all when he saw my expression. I plonked down onto the sofa, leaning forward with my face in my hands. Jay sat beside me and rubbed my back without asking me any questions. I felt like I should be wrecked but I couldn't connect with it. I knew that my parents were separated, that it had been something I imagined happening dozens of times before. But knowing it could happen didn't prepare you for when it actually did. They weren't just taking a break, they were moving on without each other, and in my mother's case, maybe with other people. Well, one other person.

There were a lot of hurtful things I imagined my mother doing, but being unfaithful wasn't one of them. And perhaps she had not been at all, but just the presence of Genie around the house was enough to apply the smallest amount of pressure to a marriage that was already on unstable footing. And I felt as though Genie had knowingly inserted herself into a precarious situation, and then decided to stay put. I wondered if it was hereditary, the ability to leave heartbreak in your wake, a move I thus far had only attributed to Dee. I couldn't understand how my mother could dislike him so intensely, and yet still live happily and in close quarters with his aunt.

And I couldn't stomach wondering these real things anymore, imagining my father sitting alone in a crummy flat surrounded by boxes, whilst my mother shared old stories with an old friend. Or lover. I didn't know. I couldn't retell the full story because I didn't have all the facts. I just had my own worries and all the memories of my mother and father staying married despite the constant friction between them. Were they ever as unhappy as I had imagined, or was this more recent than I was realising? And what could have kept them together? Why was it only now that they were breaking apart? I felt that if I could just find the answers, then maybe I could avoid making the same mistakes.

27.

I leaned into Jay and he held us both up. We found a groove that worked for us, slowly at first, neither one wanting to push the other too far, too quickly. One day I came home and there were succulents everywhere; two at the kitchen window, three in the living room, one perched on the tiny window sill of our even tinier bathroom, and another two in the bedroom. Jay was sat on the sofa reading, and looked up at me casually as I walked into the living room, my arms gesturing a little too energetically, questions all over my face.

"Why all the... everything—the succulents?"

He placed his book down carefully and I noticed the nervous look on his face for the first time.

"I was just reading that plants make things more homely and I know you had a few at your old place and I wasn't sure if they were Fifi's so I just took a chance and now I'm thinking maybe it was too much so I can just get rid of them if you want—"

I took off my jacket as he spoke, throwing it onto the kitchen table awkwardly. Then I moved myself towards the sofa, straddling him where he sat, cutting off his speed-talking as I knew it would. I felt his arms immediately wrap themselves around me in response, and I kissed the tip of his nose softly, feeling him exhale in relief.

"I love them. Although…"

He looked up at me expectantly, his face open as it always was, and I felt a stab, a whisper of something painful in my chest that reminded me of guilt. As usual I ignored it, wanting to carry on in the moments we had together, playing house and trying to get to that place that didn't feel like pretend anymore.

"Fifi was the one that kept them alive, I'll be really honest with you."

Jay grinned, pulling me closer to him as if in celebration, happy I hadn't told him I was allergic, or that I hated plants or something else circumstantial that would have taken away from his gesture. He twisted one of my thin braids around his finger, keeping eye contact the whole time, holding on to me and holding me in his gaze. I leaned in and let him kiss me; a soft kiss that I knew would lead to something else, where succulents were the last thing on our minds. I liked it that way, getting lost in what we were, our bodies taking over so that neither of us would have to think. My mind was always at its quietest then, just happy to feel things instead of pondering them, with no room to pick anything apart.

Later on he told me that he was green fingered, that his mum had taught him and that his grandfather had been the groundskeeper on a wealthy estate in Jamaica. It was in his blood, he said. I listened as he spoke more than he had before about his family, the town they were from, what they meant to him. I rested my chin on his chest as the low trickle-hum of his voice soothed me. I found myself smiling when his voice rose slightly, excited in parts and serious in others. I tried to take it all in, to feel his words surround me, bring comfort like they were supposed to. And all the while he held me tightly in his arms, his fingers tracing small circles on my back. I closed my eyes and fell asleep to the sound of his voice, wondering not for the first time, if this was what contentment felt like.

Soon we were a routine of togetherness. We set our alarms every night before bed so that we woke up together. We went food shopping every Wednesday evening because his fridge wasn't big enough for us to go less frequently. We spent Sundays at home, reading or pottering around the flat, tidying this or fixing that. Once a month I helped him put on his spoken word night *The Light,* where we had first met, and every other week we ran the *Spotlight Shows*. We flourished within our work together. We became synonymous with one another and weeks would go by before I referred to just myself in conversation, rather than "me and Jay".

When I walked in the door after work he was always there waiting for me, marking papers or reading or watching TV, but always waiting. As if he couldn't relax until he had eyes on me. I would kiss him hello, our night not really beginning until we did that. Sometimes I squeezed myself onto the sofa with him, interrupted what he was doing so that he could ask about my day. He focussed on me in the way you might pay attention to a newborn, full of love and adoration but also constantly checking that I was still alive, still okay. I found myself trying to reassure him with small gestures, picking up his favourite wine or buying tickets to some obscure Ska band that I could just about stomach but knew that he loved. And after a few months of us living together he seemed to relax a little, to trust that when he woke up, I would still be there. I leaned into his trust in return, took it as my own, tried to absorb it, to find space in it. I wondered how everyone else did it, how you want what the other person wants. Do you create that yourself or do they do it for you?

It's what I had assumed about my parents, that they were in some way dependent on each other for whatever they needed to survive. I kept waiting for that need to click into place with Jay and I, for me to feel a little bit more lost when he wasn't around, to feel like if not half, at least some of me was missing. That's how I would know we were going to go the distance.

But perhaps things changed because I became obsessed with what wasn't happening, with what wasn't working.

*

"You believe in that stuff, soulmates?"

Jay asked it with curiosity as we sat in a pub garden across from each other at a wooden table.

"I mean, I don't anymore, but when I was younger I did."

"When you were at uni?"

I nodded, tracing a finger around the edge of my wine glass.

"When you were with—Dee."

Jay frowned as he said it. I noticed it wasn't a question, that he paused slightly before saying Dee's name. These moments were a hesitation for me too—I couldn't really understand how Dee still managed to creep into things between us. Perhaps I was letting him.

"Yes, when I was young and dumb; it happens. But that's what I mean."

"What?"

He took a large gulp of his beer, suddenly parched.

"My mum, she believes in soulmates. I remember Genie telling me that years ago, and it just popped back into my head recently."

"So, she thinks Genie is her soulmate?"

I frowned, thinking about how to better frame my words.

"I don't know. But the way Genie said my parents were as teenagers, I think my mum thought my dad was hers. Like, she really believed it."

I looked up at him and he surveyed my concerned face, waiting for more.

"And this is a... good thing?"

"No, it's... well no, I guess not. Not now...but also; yes, because it means it wasn't all for nothing. That they really loved each other."

Jay rubbed his stubbled chin and finished his second beer. I was still nursing my first glass of wine, not really in the mood to drink but agreeing to come out anyway, because I had noticed how we were veering towards a rut. After six months of living together, of being in each other's pockets and adjusting our personal routines for new, coupled ones, things had become habitual but frustrating, in tiny ways that sometimes scraped the back of my teeth. Even our social outings were thinly veiled excuses for us to do more work on the *Spotlight Shows* and build our business. They were becoming much less about building our relationship. I didn't begrudge it because I loved the work, and it felt useful and purposeful, even when I battled restlessness.

"What do you think made them stop loving each other then?"

I paused mid-shrug at Jay's question, the movement feeling too nonchalant for the answer it deserved.

"I don't know that they did, maybe they just grew tired or... I don't know. Let's talk about something else."

He frowned at me in annoyance suddenly, as if I was taking something away from him.

"We can, but you brought it up, so clearly you want to talk about them."

"I really don't."

I took a sip of my wine and winced at the slightly vinegary taste, remembering why I was drinking it so slowly.

"Well, fine. But I have a theory."

He held out his hand as if asking permission to say more, giving me a small smile at the same time, that I knew I couldn't say no to. I nodded for him to continue.

"So maybe they didn't stop loving each other, it just changed into something else. Remember we had that poet that used to be a physicist, who talked about love as energy; it never disappears, it just changes shape?"

"I'm sorry, I wasn't aware we were at one of our shows."

He chuckled at my sarcastic quip and rubbed the back of his neck in apparent awkwardness.

"Just hear me out for a sec."

"Sure. So, love never ends if we treat it like energy?"

"Exactly."

He grinned at me like I had won a prize, so I continued thinking through out loud what he was saying.

"Which means you might never stop loving people, like your first loves or exes or..."

He pulled his head back in surprise at my words, his brow suddenly furrowed with endless lines.

"Right, in theory but like… I mean I'm not saying everyone still loves, or feels something for someone they used to love..."

He trailed off, staring at me, perhaps waiting for me to finish his sentence.

"No, of course not. I get you."

We both sat in silence for a moment, the atmosphere suddenly filled with tension and unspoken things. He stared at the table and I wondered if my inability to fill silences had finally rubbed off on him. So, I spoke up this time.

"So, your theory?"

"Yeah… yeah, so maybe it's like energy, and if you can

keep loving someone in different ways, then maybe there's the potential for love to go back to how it was originally. Where you fall back in love again."

He spoke in a low voice now, so that I had to lean in to hear him. I realised he had been trying to cultivate hope for me, that my parents might not stay apart. But somehow, he had gotten bruised in the process. I told him that maybe he was right, and I hoped so, and then suggested we go home. We both knew what it meant. Ten minutes later we were back in the flat, clothes removed, the sound of the neighbour's motorcycle rumbling in my left ear as Jay whispered into the other one, asking me if I liked whatever he was doing, our bodies pressing into the mattress periodically; a perfectly rehearsed rhythmic routine. Afterwards we lay together, Sunday afternoon creeping by, flecks of light from the window projected onto exposed skin. And I wondered how we got here again.

Neither of us had planned for sex to become a pacifier for us, to atone for any sins our mouths might make against our relationship. But it began to happen, and soon it just became a thing that happened all the time. It was the answer to the question that seemed to hang over us; a stop gap of reassurance that yes, we were fine. Look at how fine we were, at how much sex we have, how everything is so easy, until it gets hard, and then we make love again and smooth over the difficult bits.

Now when we talked, the end of the conversation remained unknown. Which slip up would I make this time?

Would I show my immaturity, or rise to whatever emotional challenge Jay had set for us that day? And I was consumed by thoughts of my parents and their marriage, what it was and was not. I tried to get a point of reference about it from my father, find out what drew him to my mother, and what pushed him away—although I felt that I already knew the latter answer. He was reluctant at first, choosing his words carefully.

"She was not like the other girls, so for me, that made up my mind."

He spoke softly, calling me from New York, midnight his time, his small voice paying its respects to the lateness of the evening.

"And that was it, she was yours?"

He gave a laugh that was heavy with a raspy edge.

"Not quite, but you know, the best things, they take work."

I could hear the nostalgia in his voice, the hues of sadness with a false levity behind it. Every time we spoke now, I wanted to cry, and thought that maybe he did too. It also didn't help that I kept bringing it up, their separation, but I couldn't think of anything else when it came to speaking to him. It was front and centre, present in all rooms and phone calls that we shared.

"Well, I'll let you go back to sleep."

"You're… you're visiting her, yes? Making sure she's okay?"

"Yes, Dad. I am. I mean, I will, sorry. It's not like…

anyway."

"Not like what?"

"Not like... she's alone."

The line was so clear I heard him sigh and shift in his bed, followed by an intake of breath, the kind you might take to gather composure.

"She is still your mother and she's still my wife. You'll keep treating her as such, okay?"

I felt the sternness of his voice rattle in my ears and replied with a one-word agreement, before finally ending the call. I left the semi lit bathroom to crawl back into bed, falling back asleep in minutes, suddenly calm and at ease. And an hour later, up again to get ready for work. My father's words continued to ring in my ears.

"She's still my wife."

A hopeful sign, a proclamation in my eyes. Somewhere deep inside I had always hoped that underneath all the negative quips and silent treatment, there was love between them. That maybe Jay was right after all, that it could return. But when I expressed this to him, he laughed, not cruelly but because he thought I was joking. When he realised I was being serious and was hurt by his reaction, he tried to console me, though I could see that he thought I was being naive.

"I know what you're saying but... what about Genie?"

And then we had sex, because I didn't want to talk about it anymore and as manipulative as I felt, I knew that he was letting me do it. He didn't want to fight either, not about this. So what if we were putting plasters over bullet holes?

*

My mother knew I was avoiding going back to the house to visit, to see the new reality she was living in now with Genie. They were officially living together, or as official as they could be where no one could talk about it. Genie was now stationed permanently in London. We still worked for the same place, but now I was the senior education project manager, working out of a different office, our professional connection a distant memory. It was how I wanted to keep it, though my mother suggested otherwise. She said it was useful for me to know the big boss, to take advantage of it, despite me assuring her that I was fine on my own, that I had bigger plans for our *Spotlight Shows,* and that I hoped to work for myself one day. She just stayed silent, but we both knew this was the safest topic for us, that it had always been; work and school. We knew the rules and the parameters. Talking about my father came with zero safeguards.

So, when she requested my presence on a Friday evening, specifically to talk about him, I braced myself. These conversations were always historically about something she felt he had done wrong.

"How are things with Jay?"

I leaned back into the sofa, selfishly a little more relaxed knowing it was just the two of us, Genie away at a conference.

"They're fine. They're good."

My mother squinted her eyes at me from her armchair,

looking suspicious.

"Hmm, fine and good together are not assurances."

I shrugged and tried to laugh it off, but she continued to stare at me.

"We're just, you know, things are up and down."

Our lack of familiarity talking about this subject was apparent as I wondered how much I should reveal. She continued to watch me before she spoke.

"Your father and I, we haven't handled this with you very well."

Her words nudged me out of my own head.

"It's okay, I'm… I'm an adult. You don't have to handle anything for me."

"Hmm, so you are up and down with Jay and it has nothing to do with us?"

"Well…"

Everything else I could think to say would have been a lie.

"Okay, then for that, I really am sorry. This time I want to be straight with you."

Now I was sitting up. She reached down the side of her chair and picked up a thick A4 sized envelope. She pulled out its contents in a stack and handed them to me like a gift. It didn't take me long to read the first page before quickly putting the stack down on to the coffee table in front of us. I turned to my mother, suddenly infuriated at the message she was delivering to me.

"You're getting a divorce?!"

My question came out in a petulant tone, accurately reflective of how childish I suddenly felt. But her face didn't change, as if she had been expecting this reaction.

"Ekuah, this has been a long time coming. I know you know this already."

"Mum, this is too much! You haven't even seen dad in months—have you even tried to work on it?"

Now she looked insulted, and then quietly angry. Her voice became low and weighted. She raised her index finger and pointed it at me, so that I knew exactly who her words were for.

"You are an adult, yes, but don't you ever question the decisions that your father and I make when it comes to the two of us. Okay?"

She was staring at me with eyes like daggers, waiting for me to obey, but I couldn't. My fists were clenched, and I felt so clearly that this wasn't right, that this was too big of a change. That this would mean the end of everything I knew and it wasn't fair. I realised suddenly that I was standing.

"You're not thinking clearly. You both just need time."

I moved to exit the living room but felt my mother grab me roughly by the arm.

"My friend, think very carefully about what you do next. You just sat here and told me we didn't need to handle you, yet here you are—"

"If you knew I was going to react this way, why'd you even call me?"

My voice was raised, my question anger-fuelled, and I

wasn't sure what answer I was expecting, but it wasn't the one that she gave.

"Because I didn't want you to hear it from your father and think that it was my idea alone. And... I didn't want to stop hearing from you."

Her face had quickly dissolved into sadness, and she dropped my arm from her grip. Her eyes glistened with tears and I turned my face away, unable to deal with all that emotion from her. But I didn't leave. Instead we sat back down in silence, me trying to burn the divorce papers with my eyes, her with an upturned face, sunk back into her armchair with her own eyes closed. And all I could think was, *what the hell do I do now?*

*

The weeks and months that followed for Jay and I seemed to merge into one long stream of difficult interactions. I felt angry all the time and he was the closest person available to experience my tirades. I was nit-picky about everything he did and said. Any offer of support he wanted to give to me over my parents' divorce was met with pithy remarks and silence. I knew that everything I was doing was wrong, that eventually I would hit the self-destruct button on our relationship for the last time, that there was only so much he could take; and he could take a lot. But I didn't know how to stop myself.

I was convinced that with Jay, I was just bringing our

problems out into the open, showing him what a future with me might look like. Maybe it would be hard, but if we could get through it, we could get through anything. But I was not in control, no matter what I told myself. I was dealing with everything poorly, and I watched as each of my outbursts pushed Jay to say less and less. The final straw was around the corner, I knew that, but by then I was a runaway train, an unpredictable mess of a woman who pathetically couldn't deal with the fact that mummy and daddy had decided not to be together anymore. I felt like I no longer had a blueprint for how to act with sense, so I threw all the plans away and became unreliable.

It began with Jay's poetry night, *The Light,* that after five years was practically running itself. So I stopped paying attention when he asked me to do things for it, call this poet and that one. It just dropped off my list of priorities, as if it had never been there in the first place. More than once a feature poet didn't turn up because I hadn't contacted them after promising that I would. Open mic spots filled up the time, but it was ruining Jay's credibility and he was under-standably upset.

"If I can't rely on you then please, just stay out of it."

I was hurt but had no defence. I had dropped the ball completely on a thing I knew meant so much to him. I beat myself up about it, knowing I was struggling to keep things together but thus far had not let anything major slip, except when it came to him.

The second thing was the *Spotlight Shows.* We had a

programme now, with the next year of school workshops almost fully booked. I threw myself further into it, focusing on the execution of the *Spotlight Shows* themselves whilst Jay ran the workshops and prepped the young people. I talked to more poets and eventually some musicians who had heard about what we were doing and wanted to be a part of it. At the time it didn't occur to me to discuss it with Jay; we had long established that I took care of the show and he worked on the school side of things. So when I told him the next show would be spotlighting a musician, he was confused.

"But it's about poetry, I thought we agreed we would keep it that way."

I sighed loudly as I washed the dishes, my back to him, unwilling to turn around.

"Do you know how many calls I get from performers who aren't poets? We need to expand, it just makes sense."

"With what time? And what resource? We've kept it small because we can't afford to make it bigger right now."

Eventually I turned around, ready to confess what I had been thinking about for some weeks.

"What if I quit my job? Then I'd have the time."

"Yeah right, don't be silly."

He waved his hand at me dismissively and the dragon lady in me appeared almost instantly.

"I'm being serious, please don't patronise me."

He screwed up his face and pinched the top of his nose as if he had a headache.

"I'm not trying to patronise you, I'm just asking that you

think about this for a second. It's fine to have a musician for this one, but we need to decide—"

"If I want to quit my job I will, I've got enough saved to live for at least six months without working. I've thought about this!"

He just stared at me like I was insane, his mouth partially open. Then he threw up his hands before leaving the room. I felt terrible about it but believed I had won. We went ahead with the musician—a grime artist—and it was a success, at least from the outside.

But it was that night, when we got home, 11PM just around the corner, that Jay finally had something more to say.

"Is that what you've been saving for all this time? To quit your job?"

I was undressing, standing in my bra and jeans, searching our wardrobe for pyjamas.

"Not at first, but yeah. Why?"

I poked my head out the side of the door to look at him. He was sitting at the edge of the bed, still fully dressed.

"I just thought… maybe I assumed it, I don't know. But I feel like we talked about it, about saving together, for a bigger place. Did I imagine that?"

I found what I was looking for and began to remove my jeans, not really picking up on his tone.

"No, you're right, we talked about it. But then you got that second salary increase and I assumed you didn't need me to help you save anymore, so I sort of, changed my plan."

"But the place was for both of us. I thought it was what we both wanted?"

I was in the bed now, talking to his back because he remained in his position at the other end of the bed.

"I know but… I'm not sure I want to do that anymore."

He stood up suddenly, his face every shade of angry as he turned to me.

"Then what the hell are we doing?!"

I sat up, knowing I was giving him a shocked look as if his anger wasn't justified. And then I shrugged, as if he was asking me what I wanted for dinner, not what I wanted from our relationship. He began to pace the room, the carpet making quiet squeaky sounds under his trainers.

"I thought—no, I *hoped* that you were ready for this. That eventually you'd be ready for *me*, but… you're not, are you?"

"Why, because I don't want to save for a pile of bricks that I'll be chained to for the next twenty years?"

The words were rolling from my tongue without my consent, or at least that's what I would tell myself later.

"The fact that we can't even have this conversation properly, Ekuah, tells me everything I need to know."

And then he just stopped talking, his eyes filling with tears, the first time I had ever seen him cry. I wanted to console him, to just cross the inches between us and wrap my arms around him, tell him I was being stupid, that I wanted all the things he wanted. But I knew deep down that I didn't. Not in that space, in that time. And torturing him with false hope was a step too far even for me. So I stayed stoic even though I was breaking inside. He dragged a hand under his eyes and straightened himself up. He was no longer pacing but instead stood in front of the bed, looking down at me.

"I know you're going through it right now, and you know I love you."

He swallowed, as if the words were caught in his throat. I realised my own face was wet, that tears were trickling from my eyes. I tried to wipe them away but they kept coming. He had paused for a long time, gathering the strength to keep going.

"I was willing to wait it out, because I thought we wanted the same things, but... we don't. So, I'm gonna go now."

He didn't wait for a reply, he had waited long enough. I watched him walk out the door in a blurry outline, my eyes too cloudy to see anything else.

PART THREE

PART·THREE

28.

It's tempting to just keep going. When bad things happen, it seems easier to hide behind the regular routine of things, hoping that eventually and with time, the pain will go away, that you'll be ready to face new things again. But I couldn't carry on in the same way.

Jay was gone. I came home one day, and half his clothes were missing from the wardrobe, his shaving set absent from the bathroom sink. He sent me a text, business-like, efficient with his words.

> **JAY:** I'm staying at Mike's. You can have the place for a month if you need time to find somewhere else. Contact me if there's bill stuff.

I laughed when I read it; waiting for more, wondering if someone else had written it for him. It was so cold. And then I waited for it to hit me, the big pain after the initial wrecking, but nothing came. It was curious, but not unfamiliar. I had a feeling of flatness, as if something had snapped and neither intense pain nor joy were within my reach.

I moved back in with Fifi. I broke the news about Jay and me to both parents. My mother was disappointed; my father wasn't surprised. I had no words for either. I took two weeks off work and spent the first few days finishing all the books I had started and stopped halfway through, when Jay had suggested something else to read that I would also love. I had become scatty with him, and so I needed to finish something. Something that we had shared. Perhaps it was my own way of saying goodbye; I wasn't sure. But I completed them and moved on to the next task.

I planned the next six months of *Spotlight Show* artists. This didn't feel like an old task anymore because I was mapping out something much bigger for the show.

"You're handling this surprisingly well. Should I be worried?"

Fifi questioned me one evening, as we ate Chinese food on the sofa, after she had told me a story about an awkward date she had had with a guy from work, and I had cackled for too long.

"I'm... handling it."

I didn't really have an explanation for my behaviour, but I knew that I felt different, less restricted. Though I had thought I was exercising my freedom before, when Jay and I were together, so maybe my perspective on things could not be trusted.

"Well, time off is good, I think you're doing it right. You're doing what you want to do."

I nodded, wondering if that was true. The next day, with

a week left of holiday to go, I wrote my resignation email, but I didn't send it yet. *Not yet, burn it down slowly.*

I wasn't trying to ruin things for myself, but I needed something to move in a different direction. I hadn't suggested quitting my job to Jay solely to push him away, but I hadn't told the whole truth about it either. I had only been quietly considering change, and the future, and not feeling as dissatisfied as I suddenly felt. And I had been fighting internally with myself, watching this wonderful man and the way he loved me, and wondering why I wasn't completely happy about it. I had, perhaps, been trying too hard to understand what had happened with my parents, how they had gone from love and leaving their country of birth together, to frosty exchanges. Suddenly it was a mystery to me, even though I had been watching it unfold for most of my life. Watching how they struggled to communicate properly, observing the seed of resentment that grew in silent vines around their relationship.

Jay and I did not have that problem, if anything honest communication had been our foundation. But in trying to understand my parents, I began to repeat their patterns, hoping I would find the key to understanding them hidden in old mistakes. And this was only one side of things; the other became clearer towards the end: that Jay and I were headed in different directions. I had grown up with him in some ways like I had with Dee, and as much as I wanted to slot into his life and future plans, when it came to the crunch I couldn't do it. But somewhere in the middle of loving Jay he was owed the truth from me, and I hadn't been able to give him that

My real mistake was thinking that it would be easy, and judging my parents for also not being honest with each other sooner. But the thing was done now.

I could only hope that one day Jay would forgive me. Because we were still entangled business-wise and detaching us from that was proving more difficult. The *Spotlight Shows* had begun to gain some publicity on social media, and then a small Time Out review saw our tickets selling out faster and faster every month. Jay continued to organise and run the workshops without me having to ask or really contact him at all. He had stopped attending the live shows a while back, before the break, leaving it mostly in my hands. And I had recruited Fifi to help me run them instead, which was working out better than either of us would have predicted. I wanted things to remain this way, and now I wanted ownership of it too, so I used the rest of my holiday days to put those things in motion. I made some applications for more funding, for the show and the workshops. I didn't want to tell Jay unless something came of it. So when it did, reluctantly, I picked up the phone to call him. He answered immediately, causing a wave of shock to ripple through me, the first live feeling I had had in what felt like weeks.

"Are you… well?"

He gave a big sigh in response, already regretting answering, probably.

"I'm okay. How are you doing?"

"Good. We got more funding. I thought you should know."

I reminded myself this wasn't a social call. My stomach was twisting in on itself in anguish, I forgot about his voice, how it used to vibrate me. Shit.

"Wow, that's great. So, we can pay the poets a bit more now?"

I wondered why he had framed it as a question, as if he already knew that that's not what it was for but wanted to remind me where he stood on the issue.

"No. This is to take the show on a sort of mini tour, get it some international traction. In Europe I mean."

He laughed, in a wicked tone I hadn't heard before; it sounded like a whip. I felt it across my face and crushed my nails into a fist, trying to hold my tongue and stop it lashing back. When he was done, he spoke again.

"I'm sorry, but how are we going to do that? We both work full time, it's just not feasible, Ekuah. I mean, did you think this through before you made that bid?"

The patronising tone I thought I had imagined months ago, had returned. Only now it had a justified edge of pain around it.

"Yeah, I did actually. And don't worry, I'll handle it. I'm finishing work in a month."

I thought the line had gone dead for a few seconds, until he cleared his throat, as if he had moved his face away from the phone, so that he could scream without me hearing it perhaps.

"Right. So, you were serious about… right, okay."

"It's what I want to focus on, you know?"

A big part of me wanted him to understand, to feel as passionate about the show as I did, above all else—including our relationship. I was realising how important the work had become to me.

"Listen, I can't do this right now."

"Yeah of course, we can talk it through later."

"No."

His reply was firm, the monotone of his voice having returned, as if he thought a show of emotion would take something from him. He continued.

"I'll finish out the workshops for the rest of the year, but after that, I'm out. It's all yours—that's what you wanted, right?"

I was glad we weren't in the same room, my eyes full of stupid tears, his words managing to cut through the stoic countenance I had been trying to foster. He still, for the most part, knew what I wanted, even if he didn't want the same thing.

"Yes. That's what I want. Thanks for… thank you."

"Cool."

He hung up before any goodbyes could be exchanged, and I stared at the phone without a clear thought coming to mind. My hands were restless suddenly, and I considered calling him back, demanding that he say more, that he be angry with me out loud, tell me that I was making a mistake. Maybe that would wake me up, take the quiet ache away from me, make me feel like a whole thing again. Instead I stood up and made a different call. To my father.

29.

///H|appy Birthday!"

My father grinned at me, leaning on the white table cloth as I pulled my chair in and felt my feet slide against the marble floor. We were in a place fancier than I had ever been before. All the servers were in waistcoats and we sat beneath a multi-tiered chandelier. My father waved a small envelope in front of my face and I hesitated before taking it.

"My birthday isn't for another three months—you know that, right?"

"Just open it!"

I took the envelope from him, tearing it open roughly, his face hungry for my reaction. I pulled out the card that was inside it and a colourful piece of paper fell out.

"The Edinburgh Fringe Festival? Oh my God!"

He sat back in his chair, grinning from ear to ear, pleased with my exclamations.

"Ask and it shall be given. I had my assistant register you, the venue is booked and everything, you can put your *Spotlight...* thingy on for four nights."

My heart felt like it was swelling as I stood up and walked

to the other side of the table, crouching down and wrapping my arms around his waist as he remained seated. Words escaped me, and this was all I could think to do. He squeezed my arm as I unclutched myself and returned to my seat.

"Are you going to be there?"

I asked happily, still buzzing from the news.

"I'm going to try for the first night, but I've got two weeks of studio sessions booked in around that time, so we'll see."

I nodded, obviously disappointed but trying to make the best of it. He gestured for the waitress who was hovering around us and ordered champagne. I couldn't help but look surprised and shake my head, telling him it wasn't necessary. He ignored me, and the champagne arrived minutes later.

"To my baby girl, conquering the world all by herself, at 25 no less!"

He raised his glass and I raised my own, trying to keep quiet, to just enjoy the toast, but I couldn't.

"Not completely by myself. I mean, Jay helped."

I thought I saw him roll his eyes, not a movement I would have ever associated with my father, but his face changed so quickly I couldn't be sure.

"Yes, yes, of course. There are two extra passes in there, so if you want to invite him…"

He trailed off, though I wasn't sure what response he was hoping for.

"I'll ask him but… he probably won't come."

I felt my voice weaken slightly, the shadow of us still

hanging over my head, sometimes spilling out my insides. I continued to try and cure it by ignoring my feelings and hoping that was enough. My father nodded, sipping from his glass, pensive suddenly. I watched him, thinking how healthy he looked these days, and sort of youthful, like he was more comfortable with himself and the world he moved through now. He was happy, and I hadn't expected it. I considered how hard I had tried to put distance between us, to keep away from Dee, the influence I had been so fearful of. It all seemed so pointless now. What was I so worried about?

"So, sweetheart, listen. I know you usually have poets and whatnot at these things, but it's Edinburgh Fringe—"

He stretched his arms out as he said the name, as if he knew it well and I hadn't been the one to explain to him what it was a month earlier.

"So maybe you have one of my artists close out your shows? You did say you wanted this to be a practice run for a European tour, right?"

He had me there, appealing to my better interests, the ones that had grown beyond what was immediately in front of me. I smiled, unable to help myself from eyeing him suspiciously.

"Who did you have in mind?"

He shrugged, spreading butter on a piece of bread from the basket in front of us.

"Not sure yet. I wanted you to say yes first."

He flashed me a smile before shoving the bread in his mouth. I couldn't help but throw my head back in laughter as he chomped down on it, glad that some things hadn't changed.

*

The festival was exhilarating and exhausting. In the weeks leading up to it, I reached out to the poets that had received the best feedback for their workshops with us, and booked them for three of the four nights. I left the last night open, trying to pin my father down with the name of an artist. I worried that he might choose that time to spring Dee on me, but then remembered hearing that he was on a European tour, so wouldn't be around anyway. Then a week before the festival, I got a call from my father telling me that he knew a young singer named Elsie who would love to do the show. We exchanged numbers and met up two days later to talk everything through. She was 22, played haunting melodies with just a keyboard and a loop, and had a piercingly beautiful voice.

Jay and I had long since developed a system to prepare artists for our live shows, getting some background information from them, the topics they explored in their work, and then, from almost a year of *Spotlight Shows*, we were able to give artists some idea of the kinds of audience questions they should expect. Elsie was a pro from the outset, adjusting her colourful headwrap that held maroon-coloured braids atop her head, to tell me about her Nigerian upbringing in Peckham. She sang about feeling displaced, about what being black and British meant to her, and about finding love. Her music was bits of indie with a soulful edge, and I felt goosebumps when I heard her sing. She was perfect.

And as soon as I got to the festival grounds, I went to work, trying to gather an audience, speaking to as many people as I could, and posting a litany of flyers all over people's tents, in pub windows, in bed and breakfasts and on any car windshields that I came across. After my efforts, the first two shows were about two thirds of the way full, but once word got out, our next two days were packed. It was the last day, with Elsie on stage, that struck the strongest chord with people. She was an open book, the perfect *Spotlight* artist, willing with her answers and eager for more questions.

Afterwards, I went to approach her, a crowd of people already surrounding her, asking her to sign copies of her CD that we were selling at the back of the venue. I watched the hordes of people eventually dissipate, and a familiar figure remained, talking and laughing with her. Five-eleven, black jeans and a wrinkled t-shirt, holding a plastic cup of brown liquor. She caught my eye and waved me over, and I watched him turn towards me, his eyes lighting up, matching mine. His beard was back too.

"Ekuah, I think you know Dee, right? I mean of course, your dad produced most of his album!"

I looked up at Dee and smiled without refrain. If I was beaming, I was sure I didn't care. He seemed to have the same look on his face anyway, and I felt my fingers move towards him and then retreat.

"Yeah, hi. What are you doing here?"

He finished his drink but held onto the empty cup tightly as we stared at each other. Somehow another two years had gone by since I had last seen him in person. Elsie piped up in response to my question, obviously uncomfortable with the new tension I had brought to their exchange.

"Well, he promised me he would come but I didn't believe it."

She grinned at him, hooking her arm into his before looking back at me, pleased. I raised an eyebrow but didn't say anything, letting the moment stay awkward for a little longer, knowing he couldn't stand it.

"Yeah I had a show here last night so thought I'd stay. Glad I did!"

He added the last bit almost apologetically and I smiled, amused by the whole thing. I told Elsie that she had been amazing, and that I would catch up with her next week when we were back home.

"You guys enjoy your night."

I flashed them both a smile and walked away, satisfied that I didn't feel those pangs of jealousy that I had expected. I took myself back to my bed and breakfast and held fast onto the feeling of resolution I felt over everything. I mused that time really did heal all wounds and hoped that one day I would be able to view Jay in much the same way, even though our history was far less tumultuous.

I chuckled to myself at how awkward it had been, standing there with the two of them. I laughed my way to the door when I heard a knock.

"Is Kwaku here?"

Dee stood in the doorway, apparently feeling that we

were past normal greetings. He asked the question authoritatively, his voice booming down the corridor. I was bothered by his countenance, as if tonight had been a regular catch up, rather than an unexpected reunion after years apart.

"No, my dad isn't here."

"Great. Can I come in?"

I paused, watching him, wondering if I should. I stepped aside, and he breezed through as if he owned the place. He turned to look at me after surveying the room.

"You look good, like always."

He sighed just before he said it, and then smiled softly at me, until I felt a prickle on the back of my neck as we held eye contact. It felt intentional on his part. My face was turned up slightly to look at him, our differing heights somehow suddenly important.

"Your beard is back."

I gestured to his chin before turning away and sitting on the edge of the bed. He joined me a few seconds later, the mattress causing us both to bounce softly under his weight.

"Do you like it?"

He stroked his chin and made a mock-serious face, which caused me to chuckle.

"I always liked it. You know that."

We both looked down at the floor, sitting too close for anything good to come from us making eye contact. Instead he shifted his leg slightly and tapped my shoeless foot with his Nikes.

"Your show is… something else."

"That was all Elsie. She's something else."

He grunted softly in agreement, nodding.

"She's just a friend. She opened for me on my tour last year."

It was my turn to nod now, taking in his words, trying not to focus on all the things going through my head, or the small flip my stomach made, still excited by him somehow. We sat in silence for a while, listening to the click of the air conditioning as it came on, the summer heat having only recently arrived. He cleared his throat to speak again.

"So, how are you?"

He had turned his face towards me and I gathered myself in order to look back at him, wondering why it was suddenly so difficult. We were too close.

"I'm good, I'm… knackered actually."

We both laughed, and I watched as he wrapped a hand around my lower arm, brushing his thumb back and forth on the inside of it. I gave him a slightly reproachful look, making no efforts to pull my arm away.

"Dee—"

He closed his eyes and smiled, as if recalling a fond memory.

"God, I miss the way you used to say my name."

I scoffed, I couldn't help it, and he opened his eyes again to smirk at me. I pulled my head back slightly; he smelt like rain and aftershave and I didn't like what it was doing to me.

"This is not a good idea."

"I heard you broke up with the poet."

That was all I needed to hear, to remind me of who we were, and where we were. I slid my arm out of his grip and stood up, turning away from him.

"God, my dad is such a gossip!"

I was amused, but no longer distracted. Dee stood without me having to ask and walked towards the door. Then he seemed to change his mind and turned back to me.

"Sorry if I caused offence. You know I'm crap at saying what I mean."

I sighed for both of us, reaching past him for the door handle without opening it.

"I don't know, I think most of the time you say exactly what you mean."

He squinted his eyes at me, obviously curious about something.

"He hurt you."

It wasn't a question, and I couldn't bring myself to clarify. Perhaps I was still ashamed of what I had done to Jay, how I had managed things, or mismanaged them. Dee wasn't wrong, but he didn't know everything, how much hurt I dished out. Or maybe he knew better than anyone. I stared past him at the door, letting it remain closed, unsure what I was waiting for. I let him remove my fingers from the handle, bringing each of them to his lips, kissing them lightly in turn. When he was done, he brought my hand back down to my side, and then leaned in to whisper into my ear.

"Let me make you feel better."

So, I let him.

When he kissed me it felt like breathing for the first time, coupled with the pangs of relief that come with being touched again by someone that I loved. We made it back to the bed and his hands remembered my body as if it were his own. As I wrapped my legs around his waist, I heard myself emit an involuntary moan at the familiar but still magnificent feeling of him inside me again; in my mind's eye, the room suddenly became iridescent. He whispered things into my ear, things I hadn't heard in years, and for all those moments I was his again, like a cell waiting patiently to be activated by his touch.

Afterwards, I laughed out loud, into the dark room, him beside me rolling over and snickering into my neck, both of us slightly bewildered. Not at what had happened, but at how good it had been.

"I think I need a cigarette or something."

He said it to no one, his voice resting in permanent surprise mode. I turned towards him and kissed his shoulder lightly. Then I rolled off the bed and began gathering up his clothes and mine. He didn't protest when I handed his to him, just pulled them back on and watched me do the same. When we were both done, we stood together, and he wrapped his arms around my waist as if we were 19 again, and all that I wanted was to belong to him. We kissed softly, and I found myself smiling at the memory. He pulled his head back, that question mark in his eyes again. I replied quietly.

"I was just thinking about how much has changed."

He ran his right hand up and down my back, and then pressed his face into my neck like he used to do. I think that he was trying to melt me, and I hesitated under the weight of him, suddenly. Maybe not quite everything had changed. I lifted his face with both hands, then stepped back decisively, as I had always known how to do. He looked at me, his features transparent, disarming almost. His words were spoken softly.

"This wasn't a mistake."

He looked at me seriously as he said it, wanting to make it clear where he stood.

"I know it wasn't."

I reached towards the door again, and this time I opened it. He turned to me and we kissed once more, seconds passing pressed against the door frame. I felt like I was saying goodbye to an addiction, giving it a proper farewell, as if there was such a thing. We pulled apart and he looked as if he was going to say something else, but no words came out. Instead he held onto my fingers for a few seconds, and then he let them go, giving me a wave goodbye and exiting left as I closed the door behind him.

I found myself sliding to the floor, suddenly exhausted, the adrenaline of the week seemingly leaving my body all at once. I could still taste him on my tongue; a familiar, somewhat unquenchable thirst at the back of my throat. Going back for more always meant wanting a little more than that. But that wasn't what I wanted.

30.

/// "It didn't happen how I would have wanted, but at least it's done."

My father reached down to stroke his new dog Smokey, who he'd gotten from a shelter just after moving into a newer, swankier flat in Surrey. He made baby faces at the puppy as if she were a toddler, before turning back to me. We were perched outside of a coffee shop near his flat, and he was reluctantly answering my questions about how he was. He and my mother had been legally divorced for almost a year, but it was only recently made official in both my parents minds, after the ceremony in Ghana. As per Ashanti tradition, an elder in my mother's family was tasked with publicly returning the *tiri nsa*—the head drink—to my father's family. It was a gift given that had sealed their marriage thirty years ago, so it was fitting that it should also represent the undoing of their union thirty years later. My mother and father had not been present for it, neither one in a rush to make their first trip back to Ghana in years, as single people again.

And maybe, there was a little shame in it too, because they were older, with a grown-up child. My father noted how many gruelling conversations he had had with relatives in

Ghana asking why he didn't just stay married, that it was far too late in life for all this change. He looked wearied by it, as if their questions were what he had been most worried about. I asked him as much but he just sighed, looking away from me, at the park across the road. Then he spoke into the air as if I wasn't there.

"We never talk about your mother."

I frowned, breaking into a confused smile.

"We talk about her all the time."

"No, we talk about how I am without her. We do not just talk about her."

"Well… what is there to talk about?"

He was right, and yet I still wasn't ready for the conversation. Now he was staring at me.

"I don't like you being angry at her. Our decision to separate was a mutual one."

"And Auntie Genie living in your house, was that mutual too?"

As usual, my word vomit was right on cue and I couldn't curb it. Perhaps I didn't want to anymore.

"Honestly, Ekuah, I'm surprised at you! That you of all people would judge your mother for—"

"I'm not judging her!"

I was a boiling kettle suddenly, spilling over because I had gone unchecked for so long. My father looked surprised that I had snapped at him but controlled his own anger by using a calmer tone.

"Then what is your problem with her?"

I stared angrily into my tea, catching a glimpse of my distorted reflection in the metallic face of the table. *Simmer down.* I sighed.

"My problem is, she left you. Or, she made you leave, either one. I don't care who she's with, I just hate the way she did it."

I watched as his face changed to a stoic sadness as I spoke, and I wondered if this time I really had said too much. But then his shoulders slumped, and he reached across the table to take my hand.

"My dear, what was I supposed to do? Not let her go, not let her... love who she wants to love? It's been long enough."

The words seemed to be pushing themselves out from his chest, through his throat, causing him to choke on them as they finally met the air. I winced in response, feeling his pain all the way in the back of my teeth.

"I know... I'm sorry."

I meant it as I squeezed his hand back. Seemingly satisfied with that, he tried to sit up a little straighter in his chair, nodding and composing himself again.

"She keeps asking me how you are. Make sure you see her before you go away, eh?"

He took another sip of his coffee, not needing a reply from me, knowing he'd already told me everything I needed to know. That actually, he and my mother were good, and maybe even friends. I felt a deep sense of relief at the prospect, as if a weight I hadn't even realised I was still carrying around, had lifted.

*

It was the week before the European tour of my show, before six dates in six different cities, before the weeks and months of planning and speaking to poets and musicians from those cities finally came to fruition, and before I fully went it alone for the first time. No more Jay, who had true to his word ceased all involvements with the *Spotlight* workshops once the summer term was over. He even changed his phone number, so that there were no loose ends left. At least that was the reason I imagined.

I had taken over correspondence with the foundation completely. They wanted to fund more workshops, but now we had no teacher. I also realised that it wasn't the move I wanted to make yet. But that was exciting too, because now all the decisions were mine. The responsibility was also mine, and I felt the pressure as a new kind of weight, but one that I had chosen to take on this time. I buzzed with anticipation for what the next two months would look like, this new future and life that I was carving out for myself. I began checking off my to do list before my trip, and I placed my mother at the top of it.

I heeded my father's words and went to see her, finding her glowing, a new spring in her step. She had redecorated the living room, and there were more pictures scattered around than I had noticed before. Many of them of me, as a toddler, a teenager, and a graduating student, flanked by both parents, my eyes distant, my smile well-practised.

The memory was a flashbulb one; I looked at myself as I really was then, my little broken heart captured on camera. I wondered how Dee was doing, and then I turned my attention back to my mother.

The sweet smell of cinnamon and vanilla swam in the air, and just as intoxicating and surprising, my mother embraced me when I first arrived, in a way she hadn't done since I was a child. Or perhaps she had always held me that way and I was only now able to feel it properly. Still, I wondered who this woman was, impersonating my usually formal mother.

"You look good, dear."

She smiled a kind of crooked grin, as if surprised by what she was seeing as we pulled apart, and then she looked me up and down, re-emphasising her words. I gave a sheepish grin back and tried to change the subject.

"Are you baking?"

The smell was difficult to ignore, plus my mother was good at many things but baking wasn't one of them.

"Not me, your Auntie Genie."

"Oh."

I walked back to the living room doorway and peered out of it towards the kitchen, spotting Genie with her back to me, searching for something in a cupboard, humming a Christmas tune even though it was September. My mother was already seated, looked at me in earnest.

"She's making plenty, there'll be some for you to take with you."

"I… just didn't know she was home. But it's fine."

"Ah don't worry, she won't be minding us while she's baking. I don't even think she's realised you're here."

My mother waved me back into the living room, pushing a pre-made tea towards me across the same coffee table that once held divorce papers, and most of my frustration at the time. Today though, we talked about me working freelance, and about my upcoming trip. My mother was pleased to hear that I was starting in Venice, that I would see Amelia again after the business in the courtyard, with the shooting. She grilled me for information about it, doing her usual due diligence of inventory on my life plans, making sure I was covering all my bases, doing the very best I could possibly do. Once she was satisfied, she smiled at me warmly and focused her steady gaze on me.

"I'm proud of you. You've done well. I see your father in you now much more. The way he was driven as a young man? Wow. He was a real force when we first met."

Her smile was still warm, and I felt it like a blanket over me. I hadn't heard her talk about my father in such a way before. I tried my luck for more information.

"Is that why you agreed to go out with him?"

She chuckled, placing her tea back on the table.

"Partly. We had a similar work ethic and he was hard to ignore."

I felt she was giving me the green light to venture forth with my curiosity.

"So, did you really steal him away from Auntie Genie?"

My mother paused, and then threw back her head in

laughter, accidentally nudging the coffee table with her knee and spilling some of her tea across it.

"Is that the story she told you? Hm! It's not true."

"So, what really happened then?"

She sighed a big sigh, one I felt ripple throughout the room. Afterwards she looked at me strangely, before mopping up the puddles of tea on her coffee table with a few paper towel sheets. Then she placed her cup back on the coaster and relaxed into her chair. I think she knew that I had a million questions on the tip of my tongue, about Genie, about her and my father, about everything. But she just looked at me and smiled, as if she were waiting for me to ask the real question, the one I had been dying to ask for a long time. So, I obliged.

"How did you and Auntie Genie meet?"

My mother smiled at first but said nothing, as if actively reaching into her memories, trying to find the best point to start from. The pause she took felt like it lasted for minutes, and after a while I thought she had simply decided against answering the question. And then finally, she spoke.

"Your grandfather had been in Accra for about… four months I think, when your uncles and I joined him. I was sixteen, and we had been living in Washington DC for the last few years, so returning was a shock. Everything was very different to what I had remembered. But school, it started off well enough, though I didn't have many friends until I met your father."

I couldn't help the smile on my face, witnessing the

wistful side of my mother, as she told a story she probably hadn't revisited in a long time.

"He wasn't shy about making himself known to me, always inviting me to this party and that. But my own father was very strict. He didn't know Kwaku's family yet and your uncles were sitting their exams for university, so they had no time to chaperone me anywhere."

She paused to pick up her tea again, fingering the edge of the cup, chuckling to herself and at what she was about to reveal.

"Anyway, one day word got around that one of the wealthy boys at school was throwing a big birthday party and Kwaku's band was going to play there. The week before, all day every day, your father was trying to come up with ways to get me to this party, just so that I could see him play—"Maybe he would sneak me out, or I could lie and say I had to stay late at school"—all foolish ideas your grandfather would have seen right through, so I didn't take him seriously. But then Friday, the day of the party came, and Kwaku came running up to me at lunchtime with a girl I hadn't met before. Tall, very pretty, very shy."

"Auntie Genie?"

"Yes. Your father explained that he and Genie were good friends, she had a driver who her mother let her use from time to time, and if she came and introduced herself to my father, he was sure to let me go to the party."

I relaxed into the chair, thoroughly enthralled.

"And it worked, just like that?"

"Somehow yes! Genie's parents were actually governors of the school or something, and it turned out my father had already met them, so he was satisfied I was in good hands."

I grinned, quietly impressed with the persistent and frank desires of my father to garner the attention of my mother. She shook her head and kissed her teeth at the same time, a wry smile on her face as if she had heard my thoughts.

"As for your father! I discovered later from Genie that they had recently broken up, but they had agreed to stay friends, even though she was not yet over her feelings for him. Still, she said she would do him this favour, though it hurt her to do it."

She frowned suddenly, as if hearing her own words for the first time.

"Wow, I can't believe dad was ever like that. Was the party worth it?"

"It was one of the most fun evenings I ever spent as a teenager."

I nodded, satisfied but still wanting more.

"I heard dad had a way when he was leading a band that made all the girls like him; again, according to Auntie Genie. Was it true?"

"Yes, it was, but... I didn't actually see him play that night—I spent most of the evening with Genie. We were just laughing and dancing, from what I can recall."

She beamed, not at me or anything within her immediate line of sight. Instead, her head tilted slightly and pointed towards Genie in the kitchen, through a wall somehow, as if she knew exactly where she was at all times. I felt a kinship with her suddenly, finally, over our shared propensity for human connection, for always wanting to hold on to it. I chose my next words very carefully.

"It must have been hard leaving—leaving Ghana, I mean?"

"It was. I didn't expect it but when it came to saying goodbye? *Awurade*."

My eyes widened, and I felt my heartbeat more clearly; she rarely slipped into Twi when we talked. I spoke quietly.

"I don't know how I would have coped, walking away from someone I… loved."

She sort of exhaled a soft sigh of resignation in my general direction, both of us aware of what was finally being said aloud.

"In all honesty, I didn't think we'd ever meet again. But now I realise…"

She stopped talking, her voice breaking almost imperceptibly at the end. She drew a breath and surprised me by locking me in eye contact.

"That maybe… I was waiting for our paths to cross again. And while I waited, your father and I had a whole life together. A good one, but also a difficult one."

I felt like crying suddenly and I didn't know why, so I verbalised the words jumping around my head.

"Do you regret it? The life you had while you waited?"

Her eyes widened in surprise and she grabbed my arm as if she were falling.

"Oh, my dear, no! I didn't it mean it like that!"

She watched the relief wash over my face, my eyes closed tightly for a few seconds as I tried to gather myself. She laughed at me and shook her head, still clutching my arm, as if she was afraid I might bolt from the room. I cleared my throat and she tipped her head to the side, speaking more confidently now as the mother I was familiar with.

"I just mean, you can't really plan for anything, you can just go with the choices you've made and find enjoyment in that. And if you're lucky enough to love along the way, well then, you're lucky."

Her face was full of contentment, and I felt so comfortable sitting beside her in that state, so completely full of hope. It was a welcome reminder that a reckoning had taken place, but out of the destruction much stronger things had emerged. My parents weren't together anymore, but they were happy. It was exactly what I had needed; to know that after a bad experience with love, there could be so much more.

31.

I rested my elbows on the table, feeling the warmth of the sun on my bare arms, and wished that I had more time. It was a familiar feeling that belonged solely to Venice. But this time around, I was there with the *Spotlight Shows,* Amelia was a newlywed with a new baby, and her husband was an old crush with a curl in his hair.

"Remember those *sciocchezze* plastic tables that we had? All gone!"

Vio gestured excitedly towards the café in the courtyard that we were sitting outside of. It had been redecorated, with new red brick on the inside, giving it an artsy, hipster vibe. Wood-framed, cushioned chairs had replaced the colourful plastic ones that used to be there, and the new chairs now sat strategically around dark, oak tables, with small lamps bolted to the middle of them. The rest of the courtyard looked the same, unchanged. But now the café had a new sign, with an attached canopy for people to sit under when they wanted to shade themselves from the sun whilst enjoying the best espresso this side of Venice, according to Vio. True to form, Amelia rolled her eyes from behind the counter as he spoke, before bringing over a tray of ice cold *limonatas* for the three of us. She plonked herself down opposite me, staring for a few seconds as Vio sat back down beside her. Then she stood up again to hug me where I sat, as if seeing me for the first time. I laughed, amused and touched.

"It's strange, being back here with you."

Vio said it in a matter-of-fact way, as if the statement carried no weight. Amelia mirrored my own questioning face in his direction.

"I mean, the last time the three of us were all here together…"

A hush fell over the already quiet courtyard, all of us in a moment of silence for what had happened almost seven years prior. How so much had changed since then. Amelia and Vio rekindled their friendship which quickly grew into the love I had suspected on my first visit there. Their relationship managed to weather a global distance as Amelia completed her MBA in an American university before returning to Venice, where Vio was now a local hero, having written a novel about a fictional version of the Mafia Veneta and his uncle's charity. The book gained a following and he wrote two more, which awarded him national bestseller success. In the background, Amelia convinced Vio's ageing uncle to let them take over the running of *Nuovo Modo,* which she quickly turned into a social enterprise so that they could keep it going. Her business savvy meant she was able to attract funding and make local business partnerships. She got Vio to write a few articles in some local papers about it and soon the charity grew into something that funded itself. Now they had five cafés that they co-owned with local business owners, running them as art and performance spaces, with the young people from *Nuovo Modo* being offered training and eventually jobs with them. It felt like symbiosis when I told Amelia I was considering a European tour; she insisted I start in one of their cafés in Venice.

"It feels like a lifetime ago."

Amelia spoke quietly, almost pensive as she looked past me at the fountain. I had words to say but wanted to sit in the quiet for a while, noting the way Vio gazed at Amelia, no longer hiding his feelings under teenage chiding and dismissive comments.

"And now you're married—with a baby! Is it too late to say I told you so?"

Amelia made an amused but shocked face, as if I had uttered some profanity.

"When? When did you tell us so?"

I turned to look at them seriously, unable to help the smirk that was creeping back onto my face.

"It was implied. Although I wasn't completely sure, especially with the thing that happened at *Nuovo Modo*."

I laughed, free and easy with my words, noting the way both their faces changed from puzzlement to realisation.

"Ah yes, the Great Beating outside the library."

Vio said it with mock seriousness, smirking as his eyes softened, looking Amelia's way. She batted him away with her hand, and then shook her head, laughing as he jolted his head back in pretend fear.

"*Sei ridicolo*! Although, Vio's uncle said—what did he say, *amore*?"

She tipped her head to the side, waiting for Vio to answer.

"Oh yes... he said the best love stories, *iniziare con una lotta*—they begin with a fight."

"At the time, when Vio told me, I think I laughed in his face."

I chuckled as Vio slid his fingers underneath Amelia's on the table, bringing the back of her hand to his lips and kissing it lightly. I thought she would be embarrassed, shy at such an open show of affection, but instead she tipped her head towards him in warm acknowledgement, before they both turned back to me as if nothing had happened.

"What about you, Ekuah, and that boy you loved? Is he also still around?"

Vio's questions caught me in silence, unable to reply as immediately as I would have liked. Amelia saw the look on my face and tried to change the subject.

"*Allora* Vio, that was years ago."

I gave an awkward but amused grunt, suddenly feeling nostalgic.

"He's still around, yeah. No longer in my orbit though, not anymore."

"You seem disappointed by it."

Vio leaned back, relaxing into his chair as he spoke, completely nonchalant. Amelia just stared at him, shaking her head openly. I gave her what I hoped was a reassuring smile.

"Not quite disappointed but... we were never very good at talking about how we really felt. Or, I wasn't..."

My heart was beating a little faster for some reason, catching up with my mouth and my brain, and the small truths I was admitting, under a now twilight Venetian sky.

"It's never too late to tell truths—and even if you don't know what exactly you will say, it's good to say something, if you feel it."

Vio spoke in that soft familiar tone, the one he had used back at *Nuovo Modo*, apologising for exposing us to the shooting, just before he dropped my hand when he found out about Dee. I couldn't help but smile, even though Amelia was making a face at him.

"Is that supposed to be good advice? Because it doesn't sound like it."

She twisted her chair towards him, waiting for an answer. I stayed silent. He threw his hands up, suddenly passionate.

"Yes! It's good advice, chase after what you want, seize the day—"

"But maybe she doesn't want to seize the day—did you even ask her?"

"I don't need to ask, she looked sad!"

Their voices never raised in volume, only pitch, and then they immediately switched to Italian simultaneously, as if it had been rehearsed, exchanging a back and forth that I was never going to be able to keep up with. All I could pick up were parts of phrases: "her life", "the choice", and "she is happy!" delivered emphatically by Amelia. I was amused but not bothered, aware that this was how both were showing that they cared. Eventually they stopped speaking, Amelia putting an end to it with her last words. Then Vio cleared his throat, giving me a half-hearted smile before moving to clear away our empty glasses, as if he were still the boy behind the counter whistling tunes at an inappropriate time. Once he was away from the table, Amelia dragged her chair around to my side, switching on the lamp in front of us when her journey was complete.

"He thinks everyone should want what we want."

She said it kindly, without reproach.

"Well, it does seem pretty good, what you have."

She looked surprised, and then her face cracked into a smile.

"Ah come on cous, you never wanted this, did you?"

I shrugged, and she threw her arm around me as she continued.

"I don't think so. This isn't the life for you."

"It's not?"

"No! And don't act coy, you know it isn't. You played domestic for a bit with Jay, but even with Dee it wasn't right. You're your own woman!"

She shook my shoulder with her arm as she spoke, causing me to giggle softly.

"I left Jay because I didn't know what I wanted though."

I was laughing as I said it, so it felt wrong, almost like a lie. Amelia suddenly wore a stern face.

"No, you and Jay broke up and then you discovered a

greater love for other things."

"That sounds so sad though. Doesn't that sound sad to you?"

"Why, because you're not pining over someone for once? Sounds freeing to me."

She smiled with one side of her face, wanting to know if I agreed.

"It is. But I still worry. Am I doing it wrong? I don't even have a plan. Or... a person."

Amelia scoffed loudly in my ear, causing me to frown. She ignored my annoyed face and jumped up, pulling me up with her. We stood eye to eye, and I could see in my peripheral vision, Vio coming out from behind the counter but stopping in his tracks, not wanting to interrupt. Amelia placed both hands on my shoulders, locking me in eye contact so that it was impossible for me to look away without her noticing.

"Remember when we almost died?"

I shook my head slightly in disbelief at her question. She continued to stare, expecting a verbal answer.

"Yes, of course I remember."

She pointed to the ground by the fountain, the exact spot where we had cowered on the floor, feeling the walls shake and crack around us as they were pelted with bullets.

"We were lying right here, and I thought that was it. I hadn't even had a chance to make any mistakes and now I was going to die outside because of poetry."

I cracked a smile, more out of discomfort than amusement.

"I was terrified too."

She nodded in response, squeezing my shoulders.

"We both had plans then, and in the end, or close to the end anyway, they didn't mean shit. Did they?"

She didn't wait for my reply, she just pulled me into a hug and I felt like I had travelled back in time, to the night of, Vio embracing us both, my heart beating a mile a minute, afraid it would explode in my chest. I felt Amelia's face turn and she spoke into my ear.

"You don't need one person. I'm your person. And Vio is. And your friends are, and everyone who's ever gone to your show, and met you, and loved you. They're your people."

I pulled my head back to look at her, wondering how she managed to evolve into an even better version of herself every time I saw her. We separated but she held onto my arm, linking it with hers and leaning into me.

"Plus, no one really knows what the fuck they're doing. You just happen to be showing that to an audience and making it work."

I laughed out loud, throwing my head back and cackling, the carefree feeling of the moment soothing me.

32.

Venice kicked off what became a fruitful and eye-opening trip around Europe. As planned, I was also able to run the shows in Amsterdam, Berlin, Copenhagen, Brussels and finally Paris. It was the warm reception from Venice that propelled things, especially after Vio agreed to do a short reading of his latest book, and then remained on stage as a surprise *Spotlight* guest. There were rave reviews in a few local papers, and I was able to run a second show off the back of it, which gave me the extra money to extend my trip by another month.

I felt untethered from so many things back home as I travelled, including my heartache over Jay that was shifting, and to a lesser extent my anxiety over Dee. I felt that same exhilaration I had enjoyed in Ghana, meeting new people and discovering different facets of myself. Only this time I was interacting with poets and musicians in their home cities, sleeping on sofa-beds and enjoying the benefits of having natives as tour guides. I thought about how much Jay would have loved it, how it was a shame he wasn't with me, but also how I had managed to get to these places anyway, by myself. Everything had become significant, meaningful, and

Paris was no exception.

It was the last stop at the end of what had become a three-month tour, my phone full of new contacts, a hundred emails I hadn't managed to get to yet, and bookmarked pages of all the online arts and culture publications that had written about the *Spotlight Shows*. But I was most excited about Paris, because Elsie was my final feature and I knew she would bring the house down. She was already there, on her second international tour opening for a well-known soul singer. It felt like fate that she was in the city at the same time as me, because my original feature had cancelled two weeks prior. And on the night of, she didn't disappoint, getting a standing ovation after her performance, and selling out CDs after the question portion of the night was done. She insisted that we go out and celebrate.

As we walked the streets of Paris, we discussed the show and how her career was going, and she made brief mention of my father and Dee.

"Your dad is so funny! And so proud of you, he won't stop telling people about your shows—Dee said he's not surprised what you've done with them. It's amazing!"

I laughed along as we walked past the canal below, the air thick with an atmosphere I couldn't quite name. I was a little uncomfortable, though I wasn't sure why. Eventually we found ourselves in a hookah café on *Rue de l'Éperon*. As we took our seats in front of an extra-large pipe, Elsie asked the waiter for vanilla, strawberry and apple flavoured tobacco as if she'd been there before. I looked suspiciously at the contraption in front of us as she began fiddling with it and recalled vaguely that the last time I had smoked shisha, my stomach was upset for two days afterwards. I aired a slight concern, half joking, half nervous.

"We're not really going to smoke all of that, are we?"

Elsie gave me a questioning look and then smiled at me softly.

"No, no, no—I mean, not if you don't want to."

I thought about it but didn't reply, watching as she manipulated the pipe with expert precision. She placed a circular mound of coal on a small metal plate at the top of it and we both smiled at the waiter as he brought over the three flavours she had asked for. She took the strawberry tobacco and put it in place, asking the waiter in perfect French to heat the coal with the lighter he held in his hand. The flame sparked, and I asked her the obvious question.

"You speak French?"

"*Un petit peu.*"

She imitated something small with her thumb and fore-finger, but I suspected she was just being modest. The waiter left us alone, and Elsie began to draw deep breaths through the mouthpiece attached to the pipe, the coal on top turning a bright red under the strength of her lungs. Once she could taste the strawberry, she motioned for me to join her by handing me the mouthpiece and my own plastic cover to inhale through. I hesitated, wondering not for the first time where the night would go. After a few seconds I took it from her and inhaled the smoke easily, letting it fill my lungs with a sort of hazy pleasure. I was lightheaded but suddenly filled with clouds of optimism. She relaxed into the leather seats, a slightly anxious look on her face.

"I just wanted to say thanks for inviting me to do the shows. You didn't have to, and when Dee suggested I would be a good fit—"

I almost choked as clouds of smoke billowed from my mouth whilst she was speaking.

"*Dee* told you about them?"

"Yeah—I thought you knew? Your dad asked him to do it at the Edinburgh festival, but he had a clash and thought I was a good alternative."

"Oh."

My brow was furrowed, and I looked more concerned than she might have thought was warranted after her comments, but I couldn't straighten my face fast enough. I had been right to suspect my father's weird ulterior motives, even though it had worked out for the best. Elsie turned back to the pipe and took another drag before continuing.

"Honestly, I thought you'd say no, because of your... history. But it was a nice surprise to see him at the festival, so I guess you guys are cool now?"

I decided not to take another drag of the hookah, my head in a wavy sort of place that felt on the borderline of nausea.

"Yeah, yeah, we're cool. We're... yeah."

"And... we're cool too, right? I mean, I feel like we're friends! Although that sounds really lame now that I've said it out loud…"

She shook her head in embarrassment, looking down at the table and retracing a circle someone had engraved into it, with her finger. I realised it was my turn to reassure her.

"Yeah, of course we're cool. Plus, you're basically my show stopper on this tour, so this has all just been you doing *me* a favour."

I grinned at her, blinking one too many times, spots of light from a nearby lamp suddenly catching in my eye. She gave a sigh of relief, as if she had been unsure of our mutual affection since she'd first met me.

"I'm so glad! I really thought it would be weird, after you know, you and Dee and now, me and him are… you know?"

Suddenly I was fully awake, my eyes open and clear, my hands on the table.

"…You're together?"

She looked surprised, realising quickly that she was delivering brand new information. But she didn't look away, she held my gaze, her expression now softer but more steady.

"I don't know what we are. Figuring it out, I guess. I genuinely thought you knew… this wasn't some under-handed way of telling you."

I eyed her, wondering if I should believe her. She didn't flinch, just continued looking at me in the now dimly lit restaurant we were sat in. Looking at her close up, I realised her features were not as angular as I had first thought. They were rounded, a cuteness to them that was unlikely to fade with age. Her makeup was perfectly applied, and I recalled how I had voiced my slight envy of her artistic skills earlier in the day, to which she responded by giving me a quick eyeshadow tutorial. I imagined that I should be feeling a way, perhaps indignant and deciding that I didn't want to be friends with her after all. But I did. She wasn't my enemy.

"It's okay… were you together when we did Edinburgh?"

The question jumped into the air before I had time to rephrase it, perhaps suppress it entirely. She chuckled, as if I had made a small joke.

"No, no—we were just talking then. Nothing really happened until a few weeks ago."

My whole body relaxed immediately. I didn't know if I had been more concerned about Dee's unavailability when we slept together, or how it could potentially break Elsie's heart. I could already tell from the way that she spoke about him, that she had fallen. She was in that place that seemed impossible to climb out of. But it occurred to me that she probably didn't want to.

*

I had a sore head the next day, after a night of hookah, red wine and an extended dance session at a club we happened to stumble into. Elsie and I spent most of our time in the club laughing and getting our lives on the dancefloor, until some guys we were dancing with became a little more handsy and a lot less fun. When one tried to grab my wrist, attempting to pull me off the dance floor, Elsie stepped to him, despite

the several inches in height he had on her. She readied herself
for a fight, the South London lion in her roaring in preparation. She shoved him backwards with a flat palm, causing the
dance floor crowd to suddenly widen.

"*Vas te faire enculé!*"

His friends gasped at the profanity, and I dragged her out
of the club before things got any more out of hand. She just
laughed it off, suddenly calm again, and we walked up to the
Pont des Arts, sitting on a bench and watching the sunrise.
The whole evening had been surreal, and upon returning to
my bed and breakfast, I was warmed by the thought that I
had made a new friend, drunk as I was. By the time I awoke
however, it was the afternoon, I was sober in name only, and
I wondered what would come of my night of bonding with
Elsie.

My answer came when my phone buzzed in my pocket,
as I stood staring out the window, considering calling Elsie
to find out if she wanted to get coffee. I answered without
looking at the screen, my head a pulsating ball of pain.

"Hey, Eckie."

My heart jumped into my mouth for a second and I
knew I wasn't going to be as cool with Dee as I was the last
time we had seen each other.

"Hey."

My voice croaked as if I had just woken up, which I had.
I had a lightbulb moment and began digging around my
bag, looking for painkillers, just to quieten the percussion
band in my head.

"How did the show go?"

His voice sounded strange and I paused to swallow the pills, gulping them down with some water.

"The show with Elsie? It went great, of course. You know her, she's incredible."

He sighed, and I heard the scratch of his beard against his fingers.

"She told you."

"Yes. Why didn't you?"

He laughed, and then realised I wasn't joining in so stopped.

"Since when did we share things like that?"

I wanted to snap at him, ask him why he was calling in the first place, but he was right.

"It's not about who's seeing who, it's that you knew we would be hanging out because she did my show, and you still said nothing."

"I said something to her."

I took my turn to laugh, his excuses were always based in some twisted sense that he was doing the right thing.

"Well, it's done now. I'm… happy for you. I really like her."

I left my words hanging in the air between us, listening to him breathing on the other end of the phone, maybe considering what to say next, or holding back whatever it was he really wanted to say.

"So, are you still hurting?"

I pulled at a thread on my sock, now sat in the middle

of the floor by my bag, the contents ransacked during my painkiller hunt.

"No, I'm… I'm good."

"So, I helped, yeah?"

I giggled involuntarily, hearing his own snickering on the other end of the phone. I kissed my teeth, smiling to the air in my room.

"You're an idiot."

"Hm! Eh-kwee-ah Dan-kwa! I know you need me, eh?"

He still sounded the same, even after all that time, after all the fights and the pain. And yet, there was still a part of me that couldn't stand the way things were now between us.

"Why are you calling? For real?"

He paused, for longer than was acceptable over the phone, but I knew him, he was trying to think it through and answer me properly.

"I'm just wondering when you're coming back home, innit."

33.

London was a smoke signal calling me home. It felt like I returned slowly, remaining in Paris for an extra week, walking the streets, drinking coffee, spending too much time perusing bakeries. I even saw Elsie one last time before she headed off to Berlin to do her final opener. I didn't mention that Dee had called me; it felt unnecessary, and a little cruel. I had always planned to go back to London, of course, but his querying me also felt like a beckoning. I continued to wonder what he had in store when I touched down at Stansted.

But once I was back, there was a flurry of activity: phone calls to return from artists of all kinds wanting to get involved in the *Spotlight Shows*, and a few offers for me to start up the workshops again, deliver them myself with full funding in place. I checked in on both my parents, much more relaxed about the fact that they were living their own lives now. I also caught Dee on the front cover of NME, in a crimson suit, a serene look on his face. I paid for the magazine and brought it home with me, unsure of what exactly I was going to do with it. I just wanted it, as evidence that he really had 'made it', this time, I suppose.

I used the rest of the morning to tackle the pile of unopened letters on my side table, sifting through them and picking out a handwritten note. It was a folded piece of paper that someone had torn from a notebook, and it was from Dee. Something he had dropped off himself, knowing I wasn't in the country.

> *Let's hang when you're back.*
> *Dee x*

It was curious. I had begun to believe his call to me in Paris was a one off, that he was fact finding to make sure Elsie and I were not at loggerheads, though I know there was a part of him that would have thoroughly enjoyed that. But this note was something else, something more. Even in the way that he delivered it, purposefully throwing me back to that night I sat outside his front door, scribbling a note to someone who had no plans of coming back to me until two years later. The memory made me angry, and then almost immediately afterwards, the feeling evaporated. I wondered if perhaps I was reading too much into it.

*

Dee wanted to do a *Spotlight Show*. We had played phone tag for a few days before he finally called me to propose this new venture. Apparently, Elsie had raved about it, about how inspired she had felt after each one, how she wrote down the ideas for three songs after the Paris event. And besides, he liked the idea of us working on something together, finally. I told him I needed to think about it, aware that show-wise, it was an offer I shouldn't pass up. But the preparation involved, it scared me. I would need to get him ready for audience members and get him to provide me with answers to the deep questions right off the top. This would be a conversation we hadn't had before. I explained it to him but he was unfazed, as usual. He told me to set up the prep session, and we would make it happen.

On a Tuesday evening, I found myself at his house. He had a place in Ladbroke Grove now, two floors that used to be flats, recently converted back into one house. Everything looked brand new, and I gathered that he hadn't spent too much time there since buying it. He greeted me at the door with a coy smile. We hugged each other for a few seconds and then he led me to the back of the house, into what was now his home studio. I realised that I had been paying small attention to his growing popularity as an artist, but I hadn't grasped how quickly he had elevated into star-status until I saw his home. No more furniture off the streets, no more bean bag chairs, and no more beat-up Peugeot.

We sat down opposite each other on comfy leather chairs, his recording booth behind us. I pulled out my notebook and he sipped from a mugful of tea whilst I settled into my chair. For a moment we were positioned—him relaxed, lounging in a polo t-shirt and joggers, me straight backed in jeans and a loose jumper, my pen at the ready—as if I were about to sketch his portrait. In a way, I suppose I was.

"Nervous?"

He laughed at my question, setting his tea down and rubbing his hands together.

"Nah. Hit me."

"Okay, so like we talked about, you'll do a 30-minute set, the crowd will be ecstatic, blah blah blah."

He grinned, nodding. I rolled my eyes a little but carried on.

"And then they'll pepper you with questions. The rules are simple, any questions rooted in bigotry won't be taken, everyone needs to be respectful and keep quiet whilst someone is asking a question—you get it."

"Makes sense. So, what are we prepping for exactly?"

I smiled, used to this question by now, always ready with the answer.

"Well, *Spotlight* audiences know how this works by now, and trust me, they will go in. So, if I ask the harder questions today, based around the topics you cover in your music, you'll be ready for anything when the show happens next week."

He nodded, his eyes scrunched together, thinking. Then a soft smile appeared as he readied himself. I thought briefly about how he was still beautiful, and I had to wait for the butterflies to pass, looking down at my notepad and drawing a line under my first question. My feelings for him were ever-present but very, very quiet these days.

"In an interview you said that your first hit *Young Life*

was written by an ex-lover. What happened between the two of you?"

I watched his face become a picture of surprise, staring at me with wide eyes and meeting my unwavering eye contact with his own.

"Damn, Eckie. People ask questions that deep?"

"Deeper than that, I'm just starting you off light."

My face was serious, eyebrows raised.

"Wow, okay... okay."

He leaned forward to pick up his tea and then changed his mind, sitting back again. Instead, he lifted his chin, pressing the back of his hand against it, tapping it absent-mindedly.

"So, what happened?"

I had to ask the question again, knowing I was splitting open old wounds, but better to do it now than in public for the first time.

"Well... I met her in a student bar. I don't think she thought much of me at first, but I managed to persuade her otherwise. Then I fell for her, deep like... and I was never totally sure that she felt the same. So... I just bounced after a while, didn't tell her, which was shitty of me. Eventually we got back together and that's when she showed me this poem, that became *Young Life*. Yeah."

"Do you think you were right, that she didn't feel the same way?"

"Come on, Eckie."

He smiled, shifting uncomfortably in his chair, the air

thick with tension and longing.

"One question leads to another question, that's how it goes."

"And this isn't just an underhanded way for us to have this convo, yeah?"

I rolled my eyes again and sighed, putting the notepad down.

"No Dee, this isn't me being passive aggressive—this is the show. But if you want to have a separate convo—"

"Yes."

He had cut me off and my pause only lasted a few seconds, but I felt there was no way to resume my sentence. I opened my mouth to speak and then closed it again, confused. I watched him as he licked his lips absentmindedly, waiting for me to respond. I found myself chuckling suddenly.

"Wait, wait. You want to talk about this? Us? Now?"

"I have a few questions, yeah."

"Shoot."

This was happening now.

"Was I wrong? Did you feel the same way as me?"

His voice was suddenly brimming with emotion, as if he were singing, and it cracked my chest open a little.

"More. I felt... more than that."

"Seen. But you never said it."

I frowned, the room suddenly feeling like a closed in tunnel, the two of us stuck and making no movements to get out.

"I wanted to. But... the first time you said it, you bolted

immediately afterwards. I felt like I wasn't even given a chance to respond."

"That's fair. But… I was a scared youth, innit."

"So was I!"

He chuckled, nodding.

"Did you hate me when I left?"

I tipped my head to the side and frowned, indicating that this question was an obvious one. He just smiled back, waiting for an answer.

"For a while I tried to but… in the end I was just sort of, angry. And then when you came back, I was still angry, but that was because of the reason you gave."

"That I wasn't good enough for you?"

"Yeah, it's bullshit. I never said that or thought it."

"Maybe not, but I felt it."

He looked down at his hands, his eyes drooping slightly in what I knew to be sadness, and I wondered if maybe we were taking this too far. I inhaled a deep breath and pulled my chair closer to his, leaning forwards and pointing my head in his direction, looking at the table.

"Maybe we should stop?"

He lifted his head just as I did, and our eyes met.

"Nah, this is good. It's… cathartic."

"Is it?"

He chuckled at my response and sat back again, leaning away from me.

"When you came to my birthday that time, after you got back from Ghana, I thought you were… shit. This is hard, you know."

"You—you thought I was what?"

He was smiling but clearly embarrassed, rubbing a hand across the top of his head now, the muscles of his biceps prominent as he lifted his arm.

"I thought you were… coming back to me. But you were not."

It was my turn to hang my head and think about all the things I wished I had said back then.

"It crossed my mind, but it wouldn't have been a good idea. So, I sort of… had to drop off after that. It was easier if we didn't see each other all the time."

"You must have been pissed I was working with your dad then?"

I grimaced, I couldn't help it, and I saw him catch the flash of anger in my eyes.

"Honestly, it felt like you kept working with him because you knew it would piss me off."

"Okay, for real, I did know that. But your dad's a G as well, I don't think I'd be where I am without him. Seriously."

He was giving me a piercing stare, wanting to make sure I knew that this was the full truth. I shrugged, relaxing back into the emotional haze of the room.

"He'll be happy to hear that, because you know, you're basically the love of his life at this point."

He laughed into the air, loudly and with a heavy bass in his voice. A few moments later he was nodding, and then suddenly, he stopped.

"Did he like me better than Jay?"

I felt my stomach drop and my shoulders tighten. Somehow this felt much more like a risk.

"Probably… but for very different reasons."

"And you, did you like me better?"

"Dee…"

I trailed off, looking around the room, unable to let the words come out.

"Why is that suddenly a hard question?"

His voice took on a petulant air, causing me to sigh.

"They're all hard questions. I thought that was the point?"

"And yet, you haven't answered mine."

Now his arms were folded, not protective but indignant, about what I wasn't sure.

"No, because I can't. There's no comparison."

"There is though. It's easy."

"Easy how?"

"Because I'm still here, and he's not."

I scoffed at him, the sound involuntary but appropriate. He continued to stare, and I tried not to let his words sink into my bones, though I knew that they would. And I couldn't think of a way to disagree with what he was saying.

"I don't know what you want me to say. Why are you still around then?"

"You know why."

He smiled at me softly, his hands now on the arms of his chair, back straight as if he were sat on a throne. He spoke again, maybe to save me from the uncomfortable look I had on my face.

"Look, I just wanna… get things straight, so we can both move on, whatever that means. But I feel like, I can only do that if I know how you feel, because after Edinburgh… I'm still feeling a way."

"What way?"

"Like maybe… it wasn't a thing for you, it was just fun."

"But it was—"

I stopped speaking, seeing the struggle on his face, the way he was trying to be as explicit as he could be, without saying it outright. I frowned and tried my words again.

"Yeah, it was fun, but it was also more than that, because it always is with us, isn't it?"

He paused and then nodded, his face now soft but serious.

"Yeah, it always is."

His words were crowned by frustration, and he picked up his mug of tea again, holding the cup to him tightly. I thought about how he still looked good to me in every room. How endeared I was by his sincerity, even when he was trying to hold things back. And how we never said the things we wanted to say in the moment, until now. It felt suddenly, auspiciously, like this was our last chance.

I breathed deep again.

"You know that I love you, right?"

ACKNOWLEDGMENTS

I've written many love letters to London, but this is the first one that's been published. So I want to say thank you to my hometown. You will always be my first love.

Secondly, thank you to the first boy who broke my heart, without whom this story would not have started.

Writing requires a certain type of solitude, that involves digging around in your own brain for much longer than sanity often permits. I'm thankful to the spaces I've found that allowed me to write and shape this book, including: Hubbard & Bell in Holborn, Hoxton Grill in Shoreditch and the Little Hope Cafe in Brunswick, Melbourne. A particular thank you to DHHS in Melbourne CBD, for the flexibility and space to write and work at the same time.

To those who have continued to champion me along the way with encouragement, support and herbal tea—Bubs (Bethany Adiyiah), Dad (Peter Danso), Doodle (Frankie Withers), E (Elizabeth Bananuka), Mum (Barbara Kuma-Aboagye) and Raph (Chloe Browne-Beck)—my gratitude for everything you've done for me knows no bounds.

To the wondrous friends and family who read early drafts of the book with keen eyes, providing a wealth of invaluable feedback that was the perfect mix of heartfelt and intellectual—Abs (Abi Akakpo), Becca (Rebecca Adiyiah), Tamara Jones, Tash (Natasha Ouna) and Yorkabel Soquar—you helped make Ekuah at least ten percent less annoying, and I thank you for that.

I am eternally grateful to Dapo Adeola for lending me his beautiful artwork for my book cover and perfectly encapsulating the emotional turmoil of Bad Love.

My deepest gratitude goes to the powerhouse that is Valerie Brandes of Jacaranda Books—thank you for reading my story and believing that it should be shared. And to your team of superwomen—Cherise Lopes-Baker for her delicate but generous edits, Jazzmine Breary and Magdalene Abraha for kicking down the doors for us #Twentyin2020 authors, and Kamillah Brandes for making our stories look beautiful on the outside and in—thank you to all of you for helping me begin.

And finally to my best friend and whole heart. Thank you for keeping me sane, and for keeping me.

ABOUT THE AUTHOR

Maame Blue is a Ghanaian-Londoner based in Melbourne, Australia. Her short stories and creative non-fiction pieces have appeared in AFREADA, Litro Magazine, Memoir Mag (US), Storm Cellar Quarterly (US), The Good Journal Issue 3 and Black Ballad. She blogs about mental health, relationships and blackness over at www.maamebluewrites.com.